DEAR DAUGHTER

by
Denver Wheeler

Wildflower Press
an imprint of Blue Fortune Enterprises, LLC

DEAREST DAUGHTER
Copyright © 2024 by Carter Summerville

All rights reserved. Printed in the United States of America. No part of this book may be used or reproduced in any manner whatsoever without written permission except in the case of brief quotations embodied in critical articles or reviews.

This book is a work of fiction. Names, characters, businesses, organizations, places, events and incidents either are the product of the author's imagination or are used fictitiously. Any resemblance to actual persons, living or dead, events, or locales is entirely coincidental.

For information contact :
Blue Fortune Enterprises, LLC
Wildflower Press
P.O. Box 554
Yorktown, VA 23690
http://blue-fortune.com

Cover design by BFE, LLC

ISBN: 978-1-961548-19-0
First Edition: November 2024

Dedication

For Doodles, who taught me what it means to be a good person and showed me a love I will cherish forever.

Acknowledgements

This novel is something that came to me a long time ago, but it took the courage of motherhood to be able to actually put that pen to paper! Most of the content of this book has been pulled from my professional experience as a mental health therapist, and stories like this are so important to me. We need to tell the stories of the ones left behind, the ones who aren't listened to, and the ones who are hurt beyond repair. The only way we can grow and change as a society is to look the world's ugliness in the face and support those who need it most. I hope this story has done just that, and I appreciate every single person who picked up this book and brought it into their lives and hearts. You will never know how much it means to me, readers.

To my loves, Oakley and Jurrand: you both have inspired me to be exactly who I am. I never could have had the space to grow and expand if it weren't for the unwavering love and support you both give me. Jurrand, this book wouldn't have happened if you hadn't given me everything I needed to be a confident person. You are my best friend in the world, and I love you and like you, bufnita. Oakley, you have shown me how to embrace myself for whatever that means, and it has been a truly beautiful and magical experience to watch you grow. I am beyond honored to be your momma, my beautiful Tree Flower.

A special thank you to all my early draft readers: I couldn't have shaped this book into what it became without all of you! A special mention for my beloved Aunt Kaki, my Doodles and Bon Bon, Adrienne Kisner, and my bestie Stephanie Ellison! You guys (and so many more) were instrumental in building up my confidence, and you are my stars!

Thank you to my writing group, The Chaos Scribes, for supporting me through editing and the final days of getting this book out there! Gage Greenwood, you changed my life with this group, and I am eternally grateful to have this little horror space in my life. Without this group's words of encouragement, hilariously inappropriate memes, and endless messages, I couldn't have gotten through this! Love you guys to the moon and back.

It goes without saying, but this book wouldn't be where it is today without the fabulous Narielle Living of Blue Fortune Enterprises. Thank you for taking a chance on my little story and helping me to shape it into the amazing book that it has become! I never would have had the courage to continue with this journey without you, and I am forever grateful!

Lastly, a special message for my Doodles. I wish you could have read the last draft of the book and held the book in your hands. I cherish every single second we had together, and I am the strong person I am today because of you. You taught me how to care for people and thus how to care for myself and my family. The gifts and memories that we shared will live on in me forever, and you will always be my best friend. I love you more than words could ever describe and thank you for making my life so special and full. This and everything I do in life is for you. Until we meet again!

PROLOGUE

*B*ethany would not stop fighting for as long as she lived, no matter how short a time she had left. How long had it been since the Brothers took her from the small coffeehouse in Tree Park? Bethany spent every moment wishing she'd never heard of the place. Her days at the farm blurred, each one blending into the next, and her previous life had morphed into a distant dream—one she didn't believe existed. She wasn't part of this family, but she had no place in the world anymore.

She had to fight.

A blow landed on Bethany's back, and she screamed like a demon escaping hell as she collapsed. She didn't recognize the sound of her own voice, but that didn't matter. The point of life now was to fight. She tried to breathe and crawled forward on hands and knees, desperately reaching out and grasping the leg of the bed beside her. Strong hands grabbed her ankles and yanked her back, but her hold on the bed stayed firm.

No, please, no!

As the man pulled, the bed slid across the wooden floors with them, screeching loudly.

"Let go," hissed the man behind her as he grabbed her wrists and jerked them from the bed.

His rugged and powerful body seemed to grow stronger the more she fought him. She bucked her body, causing him to let go of her wrists, and Bethany turned onto her back, looking up at the man with as much hatred on her face as she could muster. He sneered, wrapped one of his hands in her long, brown hair, and dragged her toward the door to the room. Her hands flew to her hair, trying to yank it back from him, but it was no use. She kicked and flailed, wailing at the top of her lungs as he dragged her through the doorway and down the staircase. Strands of hair ripped out of her scalp as the thud of each step reverberated through her tailbone and up her spine.

At the bottom of the staircase, the man's brother came into view, meek and mild as always. She continued to scream, and he shuffled backward, afraid of her. She had seen him as useless from the moment she met him, constantly stuttering and shaking, and she knew he wouldn't help her. Ever. She tried to get her feet under her, thrashing like a feral cat caught in a trap. The man holding her hair wrenched open the back door and dragged Bethany's body onto the porch, into the freezing cold. Moisture hung in the air as soft snowflakes from the impending snowstorm fell. Bethany could see her breath rushing out of her through her screams.

Her screams had always been pointless on this farm—Bethany supposed long ago that this family had taken her away from the real world and put her into some sort of alternate universe full of pain and suffering. Her scream morphed from a plea of desperation into a guttural and involuntary response. She had been in survival mode for so long that she no longer knew anything else. Despite her aggressive thrashing, the man had a power over Bethany she could never break. He dragged her down the porch steps and onto the snow-covered ground, again knocking the wind from her chest. Her screams died out as her lungs froze with icy air.

As they approached the small barn where Bethany had first awoken on this dreadful farm, her distant mind registered that things had come full circle. This new and feral version of herself was born in this barn, and it was about to die just outside of it.

The man pushed Bethany's head to the ground and stalked into the barn, his meek brother standing nearby, shifting from foot to foot. She took advantage of that moment to get away, knowing the weaker of the brothers couldn't put up much of a fight. She clawed her hands through the snow and into the solid dirt of the ground, desperate to get away from the barn. Her frail and emaciated body couldn't make any headway, and she was out of breath before she even moved a few inches.

The man emerged from the barn and laughed, his ominous bellows floating away into the night sky. He stood, blocking her way, holding a shotgun, and wiping down the barrel. His brother continually took small steps backward, as if hoping to fade into the dark night behind him.

"Get that dress off her," the strong man commanded his fading brother, who fell back in line and rushed toward her as fast as his limp would allow.

Bethany would never give up. She tried to crawl but could not progress with the brother's gentle hands on the zipper of her pink dress. He pulled the zipper down the length of the fabric, and the dress fell apart. He pushed Bethany's side, and her body's compliance with his gentle maneuvering surprised her. She had built her strength in her mind so fantastically, but in reality, she had none left. The brother pulled the fabric away from her arms and chest, leaving her clad only in frilly pink underwear and a plain white bra. Goosebumps covered her as her bare skin met the snow. She gave a shout of exertion, clawing the ground to pull herself forward, reigniting the strong man's laughter.

"You think you can get away from us?" he shouted through his laughter. "You think after all this time we would just let you go?"

"You can't," Bethany retorted, voice weak but spiteful. "You need me."

The man gave her an evil grin, and his brother awkwardly cleared his throat. Bethany tried to focus on her breathing as her strength waned.

"We don't *need* you! We've already replaced you, Sister! I've been watching the new one for weeks, ever since we realized you were too hot-tempered to be our sister. The new one has kind eyes and a quiet temperament, nothing like your disgusting disposition. She goes to the same house to babysit on the first Friday night of every month and walks home alone in the dark. And guess what day it is? The first Friday of January—your number's up, sweetheart!"

Bethany couldn't give up now. She pooled as much spit into her mouth as she could and spat at the man's boots. His laughter died away faster than a bolt of lightning could strike the ground.

"I would say you'll regret that," the man hissed, "but you won't feel anything when I'm done with you, you sick imposter." He tucked the rag into his pocket and raised the shotgun, aiming straight at her head.

"Any last words?" he asked with a sinister snarl.

"I'm *not* your sister," she said with resolute pride.

Bethany couldn't save herself, but she could claim back her identity in her final moments. She closed her eyes as she heard the shotgun cock.

"Fine by me!" the man shouted, and it was the last thing Bethany heard.

Chapter One

April had dreams and plans for her life—marrying someone handsome, having three adorable children, traveling to the finest cities of the world—all pleasant and lovely things. But nothing right now felt pleasant as she walked through Tree Park. The cold and dark night permeated every cell and the warmth of her cozy home and the vivacious laughter of her best friend filled her mind. She cursed herself for being out in the night—now early morning—snow, alone and shivering. Her breath swirled in the crisp air, wisps intertwining with the soft flakes floating to the ground. The clouds of the storm obscured the stars above her, and April felt utterly alone.

Tree Park prided itself on its quiet atmosphere and lay almost hidden on the edge of a large national forest, swallowed up by the trees. April couldn't think of many troubling things happening in her small town. The only event that came to mind was that a college student from a neighboring city went missing last year while visiting. April's roommate, Claire, had obsessed over the story and scoured the depths of the internet for information about the girl's disappearance, but the case went cold, and Tree Park went on as usual. Most of the locals supposed the girl had run away from her old life—they couldn't imagine anything that ominous happening right under their noses.

April's phone vibrated in the back pocket of her jeans—her mother calling. She rolled her eyes, her mother was not exactly the person she craved when feeling alone. Her mother constantly checked in on her as if she wasn't a full-grown adult, and it didn't leave room for independent adulthood. She took a deep breath and answered.

"Hello, Mom, you're up late!" April said, trying to curb the annoyance in her voice.

"Hi, sweetie!" her mother sang back at her. "Just checking in to see if you made it home alright."

"Not yet, but I'm just a few blocks away, so I'll be there soon," April replied.

"The Endersons couldn't bother to give you a ride home? The weather is atrocious—I think I need to have a conversation with Karen about this…."

"They have young kids, Mom. It's not their responsibility to get the babysitter home. I should have driven, but you know how I love to walk. Stop worrying, I'm fine!"

"I don't understand why you keep doing this. If money's an issue, you know your father and I are more than happy to help. It's dangerous to be out after dark like this."

April sighed. "Mom," she said, this time not bothering to mask her annoyance, "I told you, I enjoy watching the Endersons' kids for their date nights. The kids are adorable, and it's a nice change of pace for me. Plus, the house is a bit eerie when Claire's working late."

"Then why don't you come here when she works?" her mother huffed.

"I'm not having this argument again. It's only once a month, and this is Tree Park," April answered.

What April didn't say to her mother was that it *was* about the money. She had a great day job but babysitting once a month gave her an extra hundred dollars in income that she filed away for her dream vacation, a trip to the Louvre Museum in Paris. April knew her parents would fund her trip if she asked them, but it felt good to do something on her own. She craved the independence that her parents never let her have, and her secret rebellion thrilled her.

April had graduated from college with honors and a degree in art history. She dreamed of becoming an art curator in some luxurious foreign city, but that required further schooling. For now, she found satisfaction in working as a tour guide for the museum in the nearby national forest. While it wasn't an art museum, she genuinely enjoyed giving tours for the groups of children that came in on field trips. Plus, if she worked there for two years, the museum would help her pay for graduate school. She had a year under her belt and was on her way to accomplishing her goals.

Her parents scoffed at her choice of degree. Her mother hoped April would have studied business management or culinary arts to help with the family bakery in town. April, though, dreamed of big cities, glittering lights, and wild love affairs, and she didn't want to be stuck in Tree Park forever. She soothed her parents with the idea that she would live in her hometown until after graduate school, allowing them to hold on to their only daughter as long as they could. Part of her still felt like a failure for returning home, though.

"Fine," her mother said with resignation. "Can I stay on the phone until you get home?"

"No, that's alright. I'm almost three blocks away now, so I should be home soon. I'll text when I get in."

"Promise?" her mother asked, and April could hear both anxiety and sleepiness in her voice.

"Promise. Love you, Mom."

"Love you too, sweetie. Don't forget we're meeting at the bakery in the morning, so get right to bed when you get home."

"I won't forget. You get some sleep, too."

April hung up the phone and tucked it into the small white purse hanging across her chest. She scanned the buildings ahead of her but struggled to see through the misty, snowy air. She had hoped she would find an open shop or diner along the route, though knew this was unlikely. The snow fell faster and faster as the freezing air penetrated her coat. She desperately craved a reprieve from the chill. Everything was so dark—the power must have gone out.

Under normal circumstances, April enjoyed the walk from her place to the Endersons' and vice versa. She had a car but rarely used it as she had a soft spot in her heart for the ambiance of her small town. She imagined it was a warm spring day—the aroma of coffee wafting from the nearby coffee shop, popping into the Italian restaurant for some gelato, and seeing the beautiful trees on the edge of the national forest blooming with new life and growth.

A sudden, intense gust of wind blasted April from her springtime fantasy. She pulled up her coat sleeve and glanced down at the dainty watch on her wrist. Her grandmother had left it to her in her will, and April would forever cherish this small gift. She thought about her grandmother's bakery, now her mother's, just a few blocks away. She would spend countless hours chatting with her grandmother over her special lavender sugar cookies on slow days. As the only grandchild, she got all her grandmother's attention, and she liked it that way. When she died, a small part of April had gone away, too. The watch helped a bit, and she wore it every day. Each morning before she put it on, she would run her thumb over the engraving etched into the back and imagine her grandmother smiling at her.

It was now three minutes past twelve in the morning, and she felt as if the walk had taken hours, though in reality it had probably only been ten minutes. She pushed forward and pulled her scarf over her nose for warmth, picking up her pace and struggling to move through the deepening snow. She felt ridiculous as she lifted her feet high into the air over the snow and stomped back down with each step. She must have looked like a dog walking around with shoes on its feet.

Finally, she approached the outskirts of her neighborhood, almost home and almost to warmth and sleep. Just one more block to the market that April and Claire, her roommate, often stopped at on late nights out. Maybe they had power or a generator. Her long brown hair had gotten bunched up around her neck and scarf, and because she'd forgotten her hat, ice crystals coated her hair. She brushed it back as she picked up her pace again, almost jogging now. The potential of the warmth of the market created a newfound sense of motivation. If open, she could stop and get warm, perhaps even have a midnight snack. A tiny butterfly of hope flit and flapped around her belly as she yawned widely.

Caught in thoughts of warmth and safety, a soft thud startled April. She whirled, hands clutching her chest as her heart seemed to stop. A thick mound of snow slid from a roof and landed on the ground with another muted thud. April smiled, relaxed, and dropped her hands back to her sides, breathing hard.

"Just some snow," she whispered, flooded with relief.

She watched as another mound slid to the ground and something else caught her eye. An old-fashioned black truck sat parked on the side of the road, but she couldn't remember seeing it before. She looked at the truck harder, eyes squinting. The headlights were dark, and there seemed to be no one inside, but she couldn't quite see the interior details. Maybe the truck had been parked there the whole time. She had been so lost in thoughts and memories that it was entirely possible that she just hadn't noticed it. She started to turn back then she stopped again, blood running cold.

If the truck had been there the whole time, why wasn't the windshield covered in snow like the rest of the cars?

Her pulse quickened and warning flares shot up her spine. The headlights of the truck turned on, sudden and bright. Temporarily blinded, she shrieked and stumbled backward, losing her footing and falling into the cold snow. Feeling a mixture of urgency and panic, April scrambled to her feet as the truck's engine roared to life. Trying her best to break out into a run, April lost her balance once more. Her foot slipped, and she crashed to the ground, her head slamming against the curb.

Lying on her side, the fall and the truck's piercing headlights disoriented her. The world now turned dark and sinister. An uncomfortable pulsing started on her temple, and her purse lodged awkwardly under her head. The string dug into her shoulder, and she unwound it from her body. She placed her purse next to her, and it sank into the snow.

The world spun in ways April didn't think possible. She put her hands to her head to make the spinning stop. She tried to open her eyes but struggled to do so against the bright truck lights. She pulled her hands away from her head and felt something sticky on her fingers. Her eyes flew wide open despite the intense light.

Blood.

She reached her hand up to her head and prodded the wound, wincing in pain and trying to gauge the level of damage done. It didn't seem to be a deep gash—only a small trickle of blood dripped down her forehead, and April thanked the snow for at least being useful for that. She imagined that the wound would have been worse if it had happened during her springtime fantasy, with no snow to cushion her blow. She forgot temporarily about the truck and jumped when a small and timid voice spoke above her. She shielded her eyes from the bright light as best she could and shuffled back toward the curb.

"Ar-are you alright?"

A frail-looking man stood above her, looking down into her eyes. He appeared to be young, maybe around her age, and was remarkably thin. His skin was tight around the bones of his face, and his eyes seemed to sink into his skull. He wasn't wearing a coat, and his long-sleeved white shirt hung from his thin frame. He extended one hand to help her up, and the other hand held onto a belt loop of his pants, trying to keep them from falling into the snow. April hesitated, looking from the man's skeletal fingers to his sunken eyes. They were a warm, green color and unlike anything she had ever seen before. He was much shorter than most men she knew and grabbing his hand for support was closer than she expected. As she pulled down on his hand to stabilize herself, she felt him falter under her weight. The muscles of his arm shook as he leaned back for more leverage in raising her to her feet, still never letting go of his pants.

Standing next to the thin man, April's balance swayed as the world tilted. He kept a steadying hand on her back as she brushed snow from her now-wet jeans. His frame blocked some of the light from the truck, and she could look him in the eyes now. His face darkened with disgust and sadness, and alarm bells sounded in April's mind. Foreboding dread filled her veins.

"I-I-I'm sorry," he stuttered, his quiet voice floating away with the storm's wind and snow.

April didn't have time to process his apology before someone forced something over her head from behind and tied it tightly around her neck. It cut into her skin, and she yelped out of pain. Her jeans grew warm with the spread of her urine. The tie around her neck tightened, and breathing grew more difficult. Strong hands wrapped around her waist, and the fingers of those hands pressed into her skin. She could feel herself bruising under the fingers like an old pear. Vision obscured, April's hands flew to her neck, and she tried to pull at the tie, but her freezing fingers were stiff and numb. It was no use. She couldn't see who the hands on her waist belonged to. The hands pulled April back into a robust and firm body. The person held her close and dragged her. Her boots skidded across the icy ground as she attempted to find solid footing.

Trying to scream, April opened her mouth, but only vomit came out. The vomit caught in the sack and spread slickly across April's neck, small dribbles escaping from the sack and running down her back. Her stomach lurched again at the smell. She kicked and flailed as the person clutching her moved forward. A sudden rush of warm air surrounded her, and she knew it was from the truck. She thrashed harder at the thought of being taken away, a panicked desperation filling her entire body. April pulled her legs into her stomach, rearing and striking back, hitting the body with all her might. She heard the person let out a gruff grunt of pain as the pressure of the fingertips on her waist ceased altogether, and April tumbled to the ground, slamming her knee on the pavement and landing with a thud.

Disoriented, terrified, and still feeling sick, she tried to catch her balance and run but slipped again in the snow. She collapsed onto the road. She tried to scream, desperate for help, but couldn't summon enough air for more than a strangled, quiet squeak. Her breath came hot and heavy and in impossibly short bursts against the burlap sack, and April grew dizzier by the second. She felt like she could drown in the hot, trapped air surrounding her face. Part of April shut down and grew cold, while the other part sizzled like hot coals in a fire. Her energy waned, and she could not give any more. She heard another pained grunt close to her ear as the forceful fingers grabbed her once more. April was thin, and the fingers wrapped each of her dainty upper arms entirely.

"Grab her damn legs," the person with the strong hands hissed. This voice sounded much more masculine than the man who helped her to her feet.

"I-I-I'm trying!" exclaimed the thin man from before, sounding exasperated and upset.

The contrast between the two voices startled April, only contributing to her fear. She felt a weaker pair of hands grab each ankle, and she fought back as hard as she could. Horror settled into her stomach as she realized the strangled gasping sound came from her. The two sets of hands, the strong ones around her arms and the weak ones around her ankles, lifted her off the ground. She filled with rage as she discovered that her weak flails couldn't even break the grip of the thin man.

Someone, please, help me!

April saw stars blinking before her eyes as the two men tossed her body into what she could only assume was the black truck. The blinking grew brighter as she landed in the warmth, head smacking against something firm. A small part of her appreciated the heat, but she knew the cost of that warmth might be her life. It hardly seemed worth the price. Before her shaky grip on consciousness loosened and the darkness consumed April, she heard the sinister laugh of a deranged man.

Chapter Two

*H*eather sat at her desk, drumming her pen as she stared off into space, avoiding the paperwork in front of her. Her mind floated tiredly in a sea of nothingness. She'd worked overtime since one of the other detectives went on maternity leave, and was burning out fast. Though the Sheriff's station didn't get much activity, the paperwork seemed endless. Sheriff Steinman had refused to convert to electronic files, and the massive piles of paperwork cramped her hand. Her eyes strained to stay open as she drummed her pen. The sun had risen high in the sky, and she still hadn't slept yet. Heather's mind enjoyed the little mental check-out and her partner snatched the pen from her hand. Startled, she looked up.

"If you don't stop doing that, I will literally kill you," Nathan said as he winked and smiled down at her. He stood beside her desk, arms crossed, and shook his head at her. He set the pen down on the desk in front of her. "Can I trust you with this?"

"You mean you don't like my pen music?" Heather said, laughing and feigning emotional upset. She dramatically draped her hand over her forehead as she leaned back in her chair.

"Hate to break it to you," he said, leaning in close, elbows on her desk, "but you better not quit your day job, partner."

Nathan held her gaze, and his brown eyes sparkled in the bright light of the station's squad room. His floppy, brown hair fell in his face, and Heather could smell his musky deodorant. From the moment she met her partner, she had found him attractive; objectively speaking, he was a handsome man. His masculine but soft features gave him an aura of safety. His sensitive eyes stared right into Heather's soul anytime she met them. He was also tall and muscular, which didn't hurt. The front desk attendants treated Nathan better than the other employees; he received more than one Secret Santa gift every Christmas, which was not how the game worked. The worst part was that Nathan appeared blissfully unaware of his attractiveness and how he could use that to his advantage. In his naïveté, he genuinely believed the world to be a kind and happy place.

Heather found this ironic, given that they worked in the dark world of policing, the only police station in Tree Park. Though sometimes his fluffy worldview frustrated her, Heather relied on it. He had been assigned as Heather's first partner when she started working for the sheriff's office, but she had not been his. He had worked for a police precinct out of town for three years before moving to Tree Park and had some experience under his belt. Both new to this station, Nathan and Heather had gotten assigned to each other, much to his dismay. Heather overheard him complaining to their sheriff that he didn't want to 'work with the rookie,' and Heather used her hurt feelings to drive her to prove him wrong.

It didn't take long for Nathan to notice Heather's intelligence and how her attention to detail complimented his way of investigating. Small town work rarely had significant cases, and most of their job involved paperwork and interacting with the locals. Heather tended to focus on the smaller details of the work, like writing the reports and reviewing video footage, while Nathan tended to be the public face of the partnership. Heather solved puzzles with ease, paying close attention to the details, while Nathan's charismatic air made him better at sweet talking people. Nathan possessed a captivating charm, and it awed Heather how he could easily elicit information from people. On the other hand, Nathan admired how Heather never missed a detail, no matter how small. They made the perfect pair.

While their partnership worked out great, it was also a shame. Heather could have dated Nathan, maybe even married him. They had the same sense of humor, enjoyed the same hobbies, and were both cat people. Now and again, the idea of romance crossed her mind, but it couldn't work without significant trouble at work, and it hardly seemed worth it. Besides, Heather liked being alone. She hadn't dated anyone seriously since college, and she valued the independence she had built. She lived nearby in a studio apartment above a bookshop decorated precisely to her taste. The thought of integrating someone into or leaving that world entirely felt like a big headache.

Despite Nathan's optimistic worldview bleeding into Heather's from time to time, she couldn't see past the world's darkness. She genuinely believed it was better to stay alone than take a chance on love and have her heart broken. She'd suffered enough heartbreak in her life and couldn't risk more. Some days, she could barely cope, and after three years of working together, she was used to pushing Nathan out of her heart.

Nathan lifted himself from his leaning position on Heather's desk and walked to his own, sitting down and returning to his paperwork. Heather picked up her pen, planning to resume her paperwork as well, but a large, framed photograph on the wall caught her eye.

"Missing him today?" Nathan asked, and Heather blushed at being caught staring at her father.

"No more than usual," she said and cleared her throat, bending her face forward to allow her hair to hide her blush.

Heather saw this picture daily, but that never stopped the pain of her past from bleeding into her present. In the portrait, her father stood dressed in full regalia as sheriff. She had such fond memories of her sister, Autumn, and herself running through the station playing hide and seek under the detectives' desks. Heather loved growing up here but never imagined she would work here herself, especially not without her father.

"It's okay to miss him," Nathan said.

Heather nodded. "I think it's harder this time of year. You know, the holidays and whatnot—makes me feel his absence even more. Especially with Autumn gone, too."

"I feel that. You've been through a lot," Nathan said with a sympathetic nod.

Heather met his eyes, and concern danced between them. She appreciated his regard for her but needed to stop this. He couldn't care too much—she had so much to lose.

"I'm grateful that he died a hero," she said, though she could see Nathan didn't believe her words. He knew her better than that, knew that she would do anything to have him back.

Heather's father had been Sheriff of Tree Park for almost her entire life before he died. On the day of his death, he was called to a bank robbery in a nearby town that needed additional resources. The situation had gotten out of hand by the time Sheriff Byrd arrived, and it wasn't possible for them to regain control. Multiple officers were shot, and Sheriff Byrd died saving a woman and her son. The bullet had traveled through his stomach and lodged into his spine, severing his spinal cord and ending his life.

Sheriff Byrd's death shattered her family. Heather's mother and father had married at sixteen years old, and her mother couldn't cope. She could barely remember a life without her beloved James, and she never fully recovered, though she tried to pretend for the sake of her daughters. Autumn had seemed fine at first, much as Heather had, but then took a turn down a dark and drug-fueled path that led to her own untimely death. Heather didn't allow herself to think about it often.

Nathan started to speak, presumably to challenge Heather's word, but stopped when the phone on his desk rang.

"Saved by the bell."

Heather turned her gaze back to the photograph of her father, smiling to herself and absentmindedly listening to Nathan's phone call. Memories of her time running through this precinct as a child flooded her mind and Nathan hung up, clearing his throat. She turned her attention back to her partner and sat up straighter. Something about his cough felt serious.

"That was an... interesting call." She leaned forward with anticipation. "Remember how we got that tip about an old, black truck being in the neighborhood right before Bethany Tyler went missing?"

"Yeah?" Heather responded, anxiety kicking up a notch.

"That was a man with a really bad stutter, saying that he saw a black truck leaving a farm just outside of town. He said that it matched the description of the black truck he had seen on TV back when Bethany Tyler went missing."

"And he remembered the description of the truck almost a year later?" Heather said, suspicious.

"Said he did. He gave me an address for the farm, but when I tried to ask for his information, he hung up."

"Well, people don't want to get their names involved in big cases like this," Heather offered, trying to stay open. "Let's check it out."

"Sure thing, partner!" Nathan grabbed his coat from the back of his desk chair.

A renewed sense of energy bounced between them at the idea that a year-old cold case could come alive again. The pair walked to their patrol car, and Heather stifled a yawn. She had worked many long shifts in her time as a police officer, but this quickly approached the longest shift of her life.

"After this, I'm taking you home," Nathan said firmly. "You're pushing yourself too hard."

"Okay, Dad," she joked, punching him on the arm.

Nathan gave her a side-eyed look, got into the driver's seat of the car, and started typing the address into his GPS.

"It's a far drive, so buckle up," he continued, still sounding like a responsible father.

Heather glanced at the GPS and saw that the drive was about forty minutes. She rubbed her hands together, fingers frigid from the short, cold walk to the car. The blizzard the night before had left the air stinging cold and moist.

"Let's review the facts on the way. It's been a while," she said. They hadn't had any breaks in the case in over half a year.

"Go for it," Nathan replied.

"Bethany Tyler, 21-year-old female college student, went missing from Tree Park. She attended college an hour outside of town but was here visiting a local coffee shop, The Hungry Bean."

The Hungry Bean was Tree Park's biggest source of tourist income. It boasted "America's best coffee" and had been featured on a nationwide cooking channel show. The broadcast caused a short boost in tourism before the crowds died out, and Tree Park was forgotten, swallowed by the national forest once more. Some nearby college students still swore by it and made the trek to their small, woodsy town for a taste. Bethany had joined a group of her friends on such a journey almost a year ago to the day.

"She had coffee with her friends but had taken a separate car to leave early to video chat with her boyfriend, who lived out of state. The last her friends saw of her, Bethany was walking down the street toward where she had parked two blocks away," Nathan continued, picking up where Heather had left off.

"When her friends decided to head back about an hour later, they noticed Bethany's car was still parked down the block. After calling her multiple times without success, they contacted her parents on social media, who traveled here and reported their daughter missing," Heather concluded.

Heather and Nathan had spent the past year digging into Bethany's life and the night she disappeared but came up empty. Bethany had been a good student and a dutiful daughter; no one wanted to harm her. Bethany's family, her parents and three younger sisters, never heard from her again after that day. Bethany's boyfriend had proof that he was in his home state at the time of the disappearance, and while the public always assumed he was involved, it could never be proven. Bethany's purse and phone were never found, either.

The only point of note in the case was that someone had reported an old-fashioned, black truck in the area the night of her disappearance that they hadn't seen in the neighborhood before. The truck had been driving with its headlights off, creating suspicion. The witness didn't remember important details such as make and model or license plate number but hearing about a suspicious black truck was better than nothing.

"Now all that's left is to see how things go with this potential black truck," Nathan said. Heather stared out the window, lost in the trees rushing past the window. "What is it?"

"I still think they're connected," Heather whispered.

"Bethany and your sister?" This was a conversation they had had many times before, and Heather never liked the outcome.

"Yeah," Heather confirmed. "They both went missing in January, a year apart. Autumn vanished into thin air just like Bethany. It can't be a coincidence!"

"But Bethany was never found, and Autumn was. If the same person had taken them both, why would they dump Autumn's body so publicly and not Bethany's?" Nathan asked, sounding hesitant and annoyed.

Heather took a sharp breath in. Nathan didn't sugarcoat the topic. The first few times this came up, he had been very careful and talked with kid-gloves on, but now he got right to the point. A local jogger discovered Autumn's body on the outskirts of Tree Park in an alley behind the tallest building in town, the bowling alley. The coroner's report put her time of death at a few hours before the jogger came along. The toxicology report showed high levels of many different drugs, and the bones in her legs and her ribs were shattered. Cause of death was a contusion to the head that caused a fatal brain bleed. Given the high amount of substances and the injuries to her body, the coroner ruled her death a suicide, theorizing that Autumn had thrown herself from the roof of the bowling alley to take her own life.

"I don't know!" Heather shouted in frustration, appalled at her rising voice. "What I do know is that she wouldn't have roofied herself and the tox screen clearly showed high levels of Rohypnol. How do you explain that?"

"Heather," Nathan said, "she was on so many drugs, it's entirely possible that she was roofied on top of her voluntary use. Besides, the coroner's report said that it was unlikely that the fall was a push based on her injuries."

"I know that, but her body was also covered in defensive wounds. She could have put up a fight and fallen from the roof instead of throwing herself."

"You said it yourself, Heather—she was in an abusive relationship. The coroner stated that her defensive wounds were in various states of healing, so the idea of a fight before her death seems unlikely."

"And you can't discount the fact that Autumn and Bethany looked so similar. Same body type, same dark hair and eyes." Heather couldn't hear Nathan's justifications anymore. "Why are you doing this?"

"I'm trying to help you see the truth. You don't know what it's like to watch you torture yourself with trying to solve a solved case. I don't want that for you," he said, desperation in his voice.

It really was a no-win situation.

"Yeah, well, I don't need you to be looking out for me," she grumbled, staring out the window.

"Heather, you know I care—"

"Let's focus on Bethany, okay?" Heather could feel him wince beside her. *Was that too harsh?*

"Got it," he said quietly, and the rest of the drive passed in silence that remained even when they arrived at their destination.

The farm was relatively small, considering some of the massive farming corporations in the area. The drive into the property was long and straight, leading to a small, quaint two-story farmhouse. At the front, wooden pegs stuck out from the ground, and Heather wondered if it once held a sign with the farm's name. The anonymity made goosebumps break out across her skin. The house looked to be about three bedrooms, painted a beautiful pearl color that cracked with age. The window shutters shined a vibrant blue that popped against the surrounding white. It appeared to be an average and quiet home, and Heather wondered about the people who lived there.

To the right of the house stood a small, red barn with a large, garage-style door pulled closed. Heather saw no sign of farm animals and wondered if any horses lived in the barn. Behind the barn lay an enormous silo that Heather marveled at; she had never seen one up close, and it was much bigger than she could have imagined. Behind the house spread an endless sea of cropland, though snow covered it now instead of greenery.

As Nathan parked the car, Heather glanced to her left out his window at a small graveyard. She got out of the car and walked toward it. The snow covered the ground in a thin layer, and several small gravestones poked through the icy white. The writing on the stones lay weathered and faded, and Heather couldn't make out any legible words or names.

"Probably a family graveyard," Nathan noted. "Farmers tend to keep land in the family for generations."

Nathan seemed interested, but Heather got the chills.

"Let's go," she said, shivering the chills away and walking toward the quaint house.

The partners mounted the steps and knocked on the door, waiting patiently. An older woman and a younger man, perhaps her son, answered and stood stiff beside each other in the doorway, blocking the view into the rest of the house. The woman wore a bizarrely old-fashioned dress, and the man donned farmer's clothing. Heather could see the family resemblance through their dark green eyes. A flash of recognition passed through the man's eyes, but Heather didn't find this unusual. Her father's death and sister's disappearance cast a spotlight on her that she couldn't seem to escape, and she was used to unfamiliar people knowing exactly who she was.

Nathan took the lead and introduced himself. Upon receiving no return introductions and only blank stares, Nathan asked directly about the black truck. The woman and man glanced at each other before answering. Heather tried to read the message behind their glance but couldn't. The woman spoke.

"We do not own a black truck, have never owned a black truck, and have not seen a black truck anywhere near here." Her voice lilted with a southern accent, and her tone was curt.

The woman and man rushed the detectives off their porch, hurrying to shut the door behind them. Bizarre as the interaction felt, it was a dead end.

"Should we try to get a warrant?" Nathan mused as they walked back to their car.

Heather thought for a moment before answering. "I don't think one would stick," she said. "The truck was seen in the area but was never conclusively linked to Bethany's disappearance. Probably a prank call about the farm, honestly."

As the partners got back in the car, Heather stared at the farmhouse. Something inside of her screamed that this place had significance, but she didn't have the evidence to prove it. As she settled into her seat, Heather silently willed her sister to give her a sign, something to show her she was on the right track. If nothing else, Heather felt one step closer to answers.

Chapter Three

Claire awoke to the sound of her phone ringing from somewhere in the apartment. The vibrations echoed through the peaceful morning silence, annoying her. She groaned, yanking the comforter over her head, exposing her toes to the chilly morning air. The ringing continued as Claire pulled her legs up to her chest, curling under her comforter to avoid the cold. The ringing seemed never ending and Claire pulled herself to a sitting position. Rubbing her makeup-smeared eyes, she groaned. A burst pipe at work last night meant she'd gotten home later than usual and had only slept for less than an hour. She felt like a zombie, barely able to keep her eyes open, even while sitting up. By the time she swung her legs over the side of her bed to stand up, the ringing had stopped.

Sighing in relief at the sudden quiet, Claire flopped back down and curled herself into a ball, nuzzling her face into her warm pillow. She would need more rest to make it through her shift at the bar tonight. She hated working after a night of closing, but it was sick season, and people had called out left and right. Claire didn't mind the overtime pay, either. She began to drift off to sleep as she thought about work, and a pleasant, warm sensation spread throughout her body. She lingered in that blissful place between consciousness and sleep when her phone rang again.

"Shut up!" she yelled, throwing her comforter off her bed and stomping to the floor.

Claire stormed out of her bedroom to follow the sound of the chimes and found her phone lying on the coffee table in the living room down the hall. The closing shift had been brutal; almost no one wanted to leave at closing, and Claire couldn't even start her duties until over an hour after closing. She had stumbled in the door the night before, exhausted to the core of her bones, and hadn't even bothered to check her phone notifications. She'd tossed her phone and keys onto the coffee table and grabbed a bottle of water from the kitchen, chugging it on the way to bed, falling asleep as soon as her head hit the pillow.

Claire grabbed her phone and realized something felt off. Why hadn't April answered her phone or come to give it to her? Claire peeked into the kitchen but found it empty with no signs of breakfast. She then glanced down the hall toward April's bedroom. The door was closed. April hardly ever closed her bedroom door, especially not when home or sleeping. She often said that closing the door created a weird draft in her room, but if she left it open, the air could flow freely through. But why would she go out so early in the morning after a snowstorm? Was something wrong?

"How strange," Claire said to herself as she walked down the hall, not even bothering to check to see who was calling. As she reached April's bedroom door, the ringing stopped again.

"April, you okay?" Claire said through the door with a soft rap of her knuckles. "Are you sick?"

Silence.

"April? I'm coming in..." Panic rose in her chest.

Slowly, Claire turned the knob and pushed the door open. It creaked as it swung, and goosebumps broke out on her arms. Her obsession with true crime satisfied a deep need within her to explore the traumas of humanity, but it made her a bit jumpy at times, too. Claire's mind pictured the worst—

April, lying on the floor having choked to death on a midnight snack; April, murdered on her bed, throat slashed; April, hanging from the ceiling fan above her bed. Claire breathed a sigh of relief when the door opened and she found an empty room. In her exhausted and sleepy state, she had forgotten that April planned to meet her mother that morning at the bakery. The relief only lasted a moment before her phone rang for a third time, chimes breaking the silence once more.

Startled, Claire shrieked and dropped her phone, laughing at herself. Picking it up, she saw April's mother's name on the screen. The panic spread from her chest to her stomach. April's mother *never* called her.

Mrs. Dell cut right to the chase. "Is April with you?"

Claire noted a tone of anxiety in Mrs. Dell's voice, and she didn't like it one bit.

"She isn't with you?" Claire asked, perplexed. "She's not here, and I figured she had already left to meet you."

Claire heard Mrs. Dell take in a sharp breath. "She's late, and she never texted me when she got home. She promised she would text me when she got in and she never did. What if something happened to her?"

Claire's blood went cold as she wondered if something happened to April. Her mind swirled with intrusive images again—April dead and frozen in the snow; April kidnapped by a cult; April shot to death in the street. She took a deep breath and sent those thoughts far out of her mind.

"Let's stay calm and see if we can find her. Let me check my phone and see if I have any messages from her." Claire put the call on speaker to look at her phone.

Mrs. Dell had called twice, and Claire felt a pang of guilt at lingering in bed so long. She also had a missed call from April at midnight and a few texts from her that read:

Call me if you get this!
Boy, is it cold outside 🎲
Remind me never to walk home in the snow again...

Claire groaned when she saw the call and messages; she had told April over and over to call the bar if she ever needed anything, but April never did. She opted for sending a text and waiting several hours rather than bothering Claire at work. April felt that calling someone at work was something her mother would do, and she didn't want to be like that with Claire. She didn't want Claire to feel that she was needy or intrusive, but Claire desperately wished she had called the bar.

"Well?" Mrs. Dell barked with impatience.

"She called around midnight and sent some messages, but they were about her walk home. Nothing from this morning. Has Mr. Dell heard from her today?"

"No, he said I was being overdramatic and that our adult daughter doesn't need to check in every time she goes out and comes home, but I told him this would happen! I knew I should have stayed on the phone with her. What if she was taken like that Bethany girl last year?"

"Police have never been able to confirm that she was kidnapped, and she had a boyfriend in another state, so she could have gone to see him. The prime suspect is often the spouse or partner, so it's more likely that she left the state with him, and he killed her, though that could never be confirmed, either," Claire rambled, getting lost in the facts of Bethany's disappearance in her mind. Somehow, it made her feel better about April that she knew so many details of Bethany's case.

April found it depressing when Bethany went missing, and Claire supposed a part of her had too, though a bigger part of her had been fascinated. Morbid thoughts of what had happened to Bethany took over, and Claire spent months in an internet-fueled rabbit hole trying to glean information about the case. Claire's obsession with these cases spooked April, but for Claire, it gave her a sense of purpose to a purposeless life. Maybe one day, she would actually make a break in one of these cases. She used these cases to try to understand why people hurt each other. Maybe understanding these cases would provide answers to her own traumatic childhood.

"Claire, seriously, have you no manners?" Mrs. Dell said, sounding disgusted.

April's mother's attitude toward Claire in the past made it very clear that she didn't like her, so this response didn't surprise Claire. April and she had met after being randomly paired as roommates during their freshman year of college. The two decided to live together off campus after Claire dropped out during their sophomore year. Claire didn't do well in school, and she didn't enjoy learning the same way that April did. Given her morose hobby, she thought studying forensics could be the right path, but she found the science behind it all too complicated. If only Claire could have majored in true crime, then maybe college would have worked out for her.

April had chosen to continue with her education, never once losing sight of her career goals. Claire, however, had gotten a job working at a bar and found solace in an unexpected place. The busy bar environment became a haven for her, helping to drown out her negative thoughts about herself and the world. She acted as somewhat of a therapist at the bar and loved listening to the woes that only drunk people would be so open as to share. Between serial killers and serial drinkers, Claire found her purpose.

Above all else, April's parents' primary disapproval dealt with her sexuality. While Claire never explicitly expressed her sexual identity to April's parents, they discovered it. April's parents had once visited while Claire prepared for a date with a woman, and she remembered the look of stunned shock and disgust on their faces when her date arrived. Claire learned very quickly after moving that exploring her sexuality in Tree Park wouldn't be accepted by the residents.

"I'll check the driveway for her car," Claire continued, ignoring Mrs. Dell's admonishments. "She walked home from the Endersons', but if her car is gone now, then maybe she went to the store or something on the way to meet you."

Mrs. Dell didn't respond, but Claire could hear her exhale a sharp breath. She walked from April's bedroom to the front door and peeked out of the window next to it, stomach dropping at the sight of April's car covered in snow. It hadn't moved all night.

"Well?" Mrs. Dell asked, voice shifting from angry frustration to fear.

"It's here..." Claire trailed off, unsure of what else to say.

Mrs. Dell made a strangled sound, as if someone punched her in the stomach. "I'll call the Endersons and see if she went back to their house. Maybe the storm was too bad to walk through, and she turned around after I spoke with her. I'll call some of Mr. Dell's and my friends as well," Mrs. Dell said with determination. "I'll call you back after, Claire."

"Good idea. I'll call our friends and see if anyone's heard from her, too."

Mrs. Dell hung up without a goodbye, and Claire clutched her phone to her chest for a moment before getting to work. She called everyone in her phone who knew April. Not a single person had any information, if they answered at all. Claire shook with adrenaline at the possibilities of what happened to her best friend. She made her way to the living room couch, dragging her feet, and sunk into the deep cushions.

As the effects of this potential devastation set in, Claire's heart reached out to the Dells. She could only imagine how awful it must be for them. She wondered how her own mother and father would have reacted if someone called them and said their daughter hadn't come home. She couldn't even remember the last time she'd seen her father—not since high school, so obviously, he wouldn't care much. She tried to call her mother somewhat regularly, but it wasn't important to her to prioritize someone who never made time for her. She didn't know what drove her to do it, but before she knew it, Claire had clicked on her mother's contact in her phone.

"Claire, darling! I was just raving to my friends about you!"

"Mom," she said, voice shaking and words coming out like vomit, "April didn't come home last night, and we can't find her. I'm starting to worry, and I don't know what to do."

Laughter and a loud clattering sound boomed from the background.

"What was that, dear? It's quite loud in here!"

"Can you go outside or something?" Claire asked, feeling vulnerable.

"Call me later, sweetheart. You know how it is when I'm out with the girls! Ta-ta, my love!" With that, Claire's phone beeped—the call had ended.

Why do I do this to myself?

Claire wished she felt anything other than numb to her mother, but nothing else existed between them. Not anger or love. Nothing at all. Growing up, her mother worked two jobs to keep a roof over their heads, which meant working all day and all night, then crashing hard on her days off. While she now understood how hard her mother worked, it had driven an irreparable emotional wedge between them. Claire spent a lot of time alone, and she grew close to the woman in the trailer next to hers, Mrs. Bushy. She had taught Claire how to do her make-up, use tampons, and cook meals, and she would be forever grateful for that. When Mrs. Bushy passed away, she left her trailer to Claire, who had just turned eighteen. She sold it for college tuition and a car. Too bad she wasted the school money, and Claire turned out to be the drop-out that her mother knew she would be. At least she didn't have a car payment, though.

Anger flared up in Claire's chest as she reprimanded herself for calling her mother. She knew vulnerability was dangerous. Why did she do this to herself when the outcome was always the same? Why did she so desperately seek the love and emotional support that her mother clearly couldn't give? Caught in a moment of self-pity, Claire's heart jumped when her phone buzzed again—Mrs. Dell calling back. Pushing down her feelings of self-loathing, Claire answered. Maybe Mrs. Dell had found April safe at the Endersons' house.

"Anything?" Mrs. Dell shouted as soon as Claire answered.

"Nothing," Claire said dejectedly, and she didn't even need to ask Mrs. Dell about her progress. The sobs that echoed through the receiver answered her question.

Claire waited for Mrs. Dell to catch her breath, unsure of what to say and fearful she might make things worse. She bit back her own tears, feeling frantic and frazzled at hearing Mrs. Dell's despair.

"Mr. Dell is on his way to the bake shop now," Mrs. Dell said through hiccups. "I can't drive!"

"I'll go out and search for her along the walk to the Endersons' house. Maybe she stopped at the coffee shop or diner or something and lost track of time or fell asleep in a booth or something," Claire rambled.

"Good idea." Mrs. Dell loudly blew her nose. "We'll drive the route and look for any signs of her."

"Let's meet at the coffee shop and re-group there."

They said their goodbyes, and Claire walked back to her bedroom, setting her phone down on her dresser so she could get dressed. As she threw her short, blonde hair into as much of a bun as it would hold, she thought about Mrs. Dell. She hadn't liked Claire moving in with April. Claire wasn't too keen on it either, but she couldn't afford to live on her own. She worried about finding work in this small town and how people might treat her if she went out on dates, but following April to Tree Park made the most financial sense. Almost nothing remained from her inheritance from Mrs. Bushy and her bar salary couldn't support living alone. Claire was reluctant though, despite the financial security, as moving closer to April's parents would mean more interactions with them and possibly more negativity.

She pulled a hoodie over her pajama top, grabbed her snow boots out of the closet, and tucked her pajama pants into them. In the kitchen, she wrote April a note from one of the many notepads sitting on the counter. She taped the note on April's bedroom door and closed it, ensuring that her message would be the first thing April saw when she got home.

"When she gets home," Claire said to herself and shivered.

Claire supposed it might be "if she gets home" now.

Claire walked down the hall and grabbed her keys from the coffee table. With her hand on the doorknob, Claire took one last look back at the empty house. The bright sun reflected off the snow outside and shone through the windows in brilliant rays. Despite the cheery effect, she couldn't help but feel an unbearable emptiness. How much she wished April was sitting on the couch, reading an autobiography about Van Gogh, and mindlessly popping chips into her mouth. She could picture April glancing up from her book and smiling at her, shifting all focus from her favorite artist to her favorite friend. Claire blinked, and April's image vanished, filling her with the loneliness and despair she was trying so hard to push down. She closed her eyes, took a deep breath, and bravely turned the doorknob, opening the door to April's truth.

Chapter Four

The world came in flashes. A flash of bright light before her eyes, a flash of pure darkness bumping underneath her body, a flash of strong hands grabbing her arms. April couldn't make sense of it, no matter how hard she tried. Her head throbbed and ached with such intensity that she thought she had died and gone to hell. The flashes seemed to last for endless hours. April begged for release from her agony.

Maybe this is my new reality, doomed to live in these daunting and terrifying flashes for the rest of eternity. What if it is?

When she woke, confusion enveloped her. Covered in sweat, every part of her body ached. Her head throbbed, her back felt too stiff to straighten, a horrible smell surrounded her, and her tongue scratched around her dry mouth. What was this, some kind of massive hangover? She had never experienced anything like this. She reached out, trying to turn on her bedside lamp, and her arm caught on something.

"Ugh," she muttered, trying to bring her other hand to her caught one, but it caught too.

"What in the..." She opened her eyes to a dark and unfamiliar space, and she realized her back hurt so badly because she leaned against a wall.

Blinded by the darkness, April wondered where she could be. Instinct took over, and she tried to stand but smacked her head on something hard above her. Grunting in pain and surprise, she collapsed to the ground and lost consciousness once more.

She could have been out for a second or a day—April had no way of knowing. This time when she woke, she remembered her arms being caught and the low ceiling above her head but nothing about how she came to this strange space. Was this some kind of prank? She tried to take a deep breath, but her dry throat seized, and a coughing fit wracked her body. She looked for water as she choked and realized for the first time that she sat enclosed in a small, dark, box-like room.

Her mind and body froze as the reality of her situation sank in; she was being held captive and her hands were bound to the wall behind her. How did she get here? Panic took over as she thrashed and shrieked, desperate to escape. The chains attached to her arms clanked and rattled as her screams filled the surrounding space. Exhausting herself, the space grew smaller, walls seeming to collapse in on her. Her heavy breathing heated up her box and gave her the sense that the air had thinned. She shook all over and slid to the floor, wrists catching on the chains behind her.

The memory of the night before hit April like an old-fashioned black truck and she began to rock back and forth. "No, no, no, no, no…"

The flashes returned, but this time as memories. A flash of the phone call with her mother, promising to text her when she got home. A flash of snow falling off the roof behind her with a thud. A flash of her vomit being caught in the sack over her head. Her mind moved sickeningly fast, and April squeezed her eyes shut, desperate to wake up from this nightmare.

The flashes jolted her into action. April's hands flew to her sides, clawing for her purse where she had tucked her phone after saying goodbye to her mother. Devastation filled her limbs with lead as she realized it was gone.

"Damn it!" April shouted, voice hoarse, as she smacked her hands against the ground.

Along with the missing purse, her coat and boots were gone too, leaving her in a long-sleeved black shirt caked with vomit around the neck, soiled jeans, and wet socks. April could feel dried blood cracking on the skin of her head and remembered the blood on her fingers. She felt dizzy and sick as she remembered smacking her head on the concrete and struggling to breathe in the back of the black truck. She relived it in her mind, yet it also felt like a distant dream. She screamed as loud as she could, until her throat went raw, and her voice refused to continue. The screams died out and she waited, listening to her surroundings with as much focus as she could manage.

Silence.

Okay, April, breathe.

She took long and deep breaths, but it didn't work. The thick and moist air clogged her lungs. This was bad. She could die. People didn't steal women in the middle of the night and chain them up in a box just to let them go. People like this intended on keeping their victims until their very last breath, like the people in Claire's true crime shows.

Unable to calm herself, April tried to take a dizzy stock of her surroundings. The space was tiny; she had hit her head on the shallow ceiling. The walls lay close together, and she doubted she could have stretched her whole body out. The space was dark but not enough that she couldn't see. April wondered how she hadn't noticed the light peeking in under what might have been a door. She fixated on the dim source of light, and she anxiously ran her shaking fingers along the bottom. Her fingers couldn't fit under the narrow opening, preventing her from gaining grip. She pushed against the door and felt it give slightly before catching on some sort of lock. April lifted her feet, placed them a few inches up, and kicked as hard as possible. The door gave a bit but continued to catch on the lock with each kick. The solid wood wouldn't budge.

Her panic took over again as she kicked the door with all her might, over and over, until her exhausted legs gave out. April cried in big, heavy sobs, her breath coming so fast that she felt like she couldn't get any at all. She slumped against the wall, resigned.

As she lay slumped and desperate, a loud sound from outside her space startled April. Her heart and breath stopped. Fear pricked every cell of her body, and she bit down on her lip to stop herself from screaming. Desperation and self-preservation took over, and she stayed as quiet as a dead mouse, breath shallow and shaky.

The sound continued, a low snuffling followed by several loud bangs, and her imagination went wild with the sinister possibilities behind it. It took her racing and panicked brain far too long to realize that the sound came from an animal. She hadn't noticed before, but the air had the distinct smell of manure.

A horse?

Her stomach dropped as the realization hit her—she was in a barn. There were a few horse farms on the outskirts of Tree Park, but as she listened more intently, the sound of the horse was the only one she could hear. Tree Park may be tiny, but it still had the distinct sounds of a small town, none of which April could hear now.

She was far from home.

April let out a frustrated shout. The solid door wouldn't open from the inside, and April couldn't waste any more energy trying. She leaned against the wall again, nausea floating through her stomach. She felt like she couldn't breathe, both from the exertion of attacking the door and the hot air of the small space confining her. Her mind raced, thoughts jumping at light speed as she closed her eyes, and she floated into a trance-like state.

April first thought of her parents, wondering if she would ever see them again. She imagined her mother's warm embrace surrounding her and her father bravely holding her hand. She thought about the last time she saw them—New Year's Eve, last weekend. She spent the evening baking cookies with her mother, the special lavender ones, while her father cooked a massive feast for their small family. That night, she had contemplated whether it would be the last time she engaged in that tradition, craving the freedom of adulthood but worried about hurting her parents' feelings. Her stomach churned at the idea that she wouldn't see them again and she had taken that beautiful night for granted.

Next, her thoughts drifted to Claire. April didn't know the time, but from the light appearing under the door to her chamber, it seemed to be morning. Claire must have been so worried, arriving home from work and finding her not there. She wondered how Claire was handling her disappearance; was she scared? Did she call the police? A beat of hope skipped through her heart at that thought. She trusted Claire with her life. Claire protected her like her big sister. She always ensured that April took care of herself, sometimes at the expense of her own well-being.

April's mind then jumped to a memory from childhood. She must have been six years old, and she played in the snow, making snow angels beside her father. Hair pulled into pigtails, she found comfort in the image. Her father laughed as he tried to show April how to make a proper snow angel. She remembered the vivid look of pride in his eyes when she stood up and showed off her finished product. April's mother called from the porch with hot chocolate ready to warm their chilling bones. She ran to the porch and embraced her mother, and all was perfect in the world. Her father and mother kissed her on the top of the head, and she was safe; the snow was safe, the world was safe. Her body relaxed and a strange, tingling sensation coursed through her veins as her thoughts jumped from one thing to the next as she disconnected from the reality of her small casket.

A sudden clanking sound on the other side of her door startled April. As if blown open by a gust of wind, the door flew open, and the sun shone into her eyes, temporarily blinding her and flashing her back to the headlights from the night before. She attempted to shield her eyes from the light, but her chained hands couldn't reach them. Instead, she buried her face as far into her arm as possible to stop the stinging pain.

"Sit up," the strong man from her capture hissed down at her.

April snapped her head up at the sound of his voice. As her eyes adjusted to the bright winter sun, April finally saw the face of her second captor. He was shorter than she expected, not much taller than her, just like the first man, which caught her off guard. He wore a long-sleeved white shirt and tight jeans. He had a brown leather cowboy hat over his thick, blond hair and black gloves. He had tucked his jeans into well-worn brown cowboy boots. His stern face took on an unfriendly and flat expression. His mouth lay straight across his stubbled face, and his eyes were cold and disconnected, a glaring dark green. April shivered at the dangerous energy flowing from this man. She tried to scoot backward, terrified, but she could go no farther.

The thin man, who had helped April when she hit her head, stood just behind the deranged man. She could see him clearly now, unlike the night before when her head injury and the blinding headlights had blurred her vision. Still dressed in baggy clothing, he kept his eyes cast down. His palpable discomfort confused her. Why had he done this to her if he so clearly did not want to be doing this? He had apologized before the attack but allowed the attack to happen. His eyes flicked up to meet hers, and she could see him shaking as he shifted his gaze down. April looked back and forth between the two men. Their muscular builds and weights differed, but their family relation stood out. She could see it in the shape of their chins, the way they stood, and their shared dark green eyes.

"Brother Beau," the strong man finally spoke. "Key and cuffs."

"Yes, B-B-Brother Waylon," Brother Beau stuttered nervously, pulling a small set of handcuffs with a long chain attached out of the pocket of his overalls.

April's fear intensified at the strange names, and it maximized at the sight of the handcuffs. Brother Waylon crouched down and crawled into the chamber as April pressed herself as far into the wall as she could. Her breath quickened and the walls around her spun. She whimpered like a hurt dog as he gripped one of her wrists with his firm hand. She attempted to wriggle out of it, but it was useless—he was too strong.

"Don't do that," Brother Waylon said.

His deep and husky voice had a southern drawl, thick as molasses. Chills ran down her spine as she tried to meet his eye. When her eyes finally found his, she found nothing but deadness behind them, an ominous foreshadowing of what lay in store for her. April stopped fighting and allowed Brother Waylon to take her by the wrist.

"Much obliged," he said as he loosened her shackles and wrapped the new cuffs around her hands.

A thin chain bound April's wrists together, stringing one cuffed wrist to the other. She was free of the wall but bound to herself. Brother Waylon crawled backward from the chamber, and April scrambled into the opposite corner, attempting to hide, feeling bolder with him now gone. Brother Waylon chortled at her behavior. "Get 'er out."

Brother Beau's face crumbled in fear, and he shuddered. "B-b-but I'm not strong enough, Brother Waylon."

"Come on; it'll be good for you. You've got to work on gettin' stronger." Brother Waylon seemed to find it comical to put his brother in a difficult situation.

The two made eye contact, and Brother Waylon gave him a curt nod, communicating that Brother Beau did not have a choice. Brother Beau coughed and crouched down, crawling toward April. He grabbed her by the ankle and pulled with all his might, sliding her body forward some. She had hoped to push her weight into the floor to slow Brother Beau's progress, but her body refused to cooperate. She had been through too much, and she couldn't muster anything other than fear. Sweat dripped from Brother Beau's brow by the time he pulled April out of the chamber and into the barn. She lay on the floor, curled into a tiny ball, and cried once more.

"Stand," Brother Waylon commanded. "Against the wall and hands in front of ya." April tried her best to stand but she couldn't.

"I said stand," Brother Waylon hissed, taking a haunting step toward her, his dead eyes illuminating with fiery energy.

She shuffled to the wall with her hands and leaned against it to pull herself to a standing position, though she couldn't stand completely straight. She kept her side supported on the wall as she panted and shook, worried that she might collapse to the ground and what Brother Waylon might do to her as a result. She squeezed her eyes shut, willing her exertion to hold out and keep her body upright. The Brothers began talking in hushed whispers, turning their attention from April, not worried about her getting away.

Before being taken out, April felt desperate to escape from her small, dark chamber. Now, the world seemed impossibly huge, and she craved the solitude and darkness the hole had provided. April opened her eyes and checked out her surroundings. She was nervous and longed for escape. The barn they were in was relatively short. Four stalls, two on each side, lined the length of the barn, but only one had an occupant. The horse poked his head out of the top of the stall gate, looking at her with fascination. She noticed Brother Beau giving the horse a small smile, and she wondered if it was his horse. The nameplate on the stall read, "Faster than Wind," with the nickname "Windy" written below. Busy looking around and trying to stay upright, Brother Waylon startled her as he approached.

"Come on, Mother Loretta's waitin'." He gripped the chain between her handcuffs and pulled her forward with a rough tug.

April tripped at the force of his pull but caught herself and steadied her gait enough to stay on her feet. Brother Beau walked first, with Brother Waylon and April trailing behind, and April was grateful for Brother Beau's slow gait. As they walked into the icy wind and out of the barn, a small black cat followed by three tiny black kittens rushed past, crossing their path. She couldn't help but wonder how her luck could get any worse.

April saw nothing but the ground beneath her feet as she struggled to stay upright and limped behind the brothers. A quick glance at the landscape revealed a looming farmhouse and miles of snowy cropland. She was right in her first guess; they were deep in the country. As they made the long journey from the barn to the farmhouse, her socks soaked through with snow, numbing her toes and making her shiver. She rubbed her hands together for warmth, and something popped into her mind. She might not have a coat or boots, but she did still have her watch. Her thoughts picked up speed as she formed a desperate plan for rescue.

April bent into herself more drastically, trying to hide her hands as her chilly fingers worked at the clasp on her watchband. If someone happened across it in the snow, they would see the engraving on the back and could link it to her mother's bakery. Struggling, she finally got the watch free of her wrist and intentionally tripped into the snow. Her knees crashed to the ground with a thud, and Brother Waylon let go of her chain. Both brothers turned—Brother Waylon had a look of dooming anger, while Brother Beau looked downright terrified. April allowed her head to droop, and her blanket of long hair covered her hands as she pushed her watch down into the snow.

"Git up!" Brother Waylon shouted, grabbing the chain and yanking it aggressively.

April obeyed to the best of her ability, but the fall had taken a lot out of her already exhausted body. She limped more heavily and remained bent over, though this time not by choice. The grueling walk didn't stop a tiny bit of hope from kindling in the fires of her belly.

Chapter Five

Heather and Nathan pulled up to her apartment after their disappointing trip to the farm, feeling dejected. The conversation that had happened on the drive over and the depressing outcome of the black truck lead caused the two to remain quiet for the whole drive. They had searched for Bethany for so long that to have something happen now only to pan out to nothing frustrated them. If the case had continued to stay cold, that would have been one thing, but to have it slightly warm up and turn back to ice felt awful.

Nathan killed the engine, and the two sat in silence for a moment. Heather supposed she should say something, but she couldn't find the words. Grief mingled with disappointment and irritation, leaving her empty.

"I'll walk you up," Nathan said, but didn't move to get out of the car.

"You don't have to do that." She unbuckled her seatbelt.

Heather felt awkward over the conversation they had earlier. Nathan expressed wanting to protect her from pain and had started to say that he cared. To her, it felt too deep.

"I know I don't have to, but I'm going to," he said.

Nathan held the door to the small bookshop open for her. They both smiled as they passed the owner, Mrs. Reeves, on their way up the stairs to her studio apartment.

Heather loved living above the bookshop. While she wished she could read more, her job hardly permitted time to sleep, let alone read. The smell of books wafted up through the floorboards of her apartment and she loved the ambiance. Her father, though a busy sheriff, had been an avid reader and turned his home office into a small library. Every time she pulled open the door to her apartment and the smell of old books breezed into her face, she thought of her father and smiled. Today, however, nothing would distract her from the awkward tension she had with Nathan. They reached her door and paused, uncomfortable, in the doorway.

"I'm—" Nathan started.

"Nathan—" Heather said.

They laughed at having spoken at the same time, only adding to the tension strung between them.

"You go," Nathan said, smiling down at her.

"I'm glad you're my partner, Nathan. I think we work really well together, and I would hate for anything to get in the way of that."

Disappointment crossed Nathan's face, and she wondered what he had expected her to say.

"I'm glad you're my partner too," Nathan said, voice full of hesitation. "I would never let anything come between us."

"I hear that, but things have changed between us recently. I feel like you care too much, and I don't think it's a good idea."

"Oh, so you can just change how much I care?" Nathan asked with an angry scoff.

"That's not what I meant." Her words didn't coming out the way she intended. "I'm saying I want us to be careful, is all. My job's important to me, and I want you to stay a part of that."

Nathan took a step closer to Heather, and her pulse quickened. His dark eyes met hers, and she could feel the heat flowing between them.

Mesmerized, she couldn't look away. It was as if an invisible string between them shortened, and she had no choice but to gravitate toward him. Heather very much understood the words she had said and their importance, but her body sent her different signals. It said that she wanted Nathan more than anything else in the world.

"Nathan...," Heather said, voice barely above a whisper, mind and body frozen under his warming gaze.

The space between their bodies closed as Nathan's hands found Heather's hips and her hands found his chest. They stood together, staring into each other's souls. Heather desperately wanted Nathan to kiss her; she wanted it with every fiber of her being. As he bent toward her, Heather's phone rang, chimes breaking the silence and startling Heather from her trance. She jumped back and broke eye contact, looking down at her phone and seeing her mother calling. The phone continued to ring as Heather looked up at Nathan, but he looked away now, and she couldn't read his expression.

"Hey, Mom," Heather said as she answered the phone, embarrassed to find her voice was shaking.

She pulled her keys from her pocket and went to unlock the door, bumping her foot into a package on the stoop.

"I'll grab it," Nathan whispered as he bent to pick it up.

"Sorry, what Mom?" Heather asked, realizing she hadn't heard her mother's words.

"I said, April Dell didn't come home last night," Heather's mother said, an edge of frustration mixed in her tone.

"What? Oh my God—has anyone found her yet?" Heather walked through the door, and Nathan set the package on her coffee table, watching her, puzzled. She switched the phone to speakerphone so he could hear.

"Lucy Dell is calling all over town trying to find her. I told her I would check in with you to see if you knew anything."

"No, I don't. Has Lucy called it into the station?" Heather held Nathan's gaze, and a look of concern passed between them.

"Not yet. She wanted to see if she could find her first. Lucy said she worried she was overreacting and didn't want to make a fuss over nothing." Heather could hear the tension in her mother's voice beginning to rise.

"You want me to call it in?" Heather asked.

Her mother's voice caught as she tried to speak but then she paused. Heather's distinct memories from the night that Autumn had left flowed into her mind, and she thought of how long it had taken them to realize she was missing. Autumn would often disappear for days on end, especially when actively using drugs. It wasn't unusual for her to go silent for several days and turn up again, as if nothing had ever happened. After so many of those long weeks worrying about her sister, Heather and her mother had grown somewhat used to it and had stopped their desperate attempts to find her. Heather and her mother assumed that it was like any other bender and Autumn would return in a few days, hungover and broke. Heather blamed herself for not taking immediate action and tortured herself with the *what ifs*.

"No," Heather's mother said with hesitation. "It's not our decision to make. I just wanted to be sure you hadn't run into her or something."

Heather looked at Nathan, who shook his head to indicate that he hadn't seen April, either.

"Nathan and I haven't seen her, but you tell Lucy that we'll be on standby if they can't find her and need to call it in."

"I will. I love you, baby." Heather could tell her mother held back tears.

"Love you too, Mom."

Heather disconnected and only then realized she wished the conversation had gone on longer, her worry for April and thoughts of her sister being replaced by the sheer horror at having almost kissed Nathan. How was she going to address that? Trying hard to hide a blush rising in her cheeks, Heather made her way to the coffee table and tried to busy herself with the package Nathan had brought in from the stoop. She sat on the couch and tried to appear as focused as possible. She couldn't remember ordering anything, but sometimes her mother ordered things for her. Heather's black cat, Luna, dashed from the kitchen and rubbed against Heather's legs, hiding behind them.

"I'm gonna take off."

Luna, as if feeling the tension, bounded from Heather's legs to Nathan's. He smiled and bent down to scratch her ear.

"Alright." Heather kept her voice light, and her gaze focused on the box before her.

She knew she should address what had happened, but she had no idea how, nor did she have the energy. Her body and mind craved sleep. Perhaps Nathan leaving without talking about it was the best-case scenario. Heather needed time to think. He finished scratching Luna's ear and gently pushed her toward Heather as he walked to the front door.

She hadn't bothered to check the address label on the package before she tore into it, cardboard hinges flying open. When she saw the box's contents, her stomach turned to ice, and all the breath left her body. She tried to stand, but her knee banged against the coffee table, causing it to skid against the wood floors. The box tumbled from her hands, and Heather watched it fall in slow motion—first hitting the table, bumping a few times, and then crashing to the floor. Heather didn't realize Nathan was still there until his arms wrapped around her, supporting her collapsing frame.

"Heather? Talk to me—what is it?"

Heather couldn't find words as Nathan lowered her to the couch and bent to pick up the box. His face turned white as he looked inside. He knew Heather when Autumn disappeared. He went with her to report the case to the Sheriff. He knew the details as well as Heather knew them, and he knew exactly what this was.

Inside the box lay the shirt that Autumn wore the day she went missing—a white, flowy shirt with dandelions blowing in the wind printed across the chest and a screaming red bloodstain around the collar.

"Jesus." Nathan dropped the box down hard on the coffee table and turned to Heather. "I'll call the Sheriff," he said as he pulled his phone from his pocket.

Heather supposed some time must have passed between her opening the box and the sheriff's arrival, but it felt like mere seconds before Sheriff Steinman rushed through her door. Officers, her co-workers, filled her small apartment. She sat on the couch, trying to ignore the worry and pity on the faces of those around her. Gratitude for Nathan flooded her veins as he stepped into action, directing the officers and answering questions. Heather allowed the flurry of activity to rush past her as she continued to sit, feeling trapped in the most uncomfortable way.

She had wished for a moment like this—something that finally got everyone around her to believe the truth about Autumn's death. It was not an accident, it was not suicide, but cold-blooded murder. If she had wished so desperately for this moment to come, then why did she feel so broken now that it had arrived? Maybe a big part of her also wished the coroner's narrative told the true story, simple and easy to understand. The report laid everything out, tying her sister's life up in a coffin with a neat bow on top. This, however, ripped open Autumn's casket and allowed her lifeless body to rot in the sun.

Time dragged and by the time Sheriff Steinman sat down on the couch next to Heather, she had become nauseated and shaky with exhaustion and emotion. She looked up and met the Sheriff's eye, the man who had taken over for her father after his death and treated her like his own daughter. His face remained neutral and strong, but Heather knew him better than that. She could see the sadness etched on his face and loved him for that. Losing a father was never easy, but losing one young devastated her, and Heather appreciated the sacrifices that Sheriff Steinman had made to fill the father-shaped hole in her life. He reached out a gentle hand and placed it on her shoulder, looking her square in the eyes.

"How're you holding up, kiddo?" he asked.

Her body felt empty, but she couldn't pinpoint her emotions. She took a moment to gather her thoughts, staring blankly at the wall ahead of her. She supposed nothing had changed. Autumn was still dead—but at the same time, everything had changed. The world took on a hue of deceit as everything that those around her tried to convince her of crumbled. She couldn't think of anything to say other than the brutal truth.

"I told you it wasn't a suicide, and you didn't listen to me," Heather said, feeling a bit betrayed.

She had shared her innermost secret suspicion with only those closest to her, Sheriff Steinman and Nathan, and both had brushed her off, treating her like the crazed sister of a victim of poor life circumstances. She couldn't help but feel angry they hadn't listened to her, that they had insisted on listening to the coroner over one of their own. Conflicted thoughts passed across Sheriff Steinman's face as he decided how to respond.

"Well," he began gingerly, "this doesn't necessarily change the findings." Heather could see he wanted to continue but didn't, allowing his words to sink in before explaining.

Anger rose in her heart as she contemplated his words. He still didn't believe her. She stood up quickly, desperate to get out of this tiny apartment. Head spinning and vision darkening around the edges from the head-rush, Heather bumped into Nathan, not realizing he stood behind her.

"Let's get some air." He took her by the elbow and steered her toward the door.

Nathan gave the Sheriff a curt nod, and Heather found the whole thing annoying. Her apartment was no more than a bedroom and a kitchen, with a living space awkwardly forced in the middle, and it took them only a few steps to reach the door. She'd never had this many people in her apartment in her life. The last thing she saw before Nathan closed the door was Luna's golden eyes shining at her from under the couch, and Heather wished everyone would just leave them alone. Luna had become her closest companion in the years since Autumn's death, and all she wanted was to curl up with what felt like the only family she had left and cry herself to sleep.

Crap... I'm going to have to tell Mom about this.

Heather had never been close to her mother, even in childhood. She favored her father, and the two got along like peas in a pod. While Autumn took after their mother, she had enough of her father in her that Heather still felt connected to her. When Heather's father died, her mother retreated into herself and cut the rest of the world out. Heather and Autumn latched onto each other in their grief, desperate for an anchor in the stormy seas of their lives. From there, Heather and Autumn grew closer and closer, despite the periods of disappearances and the cruel actions that Autumn could take while high. With Autumn gone, Heather felt entirely alone, with only Luna keeping her company.

As the fresh air hit her, she breathed in deep for the first time in almost an hour and her tense muscles unwound the tiniest bit. Nathan cleared his throat beside her, undoing the progress in her muscles and reminding her he had followed her outside. She presumed he wanted to talk about her sister.

"Say it," Heather said with spite, watching the cars driving past.

"Sheriff S. is having the shirt processed and will send samples for testing; the red stain obviously looks like blood. Even if it is, though, that doesn't mean the cause of death wasn't accurate. She could have been wearing the shirt when she died, and her head wound could have bled onto the fabric. When her body was found, she was wearing only a bra and underwear, so perhaps a friend took her clothing from her body after her fall."

Heather bristled at his remarks.

"Okay, suppose that's the truth," Heather started, voice full of ire. "Why would they take her clothes in the first place, let alone save them for two years, and then send them to me in the mail?"

"Drugs make people do weird and irrational things. Maybe a friend saw her fall and took the clothes and stashed them away somewhere while high, trying to keep a piece of her alive. Maybe now they're sober and didn't know what to do with the clothes other than give them to Autumn's family."

Heather laughed out loud at that one.

"That's a lot of supposing," she said angrily, walking a few paces away from him down the street. "Also, why would she have been wearing that shirt the day she went missing and then also died in the shirt two weeks later?"

"Did she take a change of clothes with her when she left that night?" Nathan asked, and though annoyed, Heather knew it was a valid question. Autumn had never taken care of herself physically while high and often wore the same clothes for days on end.

"No..." She felt stupid at having jumped to such conclusions about her sister's case, or lack thereof, at the sight of one dirty and bloody shirt.

"I know it's a lot of supposing, Heather, I do, but it's also a lot of supposing to change the cause of death entirely based on one shirt."

Heather knew he was right but hated him for being the one to make her see.

"Did the package even say who it was from to make you believe that it was from a mystery friend?" Heather asked.

"It was unmarked, other than your first name written across the top. We talked with Mrs. Reeves downstairs, and she said it was on the stoop outside of the bookshop this morning when she came to open the shop. She carried the box upstairs and put it at your door before returning to her work," Nathan answered.

"You don't know anything then." Heather turned to go into her building.

Nathan made to follow her, and she put up her hand, stopping him.

"You should go; it's been a long couple of days," she said firmly, and she could see the hurt frustration in Nathan's eyes.

"Seriously?" he asked.

"Seriously," she said, holding her mouth in a straight line and staring at him.

Nathan shook his head.

"If you keep pushing people away like this, you're going to have no one left, Heather," he said as he turned to go, walking down the street to where their shared patrol car was parked.

"I don't need anyone!" she shouted after him before huffing and throwing the bookshop door open, startling Mrs. Reeves.

Heather gave an apologetic glance as she made her way to the stairwell that led to her apartment. Once inside, she sat on the bottom stair, laid her head in her hands, and cried. She cried for herself, she cried for Nathan, but most of all, she cried for her sister, Autumn.

Chapter Six

A thick blanket of snow covered the world outside of Claire's house, deadening the sounds around her. The sun shone bright on her face, giving her a sliver of optimism. She had to shield her eyes with her hand to see anything, but it didn't bother her. April's car sitting in the driveway last night had felt normal, but now it was eerie. She could easily imagine April stepping out of her car and rushing inside to escape the cold or singing in the car and dancing with her arms waving above her head. She could easily imagine that none of this was real. She shook her head, willing the ghost of April to vacate her mind so she could focus. Claire's unwavering determination lit a fire in her belly, and she would find her best friend.

On the podcasts Claire listened to, the family or friends kept hope and the cases alive, and she would do that for April. As she started walking down her driveway, Claire ran true crime knowledge through her mind. It was a myth that you had to wait for twenty-four hours to report someone missing; as long as the case was good enough to start right away, the police would investigate. She supposed April's case would be strong, especially since the town's sheriff knew her personally and knew how unlike her it would be to disappear. Claire knew that immediate action was key, and she had already done that. She had called everyone she knew, as had The Dells, and now, she searched on foot. She knew that creating a campaign on social media would be great for spreading the word, and the more she could do that, the more likely April would be found. She made a mental note to work on social media after she concluded her search. She had seen countless cases get solved with the power of the internet, and that idea gave her some hope.

Claire stopped at the end of her driveway and contemplated driving the route from her place to the Endersons' on her search but figured it would be better on foot. The snow had frozen overnight, and ice covered the roads despite the warm sun shining down. It took her almost double the drive time to get home last night because of it. She made her way to the front of their neighborhood, strolling and studying the neat row of houses. Claire's phone buzzed with messages—all from people who had not seen April.

Most of the geography of Tree Park was easily walkable. Claire didn't even want to think about what might have happened to April if she had gone missing in a big city. She would have faded into the background of the city's crime faster than a raindrop falling down a windowpane. Claire and April's neighborhood lay off the main street, where all the town's main activities occurred. As she got to the front of her neighborhood, she took mental stock of her surroundings. Across the street sat a 24-hour market, and she would start there. After that, if she continued straight, she would run into April's mother's bake shop, but turning right down Main Street would lead her to where the Endersons' neighborhood lay. Watching traffic, Claire jogged across the street.

Claire arrived at the market and took a deep breath of the fresh morning air before entering through the automatic sliding doors. She glanced around as she walked through the store but saw no traces of April. She might have stopped in the store, but she wasn't here now. Claire smiled as she saw the shopkeeper, Mr. Hackett, leaning against the counter with his back to her and watching a small, ancient television that he had sitting on a stool. He was hard of hearing at his age and hadn't heard her come in. She coughed loudly as she approached the counter. The old man whirled around in surprise.

"Claire, dear!" he said, hand flying to his chest, "trying to give an old man a heart attack?" Claire chuckled. She had a soft spot in her heart for old Mr. Hackett.

"Sorry, Mr. Hackett."

"What can I do for you, dear?" he asked, pushing his glasses further up his nose and frowning at Claire's disheveled appearance. "Is everything alright?"

"Actually, I'm looking for April. She didn't come home last night, and I wanted to see if maybe any of your employees saw her? She was walking home from a babysitting job around midnight and would have passed by on her way."

"She didn't come home?" he asked, worry printed on his face. "I'm sorry to say she wouldn't have been here. We lost power in the storm and closed down for the night around ten pm. Didn't open back up until five am when the power returned. I opened the doors myself, and you're the first customer so far."

Claire's mind flitted to an image of her stove from this morning, clock flashing. She hadn't noticed the power outage, and it made her heart sink even more. The bar lay on the other side of town, and they hadn't lost power over there. She had gotten home after seven am, after the power had come back on. Not only was April alone in a blizzard, but a power outage, too. Claire's heart sank like an anchor in the deepest parts of the ocean.

"Okay…" she trailed off, numbly standing at the counter. Claire had been in go mode this morning when making phone calls. Somehow while still at home, this whole mess felt like a dream. That dream now shattered, and a grim reality settled in its place.

April was gone.

"I'll keep my eye out, though," he said, laying a supportive and wrinkled hand on Claire's shoulder across the counter. "Are Lucy and August aware?"

"Yeah, I've spoken with them. I'm out searching, and they're making calls, but if we don't find her soon, we're going to the Sheriff's office. So far, it's only been about nine hours since she talked with her mom," Claire responded.

"Well, leave your phone number for me in case she comes by. I'll ask every customer if they've seen her; I promise it!" Mr. Hackett declared.

Claire nodded numbly and thanked him as she wrote down her phone number on a pad of paper on the counter. As she headed toward the door, Claire released a jaw-cracking yawn.

"Claire, wait," Mr. Hackett called, coming around the counter. He grabbed an energy drink from one of the large refrigerators lining the back wall of the market and handed it to her. "You're going to need this," he said, handing her the drink.

Claire reached for her wallet in the pocket of her hoodie, but Mr. Hackett held up a hand, stopping her.

"On the house, dear, and you keep in touch now."

The gesture moved Claire, and she nodded with gratitude. She headed back out into the cold morning, cracking open her drink and taking a long sip. She could feel Mr. Hackett's sad and worried eyes watching her as she left the market and wondered if this was her new normal. Was she destined to have sad looks follow her wherever she went as the roommate of the town's beloved missing girl? Claire didn't like that at all.

She headed down Main Street, passing the small pharmacy on her left that stood closed in the early morning hours. On the other side of the street, no light came from the antique shop. She couldn't help but think about how much April loved it there. April visited the store weekly, and the old couple who owned the shop knew her by name, remembering her when she was a little girl. Whenever they got a new piece they thought might interest April, they called her to come in and check it out before making it available to the public.

April loved antiques, and Claire always joked that she was born in the wrong century. Even when there wasn't anything specific for her to look at, she would peruse the narrow aisles, excited to learn something new or find something to research in her spare time. Claire found the shop too cluttered and always felt trapped inside. It reminded her of being cooped up in her mother's trailer. She couldn't walk through the aisles without bumping into something, the stark opposite of April's elegant and dainty footwork. April's figure was tall and slender, while Claire's was short and full, and April often had difficulty remembering their differences.

Claire's guilt lit a fire in her chest as she passed the antique shop. She should have been a better friend to April and spent more time doing things April enjoyed instead of always trying to drag April into her world. April always went with Claire to the movies, to parties, and to visit Claire at work at the bar despite hating to be in crowded or loud spaces. If she found April, she would take her to the antique shop every day for the rest of their lives if she wanted.

"If I find her..." Claire whispered and shuddered.

She chugged the rest of her energy drink and tossed it into a nearby trash can, doing her best to push away the thoughts that crept into her mind. She continued searching down Main Street, looking into the dark windows of various other shops, finding no evidence of April or her whereabouts. As she approached the Endersons' neighborhood, her heart sank. She didn't know what she had expected from this walk, but part of her felt sure she would find resolution. It was clear now that was not coming. When Mrs. Dell had talked with April, she likely had already walked past this point on the route, and Claire knew she would find nothing of April up ahead. Turning around, Claire crossed the street and jogged up to The Hungry Bean, where she planned to meet April's parents.

As she came to the door of the shop, Claire paused. Anxious hope bounced around in her belly as she imagined April inside. She wanted to open the door, but instead froze. She wanted to savor this, and she closed her eyes, allowing herself to live in a blissful moment of hope that her best friend was safe and sound. Taking a deep breath, Claire pulled open the door and the strong aroma of coffee and buttered croissants hit her.

She stood inside the doorway and anxiously scanned the tables and couches scattered throughout the shop. The Hungry Bean was almost empty—no one wanted to be out this early in the morning after a blizzard. Claire wondered if the local schools had closed, and families slept in instead of scouring the freezing earth like she was. The few patrons of the shop sipped coffee from porcelain mugs, a small touch April believed gave the shop an authentic and homey feel. She scanned each table and couch at least three times before she allowed herself to believe that April wasn't there.

Oh God. She's really not here.

Claire didn't know what to do next; she was supposed to meet The Dells here, but she also desperately wanted to run away. She had been so hopeful, and now that those hopes were gone, she felt sick. Torn between running from the building crying and finding a table to wait for April's parents, a voice calling out startled her.

"Claire!"

She looked up and saw her friend, Ryan, waving from behind the counter. Claire stared as Ryan came around the counter, and the familiar feeling of butterflies crept into her stomach. It appeared no level of crisis could stop her crush on Ryan.

April had known Ryan her entire life. The two had grown up together in Tree Park, but Claire had only met Ryan this past year. Once settled in Tree Park, Claire started working at the bar, and Ryan trained her. Claire found Ryan attractive from the moment she saw her and asked April about her, desperate for more information. April told her that Ryan had never had a boyfriend throughout high school and classmates teased her for being a lesbian because she kept her hair so short, though she never confirmed her sexuality. April and Ryan weren't close and didn't stay in touch in college, so April wasn't sure if Claire had a chance or not.

Claire's sexuality had always been fluid—she cared more about a person's heart and soul than their reproductive organs. She recognized that most people fell into the neat box of being straight and didn't get her hopes up when it came to Ryan. She could feel herself blushing at Ryan, feeling shy around her, but she wrote it off. These cute moments together as friends were better than scaring Ryan off with her feelings. Once they got to know each other better, Claire realized that Ryan's funny and sweet comments were flirts, and she could finally show her own affection a little.

Flirting became a regular occurrence for them after that. Between serving drinks and grabbing food from the kitchen, Claire would stop at the counter, and the two would exchange looks beneath their eyelashes in passing. Claire had a vivid memory of her devastation when Ryan gave her two-week's notice at the bar. She'd felt the ship of disappointment sinking in the ocean of her emotions at the idea of not seeing Ryan. Only after she had moved on and started working at the coffee shop did Claire realize the depths of her feelings; she was in love. Claire still saw Ryan frequently as The Hungry Bean was the only coffee shop in town, but it was never the same as being with each other through a long shift and talking late into the night. Nervous about such deep emotion, Claire let the friendship fade, too afraid to put her heart on the line. Every time Claire stopped for a coffee, she told herself that it would be the day she would brave her feelings and ask Ryan out on a date, but it never panned out. One look into those brown fox eyes, and Claire forgot her own name, which didn't bode well for remembering to ask someone out.

Today wouldn't be that day, either.

Ryan approached and smiled wide at Claire, tall stature contrasting Claire's short one.

"Hey! I'm so glad you came in! I have something to give you," she said, and Claire noticed something held in her hands.

Claire couldn't keep up with everything going on, and she felt like she was sinking in quicksand.

Ryan looked at her closely and hesitated. "Hey, are you alright?"

"No, I'm not. April didn't come home last night and…" Claire was sick of telling the same story over and over again just to be met with sad stares and useless responses.

"Are you serious?" Ryan gasped. "Then I guess this is a bad sign."

Ryan thrust her hands forward, and Claire looked down. Her blood froze in her veins. It was a small white purse with a metal chain, the one she had seen April stringing around her chest as she left for the Endersons' house the night before. Puzzled, she looked at Ryan for an explanation, praying she would tell her that April had left it there this morning after a nice cup of coffee but knowing in her heart the truth of it all.

"A customer found it on the street a few blocks away and brought it in not ten minutes ago. When we looked inside, we saw April's ID, but her phone was in there, too, so we couldn't call. I was going to call you the next chance I had, but then you walked through the door. I was thinking how lucky that was, but now, not so much," Ryan rambled.

"She wasn't here?" Claire asked, voice full of despair and desperation and hands gripping the purse tightly.

"No, I've been here since opening, and she hasn't come in," Ryan said with sympathy as Claire's face crumbled. "Oh God, you were hoping to find her in here, weren't you?" Ryan placed a tender hand on Claire's arm as Claire fought back the tears.

Claire ignored Ryan, despair clouding her brain. She didn't need to see the ID to know this was April's purse, but she opened it anyway. April's small wallet, house keys, cell phone, and some loose receipts were inside. She held the keys in her hands and ran her thumb affectionately over April's *Starry Night* keychain. She remembered when they had gone to see the real thing in New York City and the look in April's eyes when she had finally come face to face with the painting.

Will I ever see that look on April's face again? Will I ever see April again?
Tears built up in her eyes.
Where is she?
Is she lost in the snow?
Is she cold or hurt?
Is she even alive?

Her breath started to come in shorter and shorter gasps, and Claire panicked. She struggled to get any air and grew dizzy. Ryan was talking to her, but her brain couldn't decipher the words, almost as if Ryan were speaking Japanese. In desperation, Claire clenched her fists and shook her head. This had to be a nightmare. The world around her shattered into a million pieces, leaving her feeling as if she floated through space with no hope of grounding herself. The shattered pieces of her world became fuzzy around the edges as her body faltered and collapsed, but she could do nothing to stop it. Claire was dimly aware of falling as she saw Ryan reach out to catch her. Then she slipped away into nothingness.

Chapter Seven

When Heather awoke, mouth dry and feeling groggy, she had no idea how long she slept. She sat up and rubbed her eyes, brushing away the sleep, and glanced out the window to see the sun full in the sky now. Midday, she assumed. She looked around her apartment and saw the coffee table pulled askew, and memories of the morning flooded back.

The box.

Trying not to think of it, she stretched as Luna rearranged around Heather's shifting. She ran her fingers down the cat's long, silky body, enjoying the softness and warmth. Luna purred, and Heather smiled at her furry best friend.

"You love me unconditionally, don't you, Luna?" she cooed as Luna jumped from the bed and made her way to the kitchen, signaling that she only loved Heather if she got fed.

Heather chuckled as she reached for her cell phone charging on the floor next to her bed but memories slammed into her. The worst part about the box on her stoop had been having to tell her mother. She would never get the sound of her mother's strangled voice out of her head as she detailed the contents of the box. Her mother hadn't even tried to pretend she was fine—

she'd simply bawled and asked why on a loop until Heather ended the call, no longer able to stay awake. Looking at her phone, she had several missed calls from her mother's friends, presumably to ask about April Dell, and as she scrolled through them, the Sheriff called her.

She knew why he called. "Hey, Sheriff, any word on April Dell?"

"No news other than her parents have officially called it in. Can you swing by the station for the report before interviewing the Dells?" he asked.

"Sure thing, Sheriff. See you soon." As Heather hung up, a message from Nathan popped on her screen.

Hey, just talked to Sheriff S. I'm coming to pick you up. Be there in 15.

Heather groaned as she remembered the almost kiss before opening the box. After talking to her mother, Heather had thrown her body into bed without so much as a drink of water and drifted to sleep immediately. She had never once stopped to contemplate how she would handle things with Nathan, and now she had fifteen minutes to make up her mind.

Rushing to her bathroom, Heather took a quick shower before throwing on a pair of fresh clothes. She dashed to the kitchen, where Luna batted at her food bowl, and she filled it with Luna's favorite wet food. She leaned down and kissed Luna on the head before charging from her apartment and waiting for Nathan on the curb of the bookshop. She only had two minutes to think before the patrol car pulled up, and she had decided on precisely nothing. As she got into the patrol car, Heather tried to smile but saw Nathan's angry forward stare and stopped herself. Luckily for Heather, Nathan had decided for them both—the car ride would be silent.

At the station, they walked straight into the Sheriff's office. Strange feelings always arose for Heather while in this office—it felt like it belonged to her father, but that feeling had waned with time. She swore she could hear her father's loud, booming laugh coming from inside whenever she went through the door. These little moments kept her father alive, and she cherished them. The quaint station never felt the same without him, only having four detectives and eight beat cops, and his absence existed long past his death and replacement.

Heather and Nathan sat in the chairs facing the Sheriff's desk and waited for him to finish writing. Heather shook her head as she watched his hand moving furiously across the page. If he would switch to electronic filing, he could have emailed them this case, and they could have gone straight into an interview with the family. However, that was a hill that the sheriff was willing to die on, and Heather had long since given up on the actual battle. Maybe one day she would be sheriff, and she could make some fundamental changes here.

"Certainly hasn't been that long since I saw you two," Sheriff Steinman began, setting down his pen. "Are you sure you're up for it? I know you've both been working a lot of overtime recently, and I don't want you to fry yourselves."

"We're sure," Heather said. "It's one of our own—this is all hands on deck."

Sheriff Steinman nodded in approval, pride in his eyes. Heather wondered if he pictured her as a little girl.

"I agree," Nathan said. "Once we have this report we'll go to the family."

Sheriff Steinman handed a file to Nathan, the folder fresh and flat, and he tucked it into his bag to be filled with evidence from the family.

"Lucy Dell called me from The Hungry Bean. Jason Polley found a purse that belonged to April and turned it in at the coffee shop when he got his morning coffee."

"The owner of the farming store off Main Street, right?" Nathan asked. While Nathan had lived in Tree Park for a few years, he wasn't born and raised here like Heather.

"Yep, that's the one. Apparently, the barista encouraged him to bring it here, but you know how Jason is before he's had his coffee," Sheriff Steinman continued. "He found it on his walk from his store to The Hungry Bean. Lucy and August figured it was time to give me a call now that it's been found."

"They were right to call," Heather said. "Did the barista know where Jason found the purse?"

"That's all the information I have, so you best ask the Dells about that one. They're waiting for you at the coffee shop now, along with April's roommate, Claire Reynolds. She apparently fainted when the barista gave her the purse but declined medical attention."

Heather didn't know Claire well at all, but she had served her a drink or two down at the bar and she seemed nice. Heather had seen April in there many nights, too, and they clearly cared for each other. A pang of emotion strummed at Heather's heart for the girl. She knew exactly what it felt like to lose a best friend.

"I'm assuming you two have put together the coincidence of this by now?" Sheriff Steinman asked, eyeing Heather and Nathan.

They both nodded; how could they forget Bethany?

"Bethany went missing almost exactly one year ago," Heather said. What she didn't say was that Autumn had gone missing almost exactly two years ago, too.

"And she went missing down the block from The Hungry Bean," Nathan finished.

Two or three missing persons cases this close together in Tree Park, where things like this didn't happen, had to have a connection.

"No doubt in my mind that we're looking at something suspicious here," Sheriff Steinman said, "and no doubt that you two won't bring them *both* home."

The Sheriff picked up his pen and a new sheet of paper from a large stack and resumed his furious writing. Taking this as their cue, Nathan and Heather left the office, heading straight for their patrol car. On the drive over, Heather couldn't help but think of her sister. Autumn loved the snow, and today would have been the perfect day for her; snow piled everywhere, but the sun shining warm and bright. In childhood, Autumn would wake Heather up early in the morning, and the two would jump and play in the snow all day long. Autumn seemed to never get cold, despite Heather's shivering, and the two sisters would laugh until the sun went away and their noses froze. As she thought about Autumn playing joyously in the snow, something hit her.

"Huh," Heather mused aloud.

"What?" Nathan asked, sounding more annoyed than curious.

"I was thinking about Bethany and April," she said, leaving out the part about her sister.

"Yeah, what about?"

"How similar they look. They both have long brown hair and big brown eyes. They were about the same age—Bethany a college student and April having graduated a year ago. They both have pale complexions, too," Heather finished, leaving out the bit that Autumn also possessed all those things.

"Sounds like our guy might have a type," Nathan concluded, and Heather nodded as Nathan parked the car in front of the coffee shop.

They entered The Hungry Bean and Heather saw April's loved ones sitting at a table. They sat in silence, not looking at one another, with confusion, grief, and desperation on each of their faces. She remembered seeing those looks on the faces of Bethany's loved ones and felt a twinge of guilt in her heart that she hadn't brought Bethany home yet. She remembered her own emotions during the beginning stages of her sister's investigation and didn't wish that on anyone. Approaching the table, Heather smiled, taking the lead for once.

"Heather!" Mrs. Dell exclaimed, standing and pulling Heather in for a hug.

"Oh, Lucy, I'm so sorry. When my mom told me, my heart broke," Heather said into Mrs. Dell's shoulder as she wrapped her arms around her.

Mrs. Dell's eyes brimmed with tears as she pulled back from the hug.

"I can't believe this," she said, collapsing into her chair. Heather reached her hand out to shake April's father's hand.

"Mr. Dell, always nice to see my favorite teacher again, though I wish the circumstances were different."

While Mrs. Dell owned the town's only bakery, August was the town's only high school English teacher. Heather's father's love for books created a special interest in the subject of English for her, and she remembered those classes with Mr. Dell with fondness. He took her hand and gripped it in both of his.

"It's August now, detective," he said warmly, and Heather smiled.

"You all remember my partner, Detective Nathan Longville." Heather gestured to Nathan, standing behind her.

"We do," Mr. Dell said, reaching his hand for Nathan's.

Nathan smiled and shook Mr. Dell's hand before turning his trained eye to the purse sitting on the table. He reached into his bag and pulled out a pair of latex gloves and an evidence bag. He set his tools down on a nearby table as he grabbed the purse and set to work without a word. The reversal of roles felt awkward; usually Nathan did the interviewing and Heather faded into the background to categorize evidence. In this case, however, it made sense. Heather knew the Dells would be more forthcoming with her than an outsider, despite him living there for years now.

"Alright," Heather said, taking a seat and pulling out a small spiral notebook. "Why don't you tell me the story from the beginning?"

April's mother told Heather about the babysitting job, April refusing to drive in the blizzard, and speaking with her on the phone. She told Heather about the promise to text when she got in but how that text never came.

"I should have stayed on the phone with her," Mrs. Dell said, tears falling down her cheeks. Heather knew from experience that Mrs. Dell would blame herself for this, no matter what anyone else said.

"You couldn't have known," Mr. Dell said to his wife. "We both went to sleep after that phone call."

"Claire, where were you last night?" Heather asked, turning to Claire.

"I was at work. I left just after April and didn't get home until around seven am. The bar has security footage if you need to corroborate that—I worked late because a pipe burst and the owner needed bodies for the clean-up," Claire said, looking Heather straight in the eye.

"A junior detective, I see?" Heather said with a smile, trying to lighten the mood a bit.

"Something like that," Claire responded. "That's why we took action first thing this morning when we realized she hadn't made it home. I only slept for about an hour before Mrs. Dell called me to tell me that April had missed their meeting at the bakery."

Claire then launched into her explanation of her time walking through the town and talking with the locals about April's whereabouts, only to come up empty. Mrs. Dell next detailed her morning of calling her friends with no success, either.

"Good job," Heather said seriously and meant it. "The wider this spreads, the more information we can gather on what happened."

Heather took a moment to scribble notes onto her pad. Meanwhile, Nathan categorized the items from April's purse, photographing them from several angles, and placing them into evidence bags.

"And on your search, you came in here and were given the purse?" Heather asked the table.

"Yes," Claire answered, turning and pointing to the barista who was watching them intently from behind the counter. "Ryan gave it to me. She said a customer turned it in early this morning."

"Mr. Polley found it. He said it was lying in the snow a few blocks from here but didn't give the exact location," Ryan said as she came around the counter and joined the group, trying her best to be helpful.

"Thank you for that, Ryan," Heather said. "Detective Longville and I plan to interview Mr. Polley before returning to the station. Hopefully, he remembers the exact location of the purse."

"Something happened to our baby," Mrs. Dell interjected, putting a hand on her husband's arm. "She never stays out of touch. Someone took her, or she's hurt somewhere, or..." She broke out in sobs that cut her words off, and Mr. Dell pulled her into him.

He stroked his wife's back, fighting off his own tears and playing the part of the strong husband well. Mrs. Dell leaned into him and freed her emotions within the safety of his arms.

"We thought we couldn't have children; getting pregnant with April at forty was my life's biggest surprise and blessing. I had always wanted a daughter, someone to pass the bake shop along to as my mother had to me, and I thought I would never have that, and now I may have lost it entirely. Oh, Heather, you have to find her—you just have to!" Mrs. Dell sobbed from her place in Mr. Dell's chest.

Big, fat tears ran down her cheeks, in and out of her wrinkled skin, and snot dripped from her nose. Mr. Dell made soft, shushing sounds, and Claire looked as if she had seen a ghost and sat awkwardly upright. Heather felt her emotions tug at her. It had been difficult when interviewing Bethany's family, but this was worse than she could have imagined. These were her own people and watching them break apart at the seams in the most hurtful explosion of grief and confusion felt unbearable. Heather pushed down her own feelings and reminded herself to stay focused on the task at hand.

"Can someone send me a picture of April so I can forward it to the news station?" Heather asked, grabbing her business card from her pocket and holding it over the table.

Mrs. Dell took the card while scrolling through pictures on her phone, tears streaming down her face. She selected an image and typed Heather's cell phone number into her phone.

"We took that on New Year's Eve," August said with sadness, "so full of life and setting her resolutions for the year... I can't imagine that being the last time we ever see her."

Heather nodded sympathetically as she looked at the picture. April's bright and broad smile shone with brilliance and her straight, brown hair perfectly framed her face. She forwarded the picture to several members of the department who would need access to it, including Nathan.

"Claire, do you remember what April wore last night?" Heather asked.

"Jeans and a black coat, but I didn't see her shirt underneath it. I think she wore her snow boots, but I can confirm that when I get home and see what shoes are missing...." Claire's voice broke at the word missing.

Heather handed her business card to each group member, Ryan included.

"Thank you, Claire. If anyone remembers anything at any time, please contact me directly. Any other details about her clothing?"

"She always wears my mother's watch," Mrs. Dell exclaimed. "She never leaves home without it. I can send you a picture of that, too." She returned her attention to her phone.

"Thank you, Lucy, that's very helpful," Heather said as she wrote the detail down. "Does April have any distinguishing marks, anything that might set her physically apart from others?" Heather asked, moving on, and looking at the group to wait for an answer.

"She has a small scar on the underside of her chin from a bicycle accident when she was young," Mr. Dell chimed in, pointing to his own chin, eyes alight with emotion. "She lost control when we took off the training wheels and flipped over the front of the handlebars and scraped her chin on the pavement. It used to be bigger, but as she grew older, the scar got smaller."

Heather wrote this down in her notebook and looked at the group to see if anyone had anything else to add. She shifted her eyes from one person to another, noticing Claire looking down and not at her. Claire wrung her hands under the table and seemed very uncomfortable.

"Claire?"

"April had a tattoo," she said, voice barely above a whisper and face showing a look of betrayal. Clearly, April hadn't wanted her family to know.

"What?" Lucy shouted, shocked.

"She thought her parents were old-fashioned, and she had so many co-workers with tattoos that she thought their rationale of not being able to find work was silly. She got it a few months ago. I got one at the same time, though that was my fifth, so it was a different experience for me...."

Claire trailed off, feeling uncomfortable. Heather gave Lucy a brief glance, and she appeared angry and upset, but stayed quiet.

"What's the tattoo of, Claire?"

"It's a small minimalist Van Gogh sunflower on her right foot. She figured that was an easy way to hide the tattoo—wearing shoes and all."

"Thank you for your honesty, Claire. The important part is getting April home, safe and sound," Heather said as she looked around the group, trying to center their focus on finding April.

"You're right, Heather," Mrs. Dell said. "All that matters is that she's safe."

"Plus, if she had to get a tattoo, that's a great one to have," Mr. Dell said, sharing April's love for art and chuckling. The group laughed in response, breaking the tension, much to Heather's relief.

"Can you think of anything else important to tell me?" Heather asked, looking up. Nathan, behind her, tapped her shoulder, signaling his completion of categorizing.

"We know about the girl who went missing from here last year—everyone does," Mr. Dell said, looking at his wife. "Do you think the same person who took that girl could have taken our April?"

Heather paused. She hoped this wouldn't come up.

"Mr. Dell," she said out of habit and familiarity, "August, I mean, I won't lie to you. I don't know if the girls are connected, but if they are, we will find out."

Mr. Dell nodded, and Mrs. Dell started to cry once more.

"We'll take her purse and phone to the station. We have a great tech analyst who will review local security footage and dig through April's phone to ensure she wasn't being harassed or stalked. Later today, you'll likely see this on the news, so don't be alarmed."

"What can we do?" Mrs. Dell asked.

"Would a vigil or some sort of gathering help?" Claire said, and Heather could see she had done her homework.

"A vigil is helpful, so I would start there. Great idea, Claire. You want to spread the word to as many people as you can. Social media campaigns can be great, too, though of course they will always attract some negativity. The more people who know about April, the more likely it is that we'll find her. Once we release the information, the Facebook group Virginia Missing will receive it as well, and they will help spread the word."

Everyone nodded.

"Are there any leads in Bethany's case?" Claire asked, looking Heather in the eyes.

Heather could tell that Claire already knew the public answer and hoped for some insider information.

"No," Heather said. "The case has gone cold."

Heather felt the group sag into their sadness, their hope waning. Heather placed a supportive hand on Mr. Dell's shoulder as she realized she felt empty herself.

Chapter Eight

After her fall, the brothers led April through the snow and straight to the house. Panic grew inside her chest as they approached the back of the house. She did her best to limp up the porch stairs, but her body had grown even weaker during the walk. As she stepped onto the first step, her legs gave way, and she tumbled to the ground, this time not intentionally. She lay in the freezing snow, and the world started to dim and go black around the edges. April could have sworn that she saw beautiful stars twinkling in the air as Brother Waylon leaned down, his face meeting hers.

April's vision swam with stars that seemed to bounce off of Brother Waylon's face. She expected him to have a sinister snarl as he did last night, but instead, he looked bored and annoyed. Rolling his eyes, Brother Waylon braced himself as he pulled her up the stairs by her handcuffs. The cuffs dug into her now chafed wrists, but she didn't care. The movement of her body up the stairs gave her a sense of flying, and it felt marvelous. She wished she would continue to soar up and away from this dreadful place. She closed her eyes for what felt like a second before a blast of warm air hit her. Startled, she awoke and gasped as if coming out of the water for a breath of air while swimming. She started flailing as Brother Waylon dragged her body over the threshold.

"Quit that and git up," he said as she tried to scramble to her feet.

April swayed a bit but steadied herself with the wall behind her. Brother Waylon and Brother Beau removed their boots, and she took advantage of this moment to study her surroundings. A small hallway lay to her right, a set of stairs in front of her, and a swinging door to her left. Heavy black curtains covered each window, not allowing light to break through, giving the house a dark and eerie aura. It took a moment for April's eyes to adjust to the darkness. Her head ached and throbbed as her eyes got used to the new surroundings. Wood paneling lined with black-and-white pictures covered the walls. Most of the photographs displayed the property, and April noticed the barn appeared in better shape than she had just seen it.

Farther down, the hallway opened into the living room. She could see the back of a woman rocking in a rocking chair centered in the middle of the room. She hummed a soft tune, and the off-key notes floated down the hallway. A wood-burning fireplace lay before the chair, crackling and hissing in a way that April would have previously found pleasant but now found jarring. She couldn't make out many details of the woman but could tell she had soft, gray hair pulled back into a neat and tight bun at the nape of her neck. She must be the "Mother Loretta" the brothers had talked about.

"Brothers," a falsely sweet southern voice chimed from the living room, and the woman turned her head toward the hallway. "Is that you?"

"Yes, Mother Loretta," replied Brother Waylon. "Sister Jolene as well."

April looked around, puzzled. No one else was here—who was Sister Jolene?

"Good," the mysterious woman replied. "It'll be supper in a few hours, you hear, and I want *everybody* to be ready in time."

April shuddered at Mother Loretta's emphasis on the word *everybody* and wondered if that included her. Her stomach gave an involuntary growl at the thought of dinner. *When was the last time I ate?* April couldn't remember. The room spun again as she puzzled over Sister Jolene.

"Walk," he commanded, turning his attention back to April.

She thought she couldn't walk, but the idea of Brother Waylon dragging her again lit a fire in her gut. She nodded in silence, and he grabbed the chain between her handcuffs, pulling her toward the stairs. Brother Beau fell in line behind the hunched-over April, still never meeting her eye.

Brother Waylon started up the stairs, and April did her best to follow, feeling like the staircase walls narrowed as she climbed. A series of old-fashioned portraits lined the walls, giving her the sense of being watched. Paranoia crept in as she imagined hands reaching out from the portraits and grabbing her hair. She looked at each one as she passed, desperate to focus on something other than what waited for her at the top of the stairs.

The first frame was empty, which April found bizarre. Each portrait had a name etched in metal at the bottom, but someone had scratched this one and it was unreadable. April shuddered to think of who could have been in that frame and where they were now.

Her pace slowed as the exertion of climbing the stairs drained her weakened body. Brother Waylon gained a lead, the slack in the chain tightening, as she studied each of the portraits remaining. The second one, titled "Mother Loretta," pictured a woman who appeared to be slightly older than the brothers were now. She stared into the camera with dead, green eyes. Her hair was pulled into a tight bun, and she wore a garment that came all the way to the top of her neck, buttons fastened tight. The deadness in her eyes made April feel like she looked at a corpse and not a living woman.

The third portrait showed Brother Waylon, though he looked much younger. He stared into the camera with a smug look as he touched the front of his cowboy hat in a nod. She had grown very familiar with those arrogant eyes and seeing them on such a young person made her shiver.

The fourth portrait was of Brother Beau, and April could see that, even in his youth, he'd been sickly. His sallow cheeks sunk into his face, and his skeletal thinness existed even then. He looked at the camera with shy eyes, as if he wanted to look away and didn't like the attention, his face slightly turned away.

Lastly, April's eyes landed on an unfamiliar face, a young girl. Though she didn't smile, April could see the smile behind her eyes. She had a light and jovial air about her, and April somehow knew she was a kind little girl. Her brown hair fell straight to her shoulders, vastly different from that of the brothers. A large pink ribbon adorned the top of her head, holding her hair back from her face. She looked almost like a doll; her chubby cheeks were practically pinchable. The nameplate at the bottom read "Sister Jolene."

So that's Sister Jolene…

As they reached the top of the stairs, April dropped to the ground, strength failing her after the arduous and slow climb. Brother Waylon let her fall to the ground as he kept up his pace and turned the corner. He unlocked a series of locks lining a door frame without a backward glance. April thought for a moment about throwing herself back down the stairs, desperate for escape, but as she turned toward freedom, Brother Beau stood behind her. She had forgotten about him in his silent meekness. She made eye contact with him, and he pleaded with her with his eyes.

Behave, follow Brother Waylon, and be a good sister—is that all I am now?

April turned back toward Brother Waylon and crawled to the door, legs more dragging than aiding the process.

By the time April reached the door, sweat dripped down her brow from exertion. Her body had never experienced such weakness and dehydration, and her throat lay raw from screaming and crying. Her shaking arms gave way, and she could no longer support her frame. She lay flat on her belly, panting and wishing she would die, as strong hands pushed her forward. Brother Waylon slid her collapsed body across the wood floor and through the doorway with almost no effort at all. He moved her into the room, where he locked the chain between her handcuffs to a longer chain attached to a bed. Leaving her there, the brothers left the room.

April had no energy to hold on.

The world faded into black, and she found herself standing in a space of nothingness, alone and screaming into the void where shadows and demons floated. They laughed and shrieked, terrifying her. She curled into a ball and covered her ears, screaming at the creatures. She tried to crawl away from the terrifying beings of her nightmare, but no matter how far she went, the void extended around her. She would never escape, an animal caught in their trap, and that reality swallowed her whole. She had thought this was a nightmare, but the lines between reality and sleep had blurred too far to even tell who she was, let alone where she was. This must be the end for her.

April awoke with a start, sweating and shaking, to the sound of the bedroom door being unlocked. As each lock clunked, she looked around, desperate for a place to hide. She still laid on the floor where Brother Waylon had left her, and she slid under the bed as far as her restraints would allow. She cowered and shook, desperate to hide and protect herself.

The bedroom was medium-sized, with a large bed against one wall and windows opposite. No curtains covered the windows and April wondered why. Bright rays of sunshine floated into the bedroom creating a calm and safe aura, contrasting her captivity. As April stared at the window from her vantage point, she realized thin metal bars crisscrossed the panes of glass. The brothers had done their homework on how to keep someone locked in. The walls of the room were painted a light shade of pink and covered in faded girly posters curling at the edges. To the right of the window, a large dresser held small stuffed animals and candles on the top. Next to that, a pair of white closet doors set into the wall. Above the closet doors hung a large, rectangular sign that read: "Sister Jolene" in curlicue writing.

When the door swung open, April emitted a strangled shriek. She put her hand over her mouth to stifle her scream and better hide herself, staring wide-eyed at the bottom of the door. Cowboy boots appeared, and relief flooded her mind as she realized it was Brother Beau's limping gait and not Brother Waylon's confident one. She watched the space just behind the door, waiting for Brother Waylon to enter the room, too, but he didn't. The door closed, and Brother Beau stood silent.

Brother Waylon terrified April in a way that no one ever had. The dead look behind his eyes made him unpredictable, and she knew he wouldn't hesitate to kill her. Brother Beau, on the other hand, didn't seem like a willing part of this ordeal, and she wondered if he had the capability of hurting her. All his interactions with April thus far had been apologetic and at the command of his brother, and she doubted he would have done those things of his own free will. While she didn't feel that Brother Beau was an acute threat to her well-being, she was here because of him nonetheless and dreaded his presence in the room.

April kept her hand over her mouth as she prayed that Brother Beau wouldn't find her. Like a scared kitten in a new home, she shook as she held her breath, waiting for something to happen.

"I-I-I won't hurt you," Brother Beau said quietly, his feet shuffling.

April remained still, taking shallow, quiet breaths.

If I don't move, he won't see me.

It was completely illogical to believe that Brother Beau would simply leave the room, but nothing made sense anymore.

Just stay still, just stay still, just stay still...

Brother Beau continued to shuffle his feet, unsure of what to do or say. She believed he wouldn't hurt her, but her mind focused only on escape. If she let Brother Beau know she hid under the bed, then she would be accepting her place in his family. It might be a small and quiet rebellion to stay hidden, but it was her rebellion to make.

"I have food and w-w-water," Brother Beau said, as if trying to encourage a toddler to stop screaming.

This got April's attention. As if listening to Brother Beau's words, her stomach gave another loud growl, and her mouth wanted to start watering but instead created a horrible taste. Her body craved sustenance, and she felt herself caving. Her mind and body warred with each other. Her mind begged her to stay still while her body felt sicker and sicker from the lack of nourishment. It became too much for her, and she started to cry in loud, wracking sobs, though her eyes stayed dry. She had never been this thirsty before. Brother Beau leaned down, and she was horrified at being found. She shrank as far away from him as her restraints would allow, the cold metal digging into her raw skin.

"M-might be hard to drink and eat under the bed," Brother Beau said kindly as he pushed a plate and glass of water toward April.

The water had ice cubes, and the glass dripped with condensation. The plate had the most delicious-looking sandwich April had ever seen; the fluffy white bread smelled homemade, the cheese melted down the sides, and the thick-cut turkey looked divine. She tried to reach out and grab the food but banged her head roughly on the underside of the bed. That didn't stop her, and her hand knocked into the glass of water as she reached again. It teetered dangerously, and her heart sank as she imagined the glass toppling and her precious water gone forever. She didn't know if she would get more and knew she couldn't afford to be reckless.

April crawled out from under the bed, keeping her gaze stuck on the floor to avoid Brother Beau's eyes. As she emerged, he tried to stand from his crouched position but lost his balance and fell onto his backside. He scrambled quickly away from April as if afraid of her. She found the whole thing ridiculous.

Why is he afraid of me? He's the one who stole me away...

She had barely emerged from the underside of the bed before she snatched up the glass, spilling some off the top and guzzling it. The water felt heavenly going down, and it soothed her throat and dry mouth. She set down the glass and hungrily pulled the plate of food toward her, sinking her teeth into the delicious sandwich. April closed her eyes as the flavor hit her taste buds. She kept her eyes closed as she savored each giant bite of the sandwich she took. She ate like a savage, crouched on the ground, and chewing with her mouth open, groaning in pleasure. When she had finished, April felt incredibly empty and desperate for more sustenance.

She lifted the plate and glass and held it out for Brother Beau, too afraid to speak up but hoping he would refill it all for her. As the items left the ground, Brother Beau flinched, startling April, who dropped the items and cowered from him.

"S-S-Sorry," Brother Beau said, "I thought you m-might throw them at me." April shook her head vigorously, indicating that she would never do such a thing.

Thinking that he might call Brother Waylon for support against what he thought could be April's violence, she cried into her hands.

"No, no," Brother Beau said. "D-d-don't cry!"

April pulled her knees to her chest, wrapped her hands around her legs, and buried her face into her arms. She wanted to make herself disappear, make this farm disappear. The water had not sated her thirst, and the sandwich now sat like a brick in the bottom of her stomach. Sharp pains stabbed through her stomach, and her sobs came harder. She could hear Brother Beau shuffling but didn't have enough energy to be afraid anymore. Her exhaustion and headache mixed with the stomach pain, causing a cloudy fog to settle over her mind.

"H-h-here," Brother Beau said.

April peeked over her arms to see what he offered. He held a small, blue handkerchief. She looked up at Brother Beau's face and met his eyes. They were kind and sad, and April felt like she could trust the gesture. She snatched the handkerchief, darting her hand out and pulling it back as if he could have bitten her. She dried her tears with the cloth, finding comfort in the gesture. She began to calm as the sleepy haze in her mind worsened. Her eyes drooped as the room darkened. April reached a hand to the floor to steady herself as her stomach swam in circles, threatening to get sick.

Brother Beau placed a gentle hand on April's elbow and encouraged her to stand up. She no longer controlled her mind or body as consciousness slipped in and out. *What did he do to me?* April thought.

The flashes she experienced while in the barn came back. A flash of standing up and swaying. A flash of Brother Beau pulling the comforter over her broken body. A flash of Brother Beau gently stroking her face.

"You're different," he whispered, clear as a bell, as April's eyes closed again. "You could be her."

Chapter Nine

Claire didn't know what to do next. After the detectives left, the group remained still for a long while, but they finally decided to move on. She stood up awkwardly, as did April's parents, and said goodbye to Ryan, who gave Claire a sympathetic pat as she returned to the coffee counter. Claire tried to smile at April's parents as they walked toward the door of The Hungry Bean but found her facial muscles wouldn't cooperate. Instead, they formed a sour frown that looked as if she had smelled something disgusting. April's mother kept her face blank, and April's father smiled back. She supposed years of teaching hormonal teenagers had taught him to put on a poker face regardless of the circumstances.

The coffee shop door opened, and a crowd moved toward them with flashing lights and shouted questions.

"Are you the Dells? Do you know anything yet? Where were you last night? Any comments?"

Reporters, Claire thought.

She took a stumbling step back, grabbing Mrs. Dell. Mr. Dell stepped in front of them while Ryan shooed the reporters out the door and slammed it shut behind them. Ryan glanced at the Dells and Claire and flipped the deadbolt on the door. The three stood stunned in the quiet atmosphere of the shop. Mrs. Dell cried into her hands, and Mr. Dell paled, as if the realization of his daughter's disappearance just now hit him. Anger burned in Claire as she imagined smashing their cameras to the sidewalk.

"Are you guys alright?" Ryan asked.

Mr. Dell pulled his wife into his chest as Claire nodded, not saying a word. She looked out of the glass door and could see the reporters still swarming. Her anger grew and burned like wisps reaching out from her core to touch every part of her. The reporters' behavior disgusted her. The podcasters she listened to never would have done this to the family and friends of a victim. They honored the victims and sought to learn more about these crimes to help society. They gained consent and did the job out of the goodness of their hearts, not for a sleazy paycheck. These reporters did the exact opposite. They violated, emotionally attacked, and disregarded Claire and the Dells' already shattered feelings.

Claire shook her head, repulsed at the behavior of the people outside. She wanted to shove the door open and start pushing the reporters to the ground. She wanted to scream in their faces, intimidating them into leaving. She took a deep breath as she reminded herself that violence would help no one. Instead, she took that anger and used it to formulate a plan of action in her mind.

Claire had always felt protective of April, and in her absence, she found that protective feeling transferred to her parents. She wouldn't let these vultures hurt the Dells, if she could help it. She turned to Ryan and put a hand on her forearm, surprising herself with the bold gesture. She could see the surprise in Ryan's eyes as well.

"Ryan, can you help me push them out of the way while we get April's parents to their car?"

"Of course," Ryan said, straightening to prepare for the battle, honor and pride printed on her face.

"Can you pull your coats over your heads?" Claire asked, turning toward

Mr. and Mrs. Dell.

"We can," Mr. Dell said, removing his coat and draping it over his head. He then helped Mrs. Dell to do the same through her tears.

"Okay, good," Claire said. "Ryan and I will go first. Stay as close to us as you can, and we'll lead you to the car as fast as possible."

The four started walking for the door, Claire and Ryan leading the grieving parents, but Mrs. Dell stopped, pulling herself away from Mr. Dell.

"Wait!" she shouted, and Claire turned. "What about you?"

"What about me?" Claire asked, feeling confused.

"You walked here."

In her fiery anger and protection of April's parents, Claire had forgotten about herself. She had opted to walk, but she couldn't walk home with the reporters swarming. She imagined trying to get home, both trying not to slip in the snow and avoiding photographers and questions, and knew it wouldn't work.

"I'll figure it out once you guys are safe," Claire said.

"I can take you home," Ryan said, and Claire felt a pang of excitement at the idea of riding with Ryan.

"Thank you," Claire said, blushing.

"Nonsense!" April's mother yelled. "You'll come with us. August, tell her!" Mrs. Dell continued, tugging on her husband's arm like a frustrated toddler.

"We'll take you, Claire," Mr. Dell confirmed. "It's what April would have expected from us."

Tears filled Claire's eyes because Mr. Dell was right—April would be appalled if she heard that her parents didn't take care of Claire as their own in her absence. As appealing as it sounded to drive home with Ryan, Claire felt like she owed it to April to accept this loving gesture from her parents.

"Thank you, Mr. Dell," Claire said, choking up. Ryan smiled and squeezed Claire's hand—she understood Claire's decision.

"Alright, let's go," Ryan said.

I've got this, Claire thought as they pushed the door open.

A flurry of loud screaming, flashing lights, and microphones in their faces filled the short walk to the car. Swept up into a whirlwind, Claire's head spun. She ran around the side of the car to open the door for Mrs. Dell as Ryan opened the door for Mr. Dell. Claire gave a small smile to Ryan, who returned it before dashing down the sidewalk to the coffee shop. Sitting in the Dell's car, safe from the vultures, Claire finally took a breath and reflected on the police interview. She hadn't known what to expect from the detectives, but she knew it wasn't emptiness and looming dread. If anything, she felt worse than before, as if April drifted farther away somehow. She tried not to look at April's parents for fear she would start crying and upset them.

"Would you like to come home with us, Claire?" Mr. Dell asked, putting the car in drive and pulling away from the crowd of reporters.

Claire looked at Mr. Dell with surprise. The Dells had never voluntarily asked her over and she hadn't expected the gesture now. In her shock, she forgot to respond and sat mute in the backseat.

"Maybe we can plan that vigil together as the detectives suggested," Mrs. Dell posed, eyes brimming with tears.

Claire wondered if the poor woman would cry until all the water drained from her body and she shriveled up like a dead worm on a hot sidewalk. As Claire pondered their offer, exhaustion set into her bones and her body grew heavy. She needed a break, away from people, and worried about what might happen if she didn't take one. Plus, she could be more useful to April at home—at the Dells, she would get distracted with supporting them, rather than focusing on the next steps.

She gave some thought before she responded. "I promised Detective Byrd that I would check on April's shoes, so I should probably do that. Plus, I'll be more helpful to the vigil planning from home with my computer and whatnot."

Mrs. Dell made a sound of disapproval, and Mr. Dell nodded. The rest of the drive passed in awkward silence, and Claire wondered if she'd made a mistake.

What if the Dells take this as a personal slight?

What if they cut me out of the investigation?

Fear clouded Claire's mind, and she panicked she might somehow lose April forever by upsetting her parents. Mr. Dell pulled into the driveway and Claire took matters into her own hands.

"Where should we plan for the vigil? I can send the information to Detective Byrd so she can get it on the news. I'm going to make a social media page for April, as well, and can post it there, too."

This question seemed to soften the Dells a bit, and Claire felt immediate relief.

"I thought I could call the pastor and see if we could have it at the church," Mrs. Dell said.

"Great idea, honey," Mr. Dell said. "I'll do some cold calling to spread the word to the older folks who aren't on social media."

"That's smart," Claire said, trying to feign enthusiasm.

It didn't hit Claire until she looked out the windshield at her home, but she dreaded going inside. As much as she craved a break, Claire's world had shattered, and she didn't know how to move forward. When she walked through that door, the stark reality of April's absence would be forced in front of her, and she couldn't know how that would affect her. She sat in the backseat of April's parents' car and stared forward at the front door as if it had snakes slithering up and down its surface. Mrs. Dell sensed her hesitation.

"It will be okay," she said, like a concerned mother. "I just know it will."

Claire nodded and put on a brave face. She opened the car but didn't make any moves until she heard an approaching vehicle. She stuck her head from the car and looked down the street as several news vans approached her house.

"Better hurry," Mr. Dell said, frowning into the rearview mirror.

"Thank you for the ride. Call me about the vigil," Claire said and dashed into her house.

She watched the Dells back out of the driveway and disappear from sight, and she hoped reporters hadn't already swarmed their house, too. After their car turned from the neighborhood, she continued to stare out the window as reporters lined the small yard, waiting to see if she would emerge. With a determined flick of the wrist, she locked the door, sealing off their access to her with smug satisfaction. She opened the coat closet, eager to check April's shoes, and looked down at the rack at the bottom. Just as she had expected—April's snow boots were missing from their place on the rack. She texted Detective Byrd.

Snow boots are missing so April was wearing them last night. Her parents are contacting the pastor to see if we can hold the vigil at the church. Stay tuned for more info.

As she walked into the living room, the tension from the day bubbled from her eyes as tears fell in thick rivers down her cheeks. The time passed impossibly fast, and her stomach gave a loud rumble for dinner, but she didn't have the appetite.

I can't sit down and eat while April is lost—possibly hurt!

Instead, she grabbed her laptop from the coffee table and flipped on the television. She scrolled through the channels until she found the local news and turned up the volume.

"Breaking news out of Tree Park today, a local woman has gone missing. Twenty-two-year-old April Dell, child of Arlene's Bake Shop owner Lucy Dell and Tree Park High School teacher August Dell, did not come home this morning. According to police, Ms. Dell was last known to be walking home from a babysitting job around midnight last night, during which time she had contact with her family. Her parents notified the sheriff's station after Ms. Dell's purse was found on the ground along her route home by a local shop owner this morning. The detectives on the case are asking that anyone with any information call the number listed on the screen. There will be a vigil held for Ms. Dell this evening, and details will be released shortly," said a blonde newscaster.

Claire sighed, disappointed. When she followed other cases, she got all her information from news broadcasts and articles—the difference here was that she was already on the inside of this one and didn't need to watch the news to learn new facts. She picked up the remote to turn off the television as a breaking news alert flashed across the screen.

"We have Sheriff Steinman here, making an initial statement to the public," the newscaster continued in her serious voice as the screen faded from her face and lit up on Sheriff Steinman, standing outside of his station. The bottom of the screen featured a chyron with a phone number.

"I want to urge the citizens of Tree Park to stay vigilant for Ms. Dell's whereabouts, and I want to thank those members who have already kicked into action to help one of our own. So far, our information in this case is limited. My detectives have interviewed the family, Ms. Dell's roommate, the family she was working for last night, as well as the man who found Ms. Dell's purse this morning. At this time, we have yet to identify any persons of interest and have successfully checked the alibis of the persons interviewed. If anyone has any information, we urge you to contact the station as soon as possible, as we believe that Ms. Dell could be in grave danger. The phone number should be on your screen. Thank you again," the sheriff concluded. He turned to walk off camera when a reporter shouted a question.

"Sheriff Steinman, is there any link between Ms. Dell's case and that of Ms. Tyler?"

Claire held her breath, waiting for the answer. Two women missing in the same small town almost one year apart didn't feel coincidental. Whatever happened to Bethany may have happened to April, as well. Sheriff Steinman leaned toward the microphones.

"I cannot comment on that matter at this time. My detectives and I are working around the clock to close all the cases on our docket. Thank you, and no further questions." His brow furrowed in frustration as he left the screen at a quicker pace.

The newscaster promised to provide updates on the case at the top of every hour, but for now, she moved on, and Claire turned the television off.

Time to get to work.

She opened her computer and created a "Missing April Dell" page on every social media site she could think of. She used a social media service, so when she posted on one, it posted on all. She invited all her friends to join the pages and then shared the page's links on her personal accounts and in several other groups dedicated to true crime. She hoped these connections would prove helpful. The more people she could get involved in this case, the better. After completing that process, she checked the groups and pages dedicated to Bethany's case for any new information. Dismay flooded Claire's mind as she realized the only new posts focused on April's disappearance, and nothing that could help find her friend. While many believed the two disappearances were connected, no one gave concrete evidence to support this assertion.

Claire then shifted her focus to doing research on Tree Park's CCTV infrastructure. It appeared the only cameras in the small town monitored the traffic on the highway just outside of it. A security camera recorded at the entrance to the National Forest at the town's edge, but it was unlikely that April would have been down there as it lay on the other side of town. Claire supposed that whoever took April may have traveled out of town that way, though, and wrote on a sticky note on her computer to see if she could obtain footage. The likelihood of a national establishment giving video footage to a nobody was slim, and she wished she had completed her forensic science degree. She posted in one of her true crime groups, asking if anyone had a way to access it or had an inside person, knowing her own effort wouldn't be enough.

She contemplated calling some of the local businesses between her house and the Endersons' to ask about their security systems when a noise from the other side of the house set her on high alert. Goosebumps broke out up and down her arms. She couldn't quite place it, but it sounded like a shuffling at the door.

Is someone scratching at my door?

Her heartbeat quickened as she imagined a murderer trying to pick the lock and kill her next; or a dog scratching at the door with April's severed arm in its mouth; or April scratching at the door to be let in after escaping whatever hell she was in. Jumping into action, driven by her paranoid and dark thoughts, Claire bolted for the door.

"April!" Claire gasped, desperate for her best friend and convinced that she was outside the door.

Claire ripped the door open, and it slammed against the wall. Ryan stood at the door—April wasn't there. Bent down, she was arranging large bags with handles. She flew back with a shriek, startled.

"Ryan?" Claire asked, flabbergasted.

"Jesus, Claire!" Ryan shouted. "You scared me!"

It's not April.

She sank to the ground, her head in her hands, and cried without restraint.

"Oh, Claire." Ryan rushed to embrace Claire, closing the door behind her to prevent the reporters outside from seeing her breakdown.

Ryan wrapped her solid arms around Claire and shushed into her hair. She murmured nice things into the top of her head and just let Claire cry. Ryan's arms held her until the tears slowed and then stopped. She hiccupped, like a small child, and couldn't sort her feelings. Upset that April wasn't at the door, embarrassed to have cried like this in front of Ryan, desperate to see her roommate, and in complete shock over everything. As she became more aware of herself again, Claire pulled back from Ryan, who looked down at her with kind and compassionate eyes. Ryan gave Claire a small kiss on the forehead before opening the front door and snatching the bags through the small opening.

"I brought you dinner. I figured after the day you're having and the fainting spell, you might need a bite," Ryan said with a sympathetic smile.

The gesture started Claire's tears again. Without April, Claire felt alone in the world, but Ryan's presence proved her wrong.

"Thank you," Claire said through her tears. "I don't know what I would have done today without you."

"I'm here for you, Claire, and I will be every step of the way until we find April," Ryan said.

"And what if we never find her?" Claire asked out of desperation.

Ryan paused. "Then, I guess you'll be stuck with me forever," she said with another kiss on Claire's forehead.

Claire leaned into Ryan's warmth and closed her eyes. This one small moment hadn't brought April home, nor did it change her reality, but it gave Claire the strength she needed to continue. She pulled back from Ryan's embrace and smiled.

"We've got work to do," Claire said, feeling motivated.

I'm bringing April home.

Chapter Ten

The busy day kept Heather distracted, but now, thoughts of Nathan swirled around her mind. She clocked out of work, relieved for a break but dreading the wide-open night that lay before her. Anxiety bubbled in her stomach. She didn't even want to think about how they would come back from this.

I can't believe he was going to kiss me—can't believe I almost let him!

She spent all day pushing the thoughts of the near kiss away and focusing on the tasks at hand. April's disappearance devastated her small town, and Heather felt the effects like the aftershock of an earthquake. Her mind ping-ponged between worries for April and her loved ones, and thoughts of Autumn's disappearance and the similarities that existed. Before she heard the news about April, Heather thought of Autumn often, but now the thoughts didn't leave her mind and it wore her thin.

She paused outside the church and removed her badge, shoving it into her coat pocket. She hadn't attended the support group in a while, and her anxiety swirled. The gesture, while silly, gave Heather a sense of normalcy, though everyone in the group knew what she did for a living. It allowed her to feel like Heather the Person and not Heather the Detective. She walked in and a familiar sense of dread settled into her chest when she saw the sign on the conference room door, *Grief Process Group*.

Heather's parents raised her in the church and she spent every Sunday of her childhood in this building. When she went to college, she stopped attending church, and after their father died, Autumn refused to go, too. Her mother remained faithful and still attended church weekly, despite her daughters' choices. Heather often wondered if she might find comfort in having faith, but at this point in her life, she didn't have time to add anything. Besides, she never enjoyed church. She remembered Sunday School, full of screaming children much younger than her running through the room. She remembered the coloring pages with Noah's Ark, learning about the Bible, and watching out for her little sister and her troublesome ways.

Once, Autumn had escaped from the Sunday School room and hid in a bathroom cabinet, causing mass panic throughout the church. The entire service stopped as everyone, adults and children alike, searched for her. Heather remembered her parents' panicked faces over Autumn's disappearance. Maybe if Autumn knew the grief that laid in store for them, she wouldn't have done that to their family. Now, as Heather passed the bathroom where the child Autumn had once hidden, Heather shook her head. Fate certainly had a sick sense of humor.

She made a beeline for the coffee station, grateful for its warmth and energy. She'd grabbed another nap in the station's locker room before waking up to attend this group, but she needed more rest. The coffee helped some. Grabbing a seat, she scanned the people sitting around the circle of folding chairs in the center of the room.

Mr. Polley sat across from her, and she smiled with warmth on her face. Mr. Polley had attended this group for five years, since his wife had died, and Heather found it incredibly romantic that he had loved his wife so much. On their way to the station from the interview, Heather and Nathan had stopped off at Mr. Polley's farming goods store to confirm the details of the purse. He hadn't noticed anything unusual; he found it on his morning walk from his store to the coffee shop and thought it best to turn it in there. He couldn't remember the exact location, but his walk was only a few blocks, which narrowed it down. They had walked the route and hadn't seen anything out of the ordinary, just as Claire had reported. At least they had a general idea of where April had dropped her purse.

She continued to scan the group and Mr. Enderson nodded at her. She had paid a visit to his house just before this meeting and had found no useful information with him either. The husband and wife each corroborated that they had come home from dinner, paid April and saw her off, and then watched a movie together before going to sleep. They provided the video doorbell footage to prove it. Heather hadn't expected to find any information from the family, but it disappointed her, nonetheless. With one cold case approaching the one-year mark, she couldn't handle having another case go cold—not that it was in her control.

Welcome, everyone," Jack, the group leader, boomed, startling Heather from her thoughts. "It's nice to see everyone, especially those joining us for the first time in a while."

He gave her a smile and a wink. She smiled back. Heather's gratitude for Jack would never wane. His unwavering support with both her father's and sister's deaths helped her heal more than he would know. She remembered her younger self, scared and shaken, walking into this same church for her first meeting with this group. She felt terrified of speaking to anyone, let alone in front of the whole group, and her body language showed it. Everyone in the crowd already knew what had happened to her family, and somehow that made things worse. She sat without taking any of the drinks or snacks and watched with anxiety because everyone seemed so comfortable.

Heather had spent the entire first meeting like this, uncomfortable and confused, and felt pure relief when it ended. She sat frozen when the others stood up, packing their belongings and making their way out of the room. She wanted to wait until the room had emptied before heading to her car, feeling an irrational fear that everyone would stare at her and judge her silence during the meeting. She didn't feel comfortable until Jack came and talked with her, sharing his own loss with an open heart. She had been at college, and Jack was newer in town, and she wasn't familiar with his story. She had never been more grateful to another person in her life because Jack opened the door for her own grief to come through.

She pulled herself out of her memories and smiled at Jack. She glanced at all the faces of people who had also lost a loved one. People spoke and shared, but she couldn't process their words. Her mind turned from grief to her job, going in circles between Bethany, April, and Autumn.

"Heather," Jack said. "Lost in thought, are you?"

Heather's head snapped up, and she sat straighter in her chair, feeling like a high schooler being reprimanded for not paying close enough attention to the lesson.

He chuckled at her. "Maybe you need to talk about where you've been for the past half hour."

Heather cleared her throat and looked up at the ceiling, willing herself not to cry. "Hi, everyone. Sorry that I've been distracted; this week is always a hard one for me." Heather paused, feeling her throat grow thicker. She cleared it and continued.

"My sister, Autumn, died two years ago next month. I don't talk a lot when I'm here, but I think it's probably time that I share my story. I'm sick of watching other people tell it for me." She took a deep breath. "Autumn attended college in the city and had fun—a lot of fun. She was all about that, the fun, after our dad died."

"Rest in peace, Sheriff Byrd," Mr. Polley said from across the group. Heather smiled and thanked him for his kindness before continuing.

"Autumn had been home over Thanksgiving break when my mom caught her doing drugs. They broke out into a huge argument, but ultimately, Autumn was an adult; what could my mom do? Autumn was vicious when she was using—made you feel like the smallest speck of dirt in her life. She left and didn't return home again until after New Year's. She had stopped going to classes and we still don't know where she was for all those weeks. She hadn't wanted to come home, but my mom and I were excited that she was there, and I suppose she felt obligated. It was only a few years after we lost my dad, and holidays were still weird for us. It's that period where you want to hold on to the past, but the future is forcing itself in."

Mr. Polley nodded in understanding, and Jack said, "After my daughter disappeared, I never stopped hanging her Christmas stocking. Those first few years, I filled it with toys. Eventually, I gave that up, but I know exactly what you mean by the future telling you it's time to change."

"Exactly," Heather said. "Things were emotionally painful, and I think that made it harder for Autumn to stay clean. She tried not to use around us, but seeing us and having that reminder of Dad drove her to use. It became such a horrible cycle. We spent that New Year's alternating between arguments and trying to hold on to the family we had left. After Autumn had been home for a little while, my mom decided it was time to confront her drug use. She wanted to try to talk her into going to rehab. I told her it was a bad idea, but she wouldn't listen." Heather shifted in her chair and took a deep breath before continuing.

"Autumn took it really badly and started screaming and throwing things. She broke a vase against the TV and stained the living room wall with spaghetti. It all happened so fast that I can barely remember it now, but before I knew it, she was slamming the door on her way out. Autumn didn't have a car, and a friend had dropped her off at my mom's house, so I followed her out and offered to drive her somewhere. She refused to get in the car and walked away. I followed her for a while, but she was being so cruel that I couldn't take it anymore, so eventually, I stopped following her."

Heather's mind flashed back to that night. Autumn's mascara ran down her face, and she stumbled as she walked. Knots of brown hair clumped on the side of her head and her body shook like a leaf in the wind. Her clothes had become impossibly baggy on her thinning frame—a white shirt with dandelions and black leggings. Heather thought she looked like a junkie.

Where had her sister gone?

"Autumn, seriously, just get in the freaking car!" Heather had shouted, her frustration boiling over into pure rage. "You're acting like a child."

"We can't all be perfect like you, Heather. Leave me alone!" Heather kept urging her to get in the car. Autumn refused, shouting insults at Heather.

"You aren't Dad; you aren't the sheriff; you aren't going to save me, Heather, so just let me go! Dad was the only one who understood me, and now he's gone! I wish it had been you or Mom who died instead!"

That one stung.

Numb and shocked, she watched her sister walk away, typing on her phone and not caring at all who she hurt. Heather gave up then. She didn't follow Autumn; she didn't call out again; she just stopped. Her tears of anger turned to tears of sadness. At that moment, Heather finally accepted that she couldn't help Autumn because Autumn didn't want to help herself. She told herself that she would talk to Autumn when she was sober, try to smooth things over with some distance and a clear mind.

"That was the last time I saw her," Heather continued, voice laden with sadness. "We learned later through the investigation that a friend had come and gotten her, and they had gone to a diner in a neighboring town. The friend left Autumn there, who said she was meeting up with the guy she had been seeing, but the diner staff told the police that Autumn left alone about an hour after her friend did on foot. Police never found her phone, so we couldn't confirm who she had hoped to see that night."

Heather paused, wiping a tear from her cheek and looking at the sympathetic faces. She was grateful for all those faces—for their emotional support and for helping her feel less alone.

"I blame myself for not getting her into my car or trying to follow her, but Autumn disappeared a lot. In that moment of my own hurt, I figured it was best to let her cool off and sober up and have a conversation with her when things were calmer. Every other time she disappeared, she came back within a week or so. But this time she wouldn't."

"You couldn't have known," Mr. Enderson said, and Heather nodded.

"By the time we decided to report her missing, it had been over two weeks. Her body was found a few days after that. I think everyone did their best, but we all know how cops treat people on drugs. Heck, I've even made the mistake of discriminating against people for using drugs in my own work. My co-workers figured she ran off with some local users to get high for a longer-than-normal bender and would show up eventually. That didn't happen."

"You did the best you could with an impossible situation, and you're doing right by her now by working hard at your job and making a difference for people like our dear April," Mr. Polley said.

Heather wanted to believe Mr. Polley's words but didn't. She had let down the one person who mattered the most in this world, and a lifetime of helping and saving other people couldn't change that. Heather would never forgive herself for not reporting her sister missing that next morning, no matter how long she lived. She couldn't let go of the fact that if she had, Autumn might still be alive.

"I appreciate the kind words, sir, but they're hard for me to really feel," Heather said. "I missed my opportunity to save her and that will never change."

"Honey," Mr. Polley said, "she was a sick girl, and you couldn't have helped her. You did everything you could for your sister, and your father would have been proud."

This was the hardest part for Heather; the town believed her sister had committed suicide. In her mind, Heather imagined that she had reported her sister missing and found her before she died at the hands of whatever sadistic person took her. In everyone else's mind, they imagined Heather reporting Autumn missing and Autumn still killing herself. Heather couldn't deny her sister's poor mental health—the depression took over and her addiction spread to so many substances—but Heather didn't believe those things had killed her sister. But she didn't want to dive into that discussion with a room full of strangers and instead smiled with appreciation at Mr. Polley and allowed the group to move on.

Heather tuned out for the remainder of the meeting. Her mind floated to those weeks when Autumn was gone but her body hadn't been found. Heather couldn't sleep, couldn't eat, and barely attended work. She'd been an absolute disaster. Sheriff Steinman should have fired her, but his dedication toward her father won out, and Heather was grateful. She stayed up all night scouring social media, searching for every possible variation on Autumn's name, desperate to find an active account. Autumn always disabled her social media accounts when she ran away from home to hide her whereabouts from her family but usually turned them on when she came home. Heather never found any trace of Autumn online in those long weeks before her discovery.

Aside from scouring social media, Heather spent her days canvasing every single establishment in Tree Park and three of the surrounding towns. She banged on doors and handed out flyers, but all to no avail. No one had any idea where Autumn went. She talked with Autumn's friends, who were all either too high or too paranoid to give her any information. Heather searched high and low and found nothing. As she prepared to travel to the farms surrounding Tree Park and the National Forest, she got the call about the discovery of Autumn's body.

She raced home as fast as she could and held her crumpled mother as they identified the remains together, both heartbroken. The rest of the week flew by in a blur; between the coroner's initial findings and the funeral planning, Heather felt completely dazed. Heather wanted to know the secrets to those missing few weeks, and she resolved to never give up. She knew the truth about her sister, and she would do anything to prove it. Heather had even gone so far as to hire a private detective to investigate her sister's death, but he didn't find anything new.

As the support group wrapped up, she plastered a fake smile on her face as she said her goodbyes and braced herself for April's vigil. While she helped Jack fold and stack the chairs, he stared at her, looking away any time she met his eye. Frustrated, Heather slammed down the chair she held.

"What?" she snapped.

"You're better than the way you treat yourself, Heather," Jack said, with an open expression on his face.

"What is with everyone saying things like that today?" Heather asked, remembering Nathan's comment about wanting better for her, too.

"Maybe because it's true, and you have people who care about you and love you?"

"Whatever," Heather said, annoyed. She grabbed another chair and slammed it shut.

"Heather, look at me," Jack said.

Despite her frustration, Heather met his gaze and softened. He crossed to her and took her hands in his. They were soft and warm, just like her father's.

"Autumn is gone, but you're here. You don't have to throw away your life over something that was out of your control. As cliché as it sounds, Autumn wouldn't want this for you."

Heather crumpled, and Jack wrapped his arms around her shoulders. She cried, relieved at being able to drop the tough detective's mask. He was right—she should accept her sister's death and allow love into her heart, but she didn't know how. Something fundamental inside of her had broken. Instead of taking the valuable advice of a trusted friend, Heather vowed to work harder to find the truth for her poor sister.

Chapter Eleven

April sat in Tree Park's only coffee shop with Claire, who lounged on a couch. Warm and happy, she wrapped her hands around a ceramic mug full of hot chocolate and marshmallows. Something, though, felt off. She couldn't put her finger on it, but something wasn't right. Claire twirled the straw in her iced latte in lazy circles as she scrolled through social media. Her blonde hair shone as the sunlight from a nearby window struck her. She looked almost angelic sitting there, a perfect piece of art, but wrong in some way.

April tried to shake the feeling of wrongness, keeping her gaze on Claire. She really was the sister that April never had. Claire had supported her through thick and thin over the years. Despite her positive feeling, the unease in her stomach grew. She closed her eyes and tried to enjoy the sunlight on her face as something in the distance crashed. April sat up straighter, heart pounding.

What was that noise?

She noticed that she and Claire were alone in the coffee shop. She looked to Claire, who glanced up from her phone and smiled.

"Did you hear that?" April asked.

"Hear what?" Claire said as she returned her focus to her phone, smiling at something on the screen.

Nobody stood at the counter or sat in the other chairs. Suspicious and a little frightened, April leaned back and tried to calm her nerves. She couldn't. Something was wrong, but what? She looked up at the ceiling and studied the little cracks and faults. A second crash followed by a scream made her jump.

"That!" April yelled. "Did you hear that?" She gestured at Claire, who remained still.

Claire didn't respond but dropped her phone to the floor and glared at April. Her deep and dark gaze scared April—this was not Claire. She wanted to but couldn't look away. Another scream pierced the silence, and she rose to her feet, slowly backing up, consumed by fear. This scream sounded different, so loud and raw that it sent shivers down April's spine. Whoever made that sound experienced pain that April could only imagine feeling in her nightmares.

The voice became hoarse at the end of the scream and shouted, "You'll pay for this!"

April couldn't figure out where the screams originated from. The shop lay empty.

Silence fell. Nothing, not a sound.

"Claire?" April whispered.

Claire sat eerily still and slumped forward, bending into an unnatural angle. Her blonde hair shrouded her—suspicion and fear wound up April's legs to her belly. Paralyzed, April stood for a moment before reaching a shaking hand out to tap Claire's shoulder. Claire's body teetered before crashing to the floor.

"Claire!" April shouted, throwing herself to the ground to check on her friend.

She used all her strength to flip Claire onto her side and brushed her hair from her face. April screamed—blood covered Claire, and maggots crawled in and out of her empty eye sockets. Her skin had a sickly green hue and had sunken in around the bones of her face. Her blonde hair grayed at the roots, and several clumps fell from her head to the floor. April shoved Claire away and scrambled backward, knocking into an empty chair and sending it clattering to the floor. The world shook and spun, and she heard another distant scream. She woke from her nightmare, sitting straight up in bed.

April's breath came in hard and ragged spurts. She blinked as reality settled. Sweat glued the sheets to her body, and she pulled them away from her skin. She was in the bedroom where her captors had chained her just a few hours earlier. She could hear a noisy commotion beneath her, and her heart raced. The clashing and banging sounds of a struggle floated into April's space. She drew herself into a little ball and pulled the comforter over her head, willing the noise to die down and go away. Whatever was happening down there may be what her own future held, and she couldn't handle that. What sounded like a heavy pot clattering to the floor echoed up the staircase, and she jolted. Another scream rose through the floorboards, and she imagined with horror that hot food splattered across someone's flesh.

"Get out, NOW!" a shrill voice shouted.

Mother Loretta?

April remembered falling asleep after Brother Beau gave her food and water, remembered the gentle way he had helped her into the bed. She shuddered at the memory of his hand brushing her cheek and felt violated. She wondered if he drugged her, if her desperation for sustenance had clouded her judgment. April shuddered at her stupidity and thought of all the bad things the brothers could have done while she slept. She ran her hands over her body, trying to feel for injuries, trying to piece together if anything happened.

Relief flooded April's mind. *I don't think they touched me.*

Her clothing remained in place, and she could trace each injury to a specific memory in her mind. She breathed a bit easier and vowed to be more careful. Another clatter sounded from downstairs. This time, to April's horror, footsteps stomped on the stairs after the clatter, and Mother Loretta's screaming grew closer.

"I told you *everyone* needed to be ready for dinner. How dare you defy me!" she shouted, and the footsteps thumped up onto the landing.

April's mind began moving at warp speed, desperate to hide before that woman burst into her room.

"M-M-Mother Loretta!" Brother Beau shouted outside her door. "Sister Jolene i-isn't feeling well. She can join us for dinner t-t-tomorrow!" His booming volume shocked April—he always talked so quietly before.

Thus far, all her experiences with Brother Beau demonstrated a meek and mild manner, and this shouting frightened her.

What if he is the same as his brother deep down? What if that side of him came out while he was here with me?

Fear rising, April gripped the comforter, pulling it tighter around her body. Her rapid breath heated the space under the blanket, making April slightly dizzy, but she didn't care. Like a child hiding from a monster in the closet, she didn't want to peek out of the blanket to get a breath of fresh air. The only difference here was that a child really had nothing to fear, but April feared for her life.

"Sister Jolene is FINE!" Mother Loretta yelled as a loud bang clattered against the door.

April jumped at the sound and whimpered. She clamped her hand over her mouth, desperate to keep as quiet as she had earlier in the day. She shook and listened to the sounds.

"Mother Loretta," Brother Waylon's flat and deep voice began, "Brother Beau is right—Sister Jolene's ill, and we need to let her rest. If we don't, she won't be able to fulfill her duties on the farm tomorrow."

Brother Waylon had tried to sweet talk his mother, while Brother Beau yelled out of desperation. She wondered why the brothers wanted to keep Mother Loretta out. April didn't know why they did it, but she allowed herself a modicum of hope that maybe no one would come into the room.

Perhaps the family would go downstairs to clean up the scatterings of dinner from their fight and eat without her. Her stomach lurched at the idea of trying to eat anything else, and she placed a fist into her stomach, willing it to stay silent.

The locks clicked on the door and April felt as if the air froze and time slowed to a stop. The door swung open and slammed the wall behind it. Footsteps, the clicking of high-heeled shoes, approached and she heard labored breathing above her. She waited in horror for her to rip away April's protective blanket, but it didn't come. Instead, a warm hand laid across her shoulder through the comforter, and a relieved sigh came from the person.

"My dearest daughter," Mother Loretta whispered as she rubbed April's shoulder. "You must be sick to be sleeping this sound at this time of day."

Mother Loretta leaned down and placed a gentle kiss on April's shoulder. She did her best to remain still and quiet, squeezing her eyes shut and begging her body to cooperate as she grew dizzier by the minute. Mother Loretta's kiss lingered on April's shoulder, but she eventually pulled back. Mother Loretta's footsteps receded, and April let out the quietest sigh of relief that she could.

The footsteps paused at the front of the room.

"Brother Waylon, you'll go downstairs with me. I'm preparing a nice soup for our dearest Sister Jolene." Brother Waylon gave an affirmative grunt as his footsteps thudded down the stairs, one heavy foot at a time.

"A-A-And me, Mother Loretta?" Brother Beau asked, his meek tone returning to him.

He sounded closer to April than Mother Loretta, which surprised her. Mother Loretta's creepy touch took all of her focus, and she hadn't stopped to wonder who else had come into the room with her. Mother Loretta let out a chuckle, deep in her throat.

"Since you know so much about being sick yourself, Brother Beau, you can stay here with Sister Jolene. Make sure she is ready by the morning," Mother Loretta said through her chuckle, and her footsteps resumed.

"Wait!" Brother Beau shouted, but it was too late.

The door slammed shut and Mother Loretta laughed as she flipped the locks.

"No…" Brother Beau whispered, banging his fists on the door.

April relaxed—Brother Waylon and Mother Loretta were gone. She waited a few moments, thinking about the interaction that had just taken place. April now realized that Brother Beau's voice hadn't escalated from bravery, but from fear. Mother Loretta clearly favored Brother Waylon—she responded better to his stern words and chose him as her kitchen companion. April felt sorry for Brother Beau. Not only did his mother love Brother Waylon more, but now he was being held captive, too.

How much of his life has he spent locked away?

April crawled out from under the comforter. Her head spun from the drastic change of no air under the blanket to the chilly air of the bedroom, and she groaned.

"A-a-are you alright?" Brother Beau asked.

April opened her eyes and did her best to find Brother Beau through the haze surrounding her. Tears swam in his green eyes, and he seemed concerned for both of them. He moved toward the bed. April held her hand up in front of her; he didn't frighten her, but she feared this situation with every cell in her body.

"I'm okay," she said, her voice dry and cracking.

"G-g-good," Brother Beau said as he walked to the closet and opened it.

Inside lay an entire row full of identical pink dresses. The fabric looked soft and sweet, like a fluffy and soft cloud. The pink took on a very light hue and a white collar lined the neckline, creating a "pilgrim girl" vibe. Brother Beau pulled a dress from a hanger and bent down. Several identical pairs of shoes lined the bottom of the closet—black flats with a buckle around the back of the heel. He grabbed a pair of frilly pink underwear and a plain white bra from the dresser and walked the bundle of clothing to April.

"Y-y-you'll need to wear these before breakfast tomorrow morning.

Mother Loretta w-w-wants Sister Jolene to look her best, e-e-every single day," Brother Beau explained.

April did not know what to do or say. Her mind swam with confusion.

I'm not Sister Jolene...am I?

April felt her touch with reality fading on this crazy farm and she doubted who she truly was.

Am I really April, or has the world I knew before this been a lie? Have I spent my life in captivity, just dreaming of a world where I could be free? Was any of it real?

"Am I Sister Jolene?" April asked, quiet and hesitant, ignoring the bundle of clothing he placed at the foot of the bed.

"You are," he hissed through his teeth, with a paranoid glance at the door.

"I'm not, though, am I?" April whispered, now fearful as well. "Maybe you have me confused with someone else."

"W-w-we don't. You are Sister Jolene, regardless of w-w-who you might have been before."

"That doesn't make any sense," April grew louder and sounded like a spoiled child.

"But you'll wear the c-clothes?" Brother Beau shook all over at the idea that April could refuse to wear the clothing he had laid down on the bed. As she met his gaze, he winced and shut his eyes as if she would jump out and attack him.

Why is one of my captors afraid of me? And why aren't I that afraid of him?

"Yes, I'll wear the clothes. I don't want to die." Her emotions took over again.

April pulled her legs into her chest and cried into her folded-up knees. She cried for so many things that her brain felt flooded with the water of her tears. She cried for herself and her confusion at her new reality. She cried for the April she had once been, who was clearly never coming back. She cried for her new identity as Sister Jolene. She cried for this man sitting in front of her, the most broken person she had ever met. She cried because even if she did survive this, a part of her had truly died forever. She cried because she could do nothing else.

Brother Beau took a tentative step toward April.

"Y-y-y-y-y–" Stuck on his words, he took a deep breath and tried again. "You are different from the others."

His words surprised April so much that she stopped crying and looked up.

"Others?"

"O-other girls."

April stared at Brother Beau with a blank expression.

Other girls, she thought. *Were there other girls here? Have they done this before?* Her brain froze around those words—as if a fork jammed her circuits and shut down her mind from the inside out. She could see the gears in Brother Beau's mind turning and his discomfort at having told her something so personal.

"I'm not the only one?" April asked, barely above a whisper.

"Y-y-you are... now... but not the only one e-ever."

April stared incredulously at him. She could tell that he read the frustration on her face as he wrung his hands and whimpered as if in pain.

"T-t-the first was really sick; Brother Waylon said it was from d-drugs. She a-always threatened us with her sister, who was a cop or something. S-s-she didn't make it long, she hurt herself too badly to recover," Brother Beau said in a rush, as if the information physically hurt him to stay inside.

April felt her blood go cold as she imagined the first woman they had taken, sick from withdrawal and probably scared out of her mind as she hurt herself beyond repair. She contemplated the last bit about her not having made it a long time.

Will I make it longer than she did?

She didn't say anything as Brother Beau continued.

"The s-s-second was too much of a fighter. She was like a feral cat. We tried to make it work for far too long. S-s-she hurt me a lot, and Mother

Loretta didn't care for her much. B-b-brother Waylon took care of her, though."

Her head spun at that information.

Will Brother Waylon take care of me as well? Her breath came in rapid bursts, and Brother Beau picked up on this.

"No, no, no," he said, shaking his head. "You aren't like them. You are kind and quiet; you could save us." He took another step toward her.

She whimpered again. She didn't want to be here, let alone save this family. She wanted to go home, and she wanted to wake from this nightmare. Part of her wanted to die, understanding the first girl. She scooted back on the bed until she came against the headboard. Brother Beau continued his slow movements toward her and reached out a hand. As he approached her bedside, April closed her eyes and turned away from him. His crazed look signaled his belief that she would save him. He brushed his hand down her hair.

"My sweet Sister Jolene," he said, as April shuddered and squeaked. "You are the one."

Chapter Twelve

Arriving at the vigil felt surreal; things like this only happened on TV. Claire parked and breathed out through pursed lips, willing her pulse to slow with her breathing. Ryan placed a supportive hand on her shoulder. Her shaggy pixie-cut hair brushed her forehead, and Claire wanted to run her hands through it. She imagined it would have felt marvelous after the hellish day she'd had. Claire stopped herself and instead placed her hand over Ryan's. Her skin was soft and warm, and Claire wished they could put the car in reverse and keep driving until this nightmare was nothing but a small wisp of a memory behind them.

"Ready?" Ryan asked with a small squeeze of Claire's shoulder.

"Ready as I can be, I guess."

"Hoods up."

The two pulled their hoods over their heads before exiting the car and stepping into the barrage of reporters. As they jogged away from the car, Ryan reached out for Claire's hand. Her heart warmed in the cold night air as tingles traveled up her arm. Claire kept a solid hold of Ryan's hand as they walked through the church's doors.

She is anchoring me, keeping me grounded. I might float into a pool of useless emotions if Ryan lets go.

To her surprise, Ryan didn't let go, and the two continued to hold hands as they walked down the hall of the church. A bit giddy at the gesture—two women holding hands in a church—she liked the feeling. Mrs. Dell's bossy voice boomed from the inner chapel, and Claire smiled with a tinge of sadness.

"It's nice to hear her sounding so like herself."

As the pair walked toward the chapel, people filed out of a small conference room just ahead of Claire and Ryan. When Claire read the sign for the grief support group, her heart sank.

Is this my fate in the future? Grief support groups over what happened to April?

As the older citizens of Tree Park exited the room, she peered inside. She saw Detective Byrd helping fold chairs. She, like everyone in Tree Park, knew what had happened to both the detective's father and sister, and her heart reached out. She didn't have any sisters, but she shared a sisterly bond with April. She shuddered at the reminder that Detective Byrd's sister hadn't come home alive, and that April might not either. As the detective folded the last chair, she gave a hug to the leader of the group before heading for the door.

"Claire! Ryan!" the detective shouted over the chatter. "Ready to get going?"

Claire and Ryan nodded, and Claire blushed as she saw the detective's eyes glazed with tears, feeling as though she saw something she shouldn't. As they walked into the chapel, Mrs. Dell rushed over, huffing and puffing.

"I am so glad you made it," Mrs. Dell cooed as she wrapped her large arms around Detective Byrd before making her way down the line to hug Ryan and then Claire as well.

The gesture surprised Claire. Mrs. Dell hesitated and hugged her a bit longer than the others, and the warmth of her embrace brought on tears. The hug reminded her of Mrs. Bushy, and Claire felt desperate for some sort of maternal comfort. She wondered if Mrs. Dell would have that kind of place in her life moving forward. If they found April, perhaps this experience would bridge the gap between the Dells and Claire, and if they didn't find April, maybe she could provide the Dells with a connection to their lost daughter. For now, Claire wanted April home, and nothing more. Mrs. Dell pulled back from her hug with Claire and jumped right into planning mode.

"Okay—Ryan, I need you to help pass out the candles. They're in boxes in the storage room. Hopefully, we have enough."

Ryan nodded and gave Claire's hand one last squeeze, dropping it slowly, allowing her fingers to slide against Claire's. Claire flushed as her gaze went from Ryan's fingers, up her arm, and straight into her brown eyes. Ryan threw her a wink and a smile before disappearing down the hall. Claire still stared at the empty doorway as she realized Mrs. Dell was talking to her.

"How does that sound?" Mrs. Dell finished, waving her hand to divert Claire's gaze into focus.

"Sorry, one more time?" Claire asked, blushing and feeling awkward. How could she be thinking of romance now?

"I said, you will stick with Mr. Dell and me at the microphones. I thought it would be nice if you said a few words about April. Does that sound alright to you?"

"It does," Claire said, honored to be given a place at the vigil with April's family.

April had always been like family to Claire, more so than her own mother and father. Tears welled up, overwhelmed by the rapid-fire emotions inside her. Mrs. Dell reached out to touch her face with gentle fingers.

"April thinks of you as the sister she never had; your place is with us, regardless of our differences," Mrs. Dell said.

Claire met Mrs. Dell's eyes, and the tears were unstoppable. They spilled down her cheeks in thick rivers, and her vision blurred. Mrs. Dell used her thumbs to wipe away her tears, something Claire's mother had never done.

"Now stop your tears—we have work to do," Mrs. Dell said, resuming her loud and booming voice and moving on from the tender moment.

Claire nodded and smiled, making her way past Mrs. Dell to Mr. Dell, who untangled microphone cords on a table behind them. Detective Byrd's quiet voice echoed through the room as she offered to help Mr. Dell with his task.

"It's just me tonight; Detective Longville maxed out his overtime. I'm going to fade into the background and keep an eye on things. If you see anything or anyone suspicious, wave to me, and I'll come up with you all. I'll chat with some of April's friends after the vigil as well and see if we get anything from them," she said.

Claire wondered if Detective Byrd's tragic family drove her to become a detective. She supposed that even without tragedy, the daughter of a sheriff might join the world of policing, but she also knew that victims of families liked to stay involved in some way.

Maybe Detective Byrd finds solace in her work helping other people.

Claire, impressed by Detective Byrd's strength, felt a small connection between herself and the detective blossoming in her heart.

Claire continued with her menial tasks, going wherever Mrs. Dell directed and thankful for the distraction. She peeked at Ryan once in a while and always caught her looking back. Excitement flared in Claire's chest over the prospect of something building, but incredible guilt swam in her belly. Life should stop in its tracks during a tragedy, but the reality never went as expected. Claire stopped looking at Ryan and forced herself to focus on the work ahead of her for the vigil. Her mind sucked into her work and time flew—before she knew it, people crowded into the chapel's pews.

The Dells took their spot at the front of the church, chatting casually with the pastor and looking nervous. Ryan stood in the chapel doorway, handing out candles and directing people toward the pews. The sheer number of people in attendance shocked Claire. She'd grown up in a trailer park in a city and hadn't experienced a tight-knit community like this. The crowd filled every pew and people started gathering at the back of the church, leaning against the wall. Claire noted Detective Byrd's location in the crowd and joined the Dells.

Claire did not enjoy public speaking, never one for attention. Her stomach churned and her mind floated as the vigil started, and she couldn't focus on April's parents speaking. She tried not to think about everyone staring at her, tuning out the voices of the speakers before her.

As Mrs. Dell ushered Claire in front of the microphone, she realized it was her turn to speak. She meant to spend the beginning of the vigil planning out her speech, but her discomfort had erased that plan from her mind. On her way to the microphone, Claire's gaze caught on the large canvas photo of April on a stand beside her.

Did I really just see her last night? Claire thought, and her heart broke all over again.

"I miss you," she said into the microphone, without thinking, a deep blush covering her cheeks.

"Her—I miss her, I mean," she said, clearing her throat. "I know I saw her yesterday, but it's been forever since we went that long without seeing each other."

She paused, clearing her now-thickening throat, and she heard Mrs. Dell behind her crying. Claire forced herself to look up into the crowd, seeing the worried and concerned faces of April's friends and Tree Park's citizens. The love and concern they reflected allowed Claire's stage fright to melt some, with a strange sense of bravery taking its place.

"April would be shocked to see all of you here. She would have thought that everyone had better things to do than to gather in her honor. I think that's the beauty of her, though; she touches people's lives without even knowing it. It makes her the best kind of person…." Claire trailed off as she heard Mrs. Dells' sobs intensify.

Claire held back tears as she found Detective Byrd in the crowd. She couldn't tell from this far away, but she swore she could see her eyes shining with tears as well. She thought she could see a look of pride on the detective's face too, which drove Claire to push on with her speech.

"April is strong, stronger than I think anyone here knows, and she will come home to us," she continued, seeing a news crew toward the back of the church. A silent reporter stood beside a cameraman, with the lens pointed at Claire. Her emotions took over as she spoke again, looking into the camera.

"If you can hear this April—we love you, and we will never stop looking for you. Ever. If the person who took April can hear this, know that you picked the wrong girl. She's got an entire town behind her, looking for her. We will find her and find you, and justice will be done. That's a promise."

Claire's eyes widened in shock as the audience broke into applause, several members standing in ovation. She stood at the microphone, speechless and blinking. Mr. Dell came up from behind her, wrapping his arm around Claire's shoulder as he spoke.

"We need each and every one of you to help us bring our girl home! Lucy and I will be handing out flyers to be distributed around town and on social media. The more we spread the word, the more likely it is that we will find her. We appreciate you all so much. Some friends will be coming around to light our candles, and we will have a moment of silence for our lost little April."

Mrs. Dell took a lighter from her pocket and lit three candles, handing one to Mr. Dell and one to Claire. Claire held it close to her heart, watching the flames flicker on the wick. The Dells embraced each other as the lights above them dimmed and the space filled with twinkling lights. The beauty of the scene struck her straight in her soul, and Claire wished that April could have witnessed this. She hoped that somewhere, April could feel the warmth and love that they sent out into the world for her. The crowd fell silent as the last candle illuminated with a flickering glow. Claire imagined a strain of positive and strong energy leaving this crowd, floating high above the church, and making its way directly into April's heart and mind, wherever that may be.

"Thank you, everyone," Mr. Dell concluded, voice thick with tears, and blew out his candle.

The crowd followed suit, and the aroma of burning wicks wafted throughout the church. Once more, the crowd buzzed with activity, a quiet murmur spreading throughout. Claire smiled and left the stage, feeling dazed. She almost bumped into Detective Byrd, who seemed to have magically teleported to the front of the crowd.

"You did great," she said with a nod, and Claire appreciated her words very much. Members of the crowd surged toward the stage, wanting to help and talk to April's parents.

"Why don't we chat in the hallway?" Detective Byrd suggested, and Claire nodded, following her through the crowd.

Once in the hallway, Claire relaxed her tense muscles, finally able to breathe. She wondered where Ryan was; Claire hadn't seen her since before the speeches when she handed out candles.

"Holding up okay?" Detective Byrd asked, though her eyes said she already knew the answer.

"I guess?" Claire mused. "But I don't think it's possible to really be okay during all of this."

"You're right, it's not. It's no secret that I've been through something very similar, and I wish I had given myself the grace to not be okay. I felt like I didn't have that luxury, and it really hurt me in the long run. I thought that pushing away my emotions would make me strong enough to find my sister, but in the end, all it did was hurt me more."

Claire looked at the detective. "I appreciate that a lot," she said.

"I made a promise to myself a long time ago that I would be the person that others needed. I couldn't take a world where people who are hurting don't get what they need. It's my way of healing."

"I couldn't imagine helping anyone else through this in the future—this has been too much for me to handle," Claire said.

"You might surprise yourself," Detective Byrd said. "You seem to know a lot about this world."

Claire got quiet, grateful her true crime hobby hadn't made her sound like a complete idiot to a real detective. Now that the cat was out of the bag,

Claire pushed forward with the many questions she had.

"Do you have any leads? Any suspects or persons of interest?" Claire asked, feeling stupid in her eagerness.

"Unfortunately, no. Prime suspects are usually the housemates, those who saw the victim last, and the victim's significant other. You and the Endersons both have solid and provable alibis, and April wasn't dating anyone. We've been going through her phone today, and there's no evidence of a grudge or a problem with anyone, either."

"I was hoping you wouldn't say that," Claire said.

"Did you think of anything else about April that we might need to know? I know some of the things we talked about at the interview were difficult with April's parents there. Maybe something else might have come to mind?" the detective asked.

"I don't think so..." Claire looked down at her hands, mulling over the idea. "I already told you about the boots, and I didn't find anything unusual at the house. I created a social media page but so far have no sightings of April after she talked with her mother on the phone last night, so nothing useful at all."

"Thanks, Claire. I appreciate your involvement. I think it's going to be helpful to the case. Call me if you need anything or think of something that might help," Detective Byrd said in farewell and turned to go.

As she did, a man Claire had never seen before bumped into the detective. She reached out for Detective Byrd's elbow, stabilizing her.

"I'm so sorry!" Detective Byrd gasped, looking up at him.

He wore a ball cap pulled down over his face and kept his eyes on the floor. He looked up at Claire briefly. He had stunning green eyes rimmed with red, like he had cried through the vigil. He must have known April well if he'd been crying like that.

"Are you alright?" Claire asked, trying to be kind, just as Heather had done for her.

"N-n-no—excuse me," he said and rushed off.

Claire and Detective Byrd shared a glance, and Claire knew what went through her mind. *That was weird*. Detective Byrd jumped into action and followed the man as he rushed toward the doors. Claire fell in step behind the detective, pulling her phone from her pocket. She opened the camera app and snapped pictures as Detective Byrd followed him out of the church. Claire stayed in the doorway, wanting to hide from the reporters, but watched the detective closely. Her mind reeled as she imagined the stuttering man hitting April over the head with a baseball bat, pushing her into a hole in the ground, and burying her alive, keeping her hostage for the rest of her life.

Detective Byrd talked to him, though Claire couldn't make out what she said. Half of the reporters focused on taking photos of Claire, the poor missing girl's roommate, while the other half had turned to follow the detective. Claire could see that the detective made no headway in her attempts to speak with the stuttering man. Claire watched as he climbed into an old black truck and tried to reverse. The reporters blocked his way, and the truck jerked back and forth as he tried to get out. Claire pulled her phone up in front of her face and snapped as many photos of the man and his truck as she could as he sped past the church and turned out onto the street. Detective Byrd jogged over to Claire and ushered her inside and away from the reporters.

"Here," Claire said, showing Detective Byrd the pictures on her phone.

Claire watched over the detective's shoulder as she scrolled through. A great shot of the truck and another of the man's face through his car window pleased Claire and a glimmer of hope floated through her stomach. The poor lighting in the pictures disappointed her, but she imagined the lab could brighten them. She frowned as she realized she hadn't gotten a shot of the license plate—what a rookie mistake.

"These are great, Claire. Text me them," Detective Byrd said, handing her the phone. "I'll get them to our tech analysts right away."

Claire sent the photos to the detective's phone. "Many perpetrators return to the scene of the crime or to an event for the victim. They get a rush from seeing the damage that they've caused. What's interesting, though, is that he was crying, almost as if he was really sad for April and all of this pain."

"Maybe he knows what happened to April but feels guilty that he hasn't said anything," Detective Byrd said.

Claire nodded, an idea lighting in her mind. "Wasn't there a sighting of a black truck in the area when Bethany Tyler went missing?"

Claire saw a look of pride flash in Detective Byrd's eyes.

"You're a quick study, Claire," the detective replied, "and that's exactly why I think we need to find that man. Immediately."

The detective said goodbye, rushing out of the church. Claire's insides tingled with excitement. She unlocked her phone and uploaded the pictures she had taken to all her social media platforms, making a mental note to do a reverse image search as soon as she got to her laptop. She may not have the license plate, but she would find this man.

Chapter Thirteen

April's mouth felt fuzzy, like dust bunnies lived inside. She ran her tongue across her teeth, willing her saliva to moisten things, but instead, it was like sandpaper grating against her cheeks and lips. She tried to open her eyes, but the sun shone in blindingly bright rays, and she couldn't manage. Her body shivered with chills, and she reached for a blanket but couldn't find one. She reached farther down, and her wrist caught on her restraint, her arm jerking back. *I'm not in my bed.* Memories from the night before flooded in. *When will this nightmare end?*

Brother Beau and April had fallen into silence after his utterances of her perfection. He gently touched her hair, her face, her neck. Brother Waylon had come in, interrupting Brother Beau's creepy infatuation, with the bowl of soup that Mother Loretta had promised and a tall glass of water. April knew they might drug her again, but she had no willpower. The one glass of water earlier in the evening had not quenched her thirst, and the small sandwich left her stomach growling. April gulped down the water and gobbled up the soup, careful not to spill it on her bed or clothing, not wanting to lose a single drop. Brother Waylon and Brother Beau stood at the foot of the bed, watching her. When she finished, the two left, and Brother Beau offered her a shy smile as the door closed, locking her in again. Feeling more coherent than earlier, April noticed the drugs hitting her system. A pleasant and warm sensation spread throughout her body. She lay down on the bed, tucking herself under the comforter, and let the sensations take over her.

What else can I do?

April's body and soul emptied—this family held her trapped in this house, held her fate in their hands. She was powerless. Maybe the best thing to do was to disconnect and let time move faster. She closed her eyes. There was no point in stalling her inevitable demise, and she might as well let her dreams float her far away from here. She did her best to steer her thoughts from her reality. A sound caught her attention—footsteps approaching the door. She heard the keys jingling in the many locks, but she didn't move.

Let them come, she thought. *What difference does it make?*

She had given up, and didn't allow herself to care. She stared up at the ceiling and waited for the door to swing open. April didn't shift her gaze toward the brothers as she heard Brother Waylon's domineering footsteps enter, followed closely behind by the timid footsteps of Brother Beau.

"Up," Brother Waylon hissed.

April didn't move a muscle. She wondered what would happen if she did nothing at all. She knew that Brother Waylon wouldn't tolerate her ignoring him for long and supposed he might get rough with her. What did it matter if they beat her and threw her down the stairs if her life was over anyway?

Brother Waylon cleared his throat, and Brother Beau spoke in hushed tones. "D-d-did you give her too much?"

"No." Brother Waylon sounded annoyed. "I know what I'm doing."

"Seems like y-y-you don't," Brother Beau said with an edge.

April registered how nervous Brother Beau sounded over his concern for her, his perfect sister potentially being harmed. She could hear Brother Waylon huffing at his brother, and she felt anxious on Brother Beau's behalf. If they had locked him in here with her, April supposed they would do even worse to him too. She didn't like Brother Beau—he had participated in this whole ordeal, after all—but he didn't deserve this treatment, either. Besides, at the very least, Brother Beau gave her useful information on the family, and she didn't want to close that channel. She cast her head toward Brother Waylon standing next to her, her neck jerking and creaking with the effort.

"I'm dizzy," she said meekly, attempting to buy some time.

Brother Waylon nodded to Brother Beau, and the two approached her. They pulled her to a sitting position, and April saw stars sparkling in her field of vision as Brother Waylon unlocked her wrists and dragged her to her feet. Brother Waylon began to undress April, pulling her black shirt from her body. Too stunned to react, she let it happen. The room spun as Brother Waylon removed her jeans next. She voluntarily stepped out of the legs, afraid of what might happen if she didn't. Her heart hammered in her chest, and she thought she might get sick at any moment. Brother Waylon next removed April's bra and then underwear, and she stood stark naked in front of him. Hot tears of embarrassment and panic stung her eyes as her mind ran wild with the things he might do to her.

Will he throw me onto the bed and rape me? Will he force me to leave this room with no clothes at all? Will he carve his name into my bare skin?

By the time Brother Beau approached with her new set of clothing, April had forgotten about his existence entirely. He dressed her with care and tenderness, which made April's skin break out in goosebumps. She gagged, and Brother Beau took a tentative step backward, avoiding the spray of vomit that emitted from her mouth. Brother Waylon grunted and shook his head as if disappointed. Brother Beau looked at April with fear. She thought she might faint. Brother Waylon took a step forward, approving of April's clothing and carefully avoiding the pile of vomit on the floor, directing April toward the door.

Shaky, her sore body creaked at the forward movement. Between the stiffness of her aching muscles and queasiness, April felt like hell. Brother Waylon took the stairs slowly, leading April from the front, and Brother Beau followed close behind her. As they passed, April stole a second glance at Sister Jolene's photo on the wall.

Where is she? She couldn't be one of the women Brother Beau mentioned, so where did she go?

At the bottom of the stairs, Brother Waylon turned down the hallway and led April toward the room where she'd first heard Mother Loretta humming. The walk down that hallway stretched into an eternity as she approached the dimly lit room at the end. The Brothers stopped, each securing a hand around April's wrists to prevent her from running. She raised her glance from the rug on the floor to the oversized rocking chair where a woman sat.

Mother Loretta.

She rocked in the chair, and April heard the click of knitting needles in her lap, though she couldn't see them. Her gray hair was pulled into the same tight bun April had seen before, but now she could see tiny, frayed tendrils sticking out from her scalp. The room was small and smelled of dirt and earth, and April shuddered. She glanced stealthily around the room, taking stock and inventory. Frost covered the only tiny window and the wood floors creaked as Mother Loretta rocked. A small table stood to the right of the rocking chair, with a loveseat to the right of that. A long, thin bookcase pressed against the wall next to the sofa, though more dust than books lined its shelves. In front of the rocking chair lay a fireplace with a stone hearth. A fire burned, radiating heat. The logs crackled, and April wondered if this place would have felt cozy under different circumstances.

Brother Waylon spoke in a flat tone, startling April. "Mother Loretta."

Mother Loretta stopped rocking, and the clacking of her knitting needles also ceased. Wordlessly and without turning, she reached out her hand and laid the bundle of needles and yarn from her lap onto the table next to her. Slowly, she stood up, smoothing down her long skirt. She moved without sound as she made her way around the rocking chair to stand in front of April. She seemed to float above the wood floors, and April's arms broke out in goosebumps.

April focused on Mother Loretta's dress, afraid to meet her daunting gaze.

She wore a long-sleeved gown that looked like something from a historical fiction novel. The dark gray fabric matched her hair in an eerie manner and gave her the appearance of wearing a burial shroud. Her creepy look and the earthy smell of the room created a sense that this woman had died years ago and escaped her grave. April could hear the click of high-heeled shoes as Mother Loretta approached, but her voluminous skirt hid them from view. Mother Loretta reached out a finger as she approached and placed it underneath April's chin. Slowly, she applied pressure, drawing April's pale face up. April couldn't stand straight, but somehow this gesture mesmerized her into lengthening her spine.

Mother Loretta's face appeared younger than April expected—nothing like the undead ghoul that April pictured gliding toward her. Soft age lines fanned her eyes, and deep frown lines were etched in her forehead and around her mouth. Her skin appeared soft and smooth, despite the lines. Her small nose pressed up slightly, just as Sister Jolene's had in the picture in the stairwell. She held her lips pressed tight, and they blanched white from the effort. April reluctantly met Mother Loretta's stare and found the darkest, deepest pools of green she had ever seen, pupils hidden in the low light. There appeared to be nothing behind those eyes but deadness, and an involuntary shudder traveled down her spine in response. Mother Loretta's mouth pulled up in a soft smile, and her gaze softened.

"Sister Jolene, my dearest daughter, are you feeling better?" she whispered, her voice tinged with sadness and pleasure, and she brushed April's lips with a gentle thumb.

Mesmerized by the moment, April couldn't decide between screaming out of sheer terror and fainting on the spot. She nodded, afraid to actually speak, and that seemed to be sufficient. Mother Loretta took a step back, reluctantly dropped April's hand, and looked her over.

"You look…thin…" she said after pondering April's appearance for a few moments, and her mind flashed to Sister Jolene's plump, round cheeks.

"The horses won't mind less weight, but I am concerned about your ability to complete your other duties. We wouldn't want you to wind up like Brother Beau, now, would we?" Mother Loretta hissed.

She shifted her gaze to Brother Beau, and April felt his hand grow slick with sweat as his grip on her wrist tightened and his fingers trembled. Mother Loretta's gaze on Brother Beau lost the soft touch—instead, it turned cold and detached.

"Protein shakes," she said casually, shifting her scrutiny from one brother to the other.

Brother Waylon gave her a curt nod.

"She'll do," Mother Loretta said, "though hopefully she's learned her lesson about her naughty behavior. I would hate to continue to punish her as we have been all these months."

Mother Loretta turned her attention to April. Frozen in fear, she didn't want to disrupt Mother Loretta's decent mood. She didn't want the punishments the other girls had received—from the look on Brother Beau's face as he talked about them, it had been horrific. As Mother Loretta watched April with a sad love, April wondered for what felt like the millionth time what was going on here.

Doesn't she realize I'm a new girl?

"Come with me, my dearest daughter," Mother Loretta crooned as she grabbed April's hand and led her down the hall.

Brother Beau's hand tightened on her wrist in a squeeze of solidarity. She stole a glance at him, and he gave her an encouraging nod. Brother Waylon picked at his nails, not bothering to look up.

Mother Loretta led April straight down the hall, passing the stairs and through the swinging door to the kitchen. Stalks of wheat decorated every surface in the room, just as April would have imagined a farmhouse kitchen. Wheat wallpaper lined the walls, dish towels with cartoon wheat stalks hung from the dishwasher and stove, and wheat magnets adorned the fridge. A cuckoo clock chimed as they entered the room, and a tiny farmer popped out holding a stalk of wheat. On the counter next to the fridge sat a set of eerie, faceless dolls resembling the family—a mother and her three children. Beside the door hung an old-fashioned corded phone. A large kitchen table stood in the center of the room, and April's blood ran cold when she saw the shackles attached to a wooden chair.

"Sit, please, Sister Jolene," Mother Loretta crooned.

April feared Brother Waylon; the deadness behind his eyes communicated he would show no mercy. She wasn't afraid of Brother Beau, at least not in the same way as his brother. Brother Beau had gone along with her kidnapping but seemed to do so only out of the desire not to be killed by his family, plus he had a fondness for her that the others seemed incapable of. Mother Loretta, however, was a complete wild card.

When April sat, Mother Loretta locked her to the chair before fiddling around in the cabinets and fridge. Part of April felt grateful for the chair; her muscles were shaking and weakened. The other part, however, felt paralyzed with fear. She watched Mother Loretta but couldn't figure out what she was doing. Her fear rose with each rapid beat of her heart, and she longed for the quiet bedroom upstairs. She knew that panicking would only lead to disaster, and she tried to take a deep breath, but it caught in her throat. The kitchen grew fuzzy around the edges, and stars twinkled in front of her.

Where am I?

April was a little girl in her mother's bakery, and the air smelled warm and sugary. Her mother's loud laugh echoed from the kitchen behind the storefront. She walked to the back and saw her grandmother wiping a plop of cookie batter onto her mother's nose. The two laughed together as they tossed the batter at each other, blissfully unaware of April's presence in the doorway. Her mother, however, caught sight of her and grabbed her daughter around the waist. April shrieked with joy as her mother spun her around and her grandmother wiped batter on her nose. April scraped the batter from her nose, sticking her sticky fingers into her mouth and enjoying the sweet taste of lavender and sugar. It had been one of her favorite days at the bakery.

Mother Loretta placed things on the table in front of April.

"I know your hands are bound, but you can still observe. Though we've baked a lot together, you've been forgetful lately and I think a lesson is in order." Mother Loretta added ingredients to a bowl.

"I can bake," April said timidly, not sure what came over her at that moment; she thought she had resolved to stay quiet, but the words came out of her mouth anyway.

Mother Loretta looked up, face somewhere between shock and love.

"You sound much improved; that rasp in your voice is gone! Hopefully, your stint with foul language is over now, too," she warned but returned to her ingredients. "If you can prove to me that your behavior is improving, perhaps we can cook together sometime soon."

April nodded, watching Mother Loretta's hands at work. She chanced a glance out of the small window above the sink. She couldn't see anything except the bright sun shining from her vantage point.

"I know you're anxious to get outside to your work," Mother Loretta crooned. "Brother Beau will take you out when we finish in here, and you can get straight to work."

"On what?" April asked, again speaking without thinking.

The moment the words left her mouth, regret washed over her like a flood. Sister Jolene wouldn't have asked such a stupid question. Sister Jolene would have known her list of farm duties. Mother Loretta had just complained about Sister Jolene being so forgetful lately, and April had done exactly that. Her breath shortened in anticipation of what would come next as Mother Loretta stopped fiddling with the bowl in her hands. She moved as if in slow motion, and April couldn't tell if it was real or her damaged mind turning the world into slow motion. Mother Loretta's eyes met April's—pure fire shone from the depths of the mossy green irises. April wanted to scream and break out of her restraints, but her paralysis returned.

"On what?" Mother Loretta hissed, throwing her whisk down to the table and splattering batter over the wooden surface. "So, you've gone from a dirty, ungrateful wretch to an absolute imbecile?"

April tried to hide her face in her shoulder. Mother Loretta reached down and slapped April across the face, stunning her. She tried to bring her hands to her face, but they caught on the chair restraints. Her cheek stung.

"I'm sorry," April shouted, tears brimming, trying to right her wrong with frantic desperation.

"I'm sorry, who?" Mother Loretta shouted back, spittle flying at April's face.

"I'm sorry, Mother Loretta!" April's tears flowed down her face, cheek throbbing at the smack.

"Dearest daughter," Mother Loretta said as she crouched down to meet April's eye level. "You know I don't want to treat you this way. I need for you to be how you were before; I need for the changes to stop. If you can be the sweet girl that I remember, then we won't have these issues." Mother Loretta ran her hand over the cheek that she had slapped.

"I'm sorry, Mother Loretta," April whispered again as she rocked in her chair.

"I'll get you some ice for that cheek before Brother Beau comes to take you for your farm work."

April wouldn't upset Mother Loretta again. She was a terrible combination of her two living children; she had the deadness and unpredictability of Brother Waylon while also having the kindness and unhinged love of Brother Beau. Somehow that made her the most terrifying person April had ever met. Mother Loretta pulled ice cubes from the freezer and put them directly on April's red and pulsing cheek. The freezing temperature of the ice burned worse than the slap had, and the cube stuck to her dry skin, ripping it a bit with each small movement of Mother Loretta's hand. Despite the pain, April did not dare move a muscle, afraid to meet a fate worse than a slap.

Chapter Fourteen

Heather's morning had gone beautifully, and it only took one call from the Sheriff to ruin it. Her run-in with the stuttering man at the vigil had ignited a fire in her soul that she had missed for so long. Finally finding progress in Bethany's case and possibly linking Bethany and April—Heather soared over the moon with pride. A man with a stutter had called in the tip about the black truck location for Bethany's case, and now a man with a stutter driving a black truck attended April's vigil—it couldn't be a coincidence. Heather had rushed to the station with the pictures from Claire and given them to Alan, head of technical analysis. He had quickly processed the information, waiting for a hit. The moment they got the information on the man's identity, Sheriff Steinman could pursue a warrant and close both cases, hopefully with both girls alive and well.

Autumn's case could be closed, too, a quiet voice inside Heather's head whispered, and she shook it away.

She knew what she believed about her sister but didn't want to pull focus from Bethany or April. While she craved the closure Autumn deserved with deep desire, she knew her sister would never come back. Heather could still save April and Bethany, and she had to keep them at the forefront of her mind. She couldn't live with another death on her conscience.

After giving the photographs to Alan, Heather went home. Alan said it would take time for him to glean any new information, and her exhaustion penetrated bone deep. She walked through the door and crashed onto her mattress, sleeping through the entire night in black dreamlessness. She now sat on her couch, dressed for the day and sipping tea while running her fingers through Luna's fur. Her phone remained silent through the night, and she'd had rare time for a lengthy shower, lavishing in the warmth. Part of her wanted to go to the station, but the other part enjoyed the morning, knowing she deserved it. If something pressing came up, they would call, and she couldn't be a great detective without the bare necessities of self-care.

As she took another long sip of her tea, she contemplated calling Nathan. *I do need to update him about the stuttering man and the black truck at the vigil. Maybe Alan told him. Maybe I made a mistake by not calling him when it happened.* Her phone rang, and the screen said Sheriff.

"Sheriff, any news on the identity of the man from the vigil?"

"Not yet," Sheriff Steinman responded, sounding curt and almost sad.

Heather's blood stopped. *Something's wrong.* She put her mug of tea on the coffee table. Luna jumped from her lap and bounded away, almost as if escaping what would come next.

"What is it?" Heather asked.

"We got a report of a body on the edge of town. The man on the phone said it had been dumped on the outskirts of the National Forest. I'm heading there now, and I want you to meet me. I already called Nathan, and he's on his way to pick you up."

Heather stood, picked up her mug, and carried it to the sink, preparing herself for Nathan's arrival.

"Any idea who it is yet?" she asked.

"No—we can confirm that when we get there. Another thing, Heather—the man on the phone had a pretty serious stutter."

It was inevitable, she thought. *It has to be April or Bethany.*

Either it would be Bethany, and the work she had done over the past year to find her had failed, or it was April, and she would have to watch the loss of another one of their own rock her town to its core.

"Got it, Sheriff."

As soon as Heather hung up, her phone buzzed with a text message from Nathan.

Here.

Heather stared at her phone; Nathan usually sent longer messages, and the one-word text hit her hard. She didn't have the mental capacity to wonder how he felt about the near kiss or the lack of information on the case. Instead, she threw down some food for Luna, spilling some bits on the floor and not caring, before rushing out of her apartment and down the stairs.

She jumped into Nathan's patrol car, and he sped off, flipping the sirens on and accelerating fast, throwing Heather back into her seat. The drive was short, but with Nathans's speed, they made it in a flash. The National Forest loomed ahead, trees looking haunted and as if they could swallow the car whole. As they approached the outskirts of Tree Park's entrance to the forest, the flashing lights of the sheriff's car came into view. The sheriff and another officer stood near the car. Her heart dropped when she saw the sheriff had removed his hat and held it over his heart.

As Heather stepped from the car, she met the sheriff's eye and saw the same sad look that he had given her on the day her father died and the day that they found Autumn's body. She couldn't read in that expression who the body belonged to, but she knew it was one of them. Her mind hoped it was an older resident of town that had passed away from natural, unavoidable causes, but in reality, she knew. The stuttering man wouldn't have reported a nobody. Heather and Nathan stopped in front of the sheriff and waited for him to give them their next directive.

"I've already ID'd the body, but I want confirmation that I'm seeing things clearly." He gestured toward the scene and took a step back.

He didn't want to taint Heather's or Nathan's identification and let them make the discovery for themselves. The other detective on the scene started photographing various pieces of evidence and combing the scene for anything suspicious. The body lay just ahead of them, surrounded by caution tape wrapped around several nearby tree trunks.

They stopped outside the caution tape, giving their names to the person with the clipboard. They put on paper booties, so their shoes didn't leave any imprints or disturb the scene. The person instructed them where they could walk—this was, after all, an active investigation.

Heather felt like her legs were filled with sand as she made her way along the edge of the tape and toward the body. The dead woman lay on her stomach with her head turned away from where Heather and Nathan stood. She could see a large bullet wound in the back of her head, clearly alerting to the manner of death and solidifying the homicide suspicions. She couldn't have shot herself execution style. The bullet had blown away and burned the hair around it, but the wisps towards the bottom of her neck and her ears were dark brown. The strands seemed greasy and uncombed, as if they hadn't been cared for in months.

The woman was mostly naked, clad only in a plain bra and frilly pink underwear, both of which looked worse for wear. Bruises, cuts, and burns covered her body. A large bruise on the cervical area of the spine resembled fingerprints, and several burn marks surrounded her elbows and hands. Her body was thin and emaciated, and ribs protruded from the skin on her sides. Clearly, this woman had not been able to take care of herself, nor had anyone taken care of her. Her skin was pale and had a sheen to it.

The cold weather has probably slowed decomposition, Heather thought. *I'm not sure I recognize her.*

She noticed the woman had harsher injuries on her ankles and wrists and thought she might have been bound or held captive for an extended period of time, certainly longer than April had been missing. The wounds were red but calloused over, not fresh. When she saw the woman's feet, it hit her.

"No Van Gogh tattoo," Heather said, pointing down.

Nathan nodded in agreement.

"It's not April," he confirmed with a look at the sheriff, who kept his face neutral.

That only left Bethany.

Nathan placed a supportive hand on Heather's arm as they moved toward the woman's face. A deep bruise covered the center of her stomach and it yellowed around the edges, indicating some healing. Heather's eyes traveled up the woman's torso, over her unmarked breasts and bra, and directly to her face. There was a blown-out bullet hole in her forehead, and the top of her scalp was brutally destroyed.

"It's Bethany Tyler," she said, confirming what the others already knew.

Heather felt numb. This was her first serious case as a detective, and it was the first crime scene body she'd seen in person. Heather had gone with her mother to see her sister and her father at the funeral home, but this was different. At the funeral home, the bodies had been cleaned and dressed up nicely—they looked as if they might wake up any second. Bethany's body looked broken and destroyed, defiled by some sadistic perpetrator.

"Just as I thought," Sheriff Steinman said from his stance near his car. "Though it can be tough to tell with a bullet wound such as that one." He hung his head for a moment.

"Doesn't look like she's been dead long," Nathan mused, frowning at the body.

He's right, she thought, studying the body.

They hadn't moved the woman, but the medical examiner would determine any pooling of blood. Rigor mortis had set in but there was no bloating. Of course, the cold weather would account for some of the delayed decomposition, but Heather thought it had been little more than twenty-four hours. With this thought, she shattered internally.

She just died. We could have saved her.

"We better go talk to the family before the story gets out," Heather said, voice cracking. She cleared her throat. "Probably need to call April's family as well. They'll be panicked that it's her once it hits the news."

"I agree," Nathan said, looking at the horizon where a fleet of news vans approached.

Sheriff Steinman nodded. "I'll stay behind and see her off to the morgue and handle the crowd control. Call me when y'all are done talking with the family. I know it's a long drive, but I want you to come straight to the station when you're finished. This isn't the break we wanted, but maybe now we have a real chance at solving this thing."

"Maybe even a chance for April," Heather said, trying her best to focus on her work and draw herself out of her emotions.

As she and Nathan walked away from the body, Heather paused. Looking at Bethany's destroyed body, her emotions crept in, like a trickle of freezing water from an icicle. She knew she was close to exploding as they filled her entire soul. Bethany's brown eyes stared lifelessly into nothingness.

"I'm so sorry," Heather whispered.

She was desperate to get the image of this broken woman out of her mind when something caught her attention. Bethany's bra and underwear. Her mind flashed to the crime scene photos she looked at after Autumn died. By the time the authorities had alerted Heather to Autumn's death, the body already lay in the morgue. Heather rushed to get her mother and then rushed to the morgue and when she'd seen Autumn's body, a white sheet covered her from the neck down. She had been determined to figure out what had happened and, against recommendations, had looked up the case on one slow and quiet night. She had looked at the photographs of Autumn, body laying at the bottom of the bowling alley clad only in a white bra and frilly pink underwear.

She grew cold as the realization hit her; *Bethany is wearing the exact same undergarments.*

She made her way over to Nathan, who opened the car door for her. Reporters crowded the roadway as another officer from the station arrived to hold them off. She threw herself into the patrol car and landed on the seat with a thud. As Nathan drove their car away from the forest, a medical examiner's van from the closest city pulled in.

Maybe someone will see the similarities.

Once they were on the highway, Nathan looked over at her. She did her best to keep a neutral expression on her face. The emotions crept in faster and faster. Sadness for Bethany and her family. Sadness for the future that Bethany could have had that was now gone forever, destroyed in the woods alongside her. Fear about the possibilities for April and her family. And what about the underwear? Who could she trust with this information? She slid her hands under her legs to hide the shaking that had hit her. As the forested scenery gave way to suburbia, her sorrow abated, only to be replaced by anger.

We've spent countless hours working hard to bring Bethany home, all for nothing. All because some scumbag decided to use her in his sick game, or whatever he's doing.

And she'd missed it, whatever clues there might have been. If she had worked harder, searched deeper, she could have saved Bethany. The realization had dawned on her at the dump site, but now it came crashing over her. Not only that, but the anger at no one believing her about Autumn barreled in as well. She begged both Nathan and the Sheriff to take her seriously for months, and no one would listen. The anguish hit her like a truck—Heather roared with anger. Her voice sounded primal, and she punched the door of the patrol car. Her knuckles screamed out in pain as she wailed over and over.

Nathan was shouting, but Heather couldn't hear what he was saying through her primal screams. He pulled over to the side of the road and got out. She almost fell from the car as her last punch hit only air. Nathan caught her before she did, and she let her body slump into his.

"We could have saved her!" Heather shouted into his arms. "We should have saved her. We failed her, and now she's dead!" Heather didn't know if she was talking about Bethany or Autumn at this point.

"I know," Nathan said, and she could hear the emotion behind his words.

"We could have saved her, and we let her die," Heather repeated.

We could have saved her. Bethany is dead. Autumn is dead.

Heather continued crying and let it run its course. She was sick of pretending to be strong; she was sick of holding back tears; she was sick of everything. Jack was right. She needed to take care of herself, but maybe she was too late. Everything in her and around her had broken, and she would never recover. Nathan wrapped his arms around her, giving her the stability she needed. She wanted to stay in his arms forever. She marveled at the fact that she couldn't remember a time that she felt this safe. She supposed it was when her father was still alive, and it broke her heart that she had lived all these years in a perpetual state of grieving and fear. She shifted her weight and hugged him, squeezing him back.

"We did everything we could," Nathan said, pulling away from the hug to look into her eyes.

He was right. Cases don't get solved without the necessary clues, and she hadn't had any with Bethany or Autumn.

"And now we have to do everything we can to bring Autumn home," Heather said.

Nathan winced and looked at Heather with more sadness in his eyes than ever before. "You mean April?" He brushed a piece of her hair from her face.

Heather covered her face with her hands and groaned. *How could I have said that?* She wanted to tell Nathan about the undergarments, but she feared he would give her that sad look as he told her she was crazy and seeing connections that weren't there. For now, she'd keep this to herself.

"Of course, I mean April," Heather lied, fully meaning that she would do everything in her power to find out the truth about her sister's death.

Nathan nodded and pulled her into another embrace. Embarrassed, she buried her face into Nathan's shirt, blocking out all the light of the world. She took a deep breath, inhaling his musky aroma. For this moment, she would allow his scent and his feel to be everything to her. In the next moment, she would put all this emotion in a tiny box and get to work. She had a girl to save, a girl to avenge, and a sister to vindicate.

Chapter Fifteen

Claire hadn't yet slept when the morning sun shone through the windows. Not only was it morning, it was *late* morning. Had she really spent all night online? She rubbed her eyes and looked at the clock in the corner of her laptop screen, blinking hard at the time. Could that really be right? She closed her laptop and set it down on the coffee table in front of her. She had stayed late at the vigil to talk with as many members of their community as she could about April and to help the Dells clean up. By the time she'd gotten home, it was late, but that didn't stop her from going online, desperate for answers.

The notifications on her phone after posting the pictures of the stuttering man came in a constant stream, and she eagerly grabbed her laptop the second she got home. She sifted through the notifications like a squirrel digging for seeds. She tried to go through each notification slowly but couldn't. She raced through each comment, share, and like, and before she knew it, the trail ended.

This can't be happening, she thought in despair. *Not a single person can identify the man from the vigil.*

Claire went through each notification at least three times before accepting nobody knew this guy. She then placed the photos she'd taken into a reverse image search. For the picture of the man, no results popped up. For the truck, only pictures of arbitrary black trucks for sale and car advertisements came up.

Maybe I missed something.

Claire repeated her electronic footsteps from before the vigil, looking for any trace of April's whereabouts on the internet and checking all the same sources. She hoped that something new might pop up but knew in her heart there would be nothing. When people disappeared without a trace, evidence didn't magically appear within the first few days. Heck, Bethany's case hadn't made any headway in the near year since she disappeared.

Claire's mind shifted to Bethany. Perhaps the key to finding April lay in the secrets of Bethany's disappearance. She traced her familiar lines of inquiry, this time related to Bethany, and checked all the pages she had flagged. All the new information dealt with April's case and people speculating if the two cases were connected. So far, she had a big fat nothing.

Claire felt disheartened once more, but a new notification came through. An employee from the National Forest uploaded a screenshot of a blurry black pickup truck. Hope pulsed through every vein in Claire's body as she clicked on the image. They had posted anonymously, not wanting to lose their job, and she couldn't contact them for more information. She sighed in frustration and saved the picture to an email, forwarding it to Detective Byrd and hoping that maybe the sheriff's office could do more than her.

The research and searching took hours, but sitting here now, Claire felt like it had been mere minutes since she arrived home from the vigil. She stretched her arms above her head and felt her aching muscles relax some. Her back popped and cracked, and she settled into the couch, staring at the black television screen. Her boss told her to take as much time as she needed, and Claire contemplated calling out of work tonight.

Would work be better than sitting here, waiting for something to happen?

On a normal Sunday morning, Claire would have slept in and caught a late brunch with April before work. Now, she sat alone in the house, paralyzed by the lack of information in the case. She considered leaving her house, but where would she go? Instead, she settled for a mental check-out and flipped on the television. The channel remained on the news station she'd watched the day before. The screen lit up with the face of a young woman, one that Claire recognized but didn't know. Tears fell down her cheeks and a reporter nodded with sympathy.

"Take your time, Angela," the reporter said.

The name rang a bell for Claire, Angela Grabel, April's high school bully. Anger flashed in her chest like a torpedo as she realized that April's high school bully, the girl who teased her for being an art nerd, stood crying on television about her disappearance. Claire stood up from the couch, propelled by anger.

"I just can't believe this is happening to one of our own," Angela sobbed at the reporter. "I don't know what I'm going to do without her."

"What the hell!" Claire shouted at the screen. "You didn't even know her!"

Her anger bubbled further as she recalled a story April had told her. When April was a freshman, she'd been excited to start high school and wasn't nervous because her father taught there. Though she would only see him for English class, April felt like she would be safe. She had decorated his classroom, selecting new works of art for the walls. During her first day of English with her father, he had proudly thanked her for the art, and Angela made a snide comment. Devastated, April made her father remove the art from the walls, fearful that she might get teased again. April told Claire that it hadn't stopped there, and Angela had continually teased her throughout the remainder of her high school years.

One of the drawbacks of returning to your hometown was the possibility of seeing people you might not want to. They hadn't run into Angela much. April worked out of town, and the two of them didn't spend much time in Tree Park on weekends, but that didn't stop April from being anxious about it. Claire wondered how April would have reacted to seeing Angela talking about her now. April had a kind heart, she would probably brush it off. Claire, on the other hand, was the exact opposite. She wanted to punch Angela in her mousy little face.

Claire curled into a tiny ball on the couch, anger melting as her mind started to shut down. Claire had always used sleep as an escape. In her mother's trailer, she would nap after school just to make the time go faster. Peaceful sleep felt easier than loneliness and wishing her mother would come home from work or her father would come back from wherever he had gone. She didn't have friends and figured that dreaming up some would be the best option for her. She would lay on the small futon that they used for a couch, close her eyes, and dream up the most fantastical situations that would whisk her out of her trailer and into a new world entirely. Claire had gotten so good at dreaming that she often worried one day she would go to sleep and never wake up, her subconscious preferring dreams to reality.

Sleep gave Claire a pleasant escape—the nightmares, however, plagued her. Trapped within evil and destruction, she'd wake on the futon, sweating and breathing hard, utterly terrified.

This time, luck was against her as she drifted into the nightmares.

At first, everything was dark. She tried to see but was blind.

"Hello?" Claire called, and her voice echoed back at her.

Her vision started to clear, but not enough to make out her surroundings. She put her hands down beside her and touched something soft. She curled her fingers and pulled at the soft strands, bringing it up to her eyes. Green strings of grass filled her hands and dirt caked under her fingernails. The grass floated from her hands and into the sky, giving its surroundings full color. Claire blinked and could now see that she sat in a large, green field. The wind gently blew, and stalks of grass waved. The air carried the bitter musk of dirt and the sweet scent of wildflowers. Her hair fluttered in the wind, and she tried to relax. She could feel the pull to close her eyes and let the wind take her away, but something inside of her refused.

But she was in a nightmare, trapped in this place, and everything around her started to rot. The grass turned brown and singed at the tips. The air smelled foul, as if something had died, and drops of blood sprinkled from the sky like rain. The small flowers surrounding Claire turned into Venus flytraps and snapped at her skin. One caught her elbow and ripped her flesh, blood pooling in the tiny wound. She stood up, and the wind started howling, whipping her hair around her face, strands smacking her in the eyes. She called out with effort as she tried to push against the wind and escape the terrorizing field, little droplets of red staining her clothing and hair.

The wind strengthened as Claire's effort increased. The nightmare world overtook her, and she realized she couldn't win. She collapsed to the ground with a grunt of pain and felt herself giving up and fading away. As her body flattened down to the ground, she heard the sinister sound of an engine revving. Snapping her head up, the bright headlights of a black truck blinded her. She shielded her face as she looked at the truck, noticing dark brown mud covering its wheels and sideboards. She craned her neck, trying to see the driver, but failing.

Claire awoke, screaming. She sat bolt upright, heart racing harder than ever before.

"It was just a dream," she whispered. The jingle of a breaking news alert from the television caused her to sit up.

Under normal circumstances, breaking news rarely indicated something good, but with April missing, this alert terrified Claire. A reporter stood somber with her microphone, the trees of the National Forest swaying in the background.

"Breaking news from our small town of Tree Park today. The body of a young woman has been found. Police are working to identify the body as we speak, and we will update once we have confirmation. Speculation is that it could be either April Dell or Bethany Tyler." Claire's legs went weak beneath her as she crumbled to the floor, knees thudding hard. Her hands flew to her mouth.

Oh God, I'm going to be sick. It can't be her... please no...

Everything shimmered as if the living room had filled up with water and it filled her lungs. A loud ringing started in her ears, and she stopped hearing the reporter. Bethany and April looked alike, it was true, but she knew that the odds of Bethany's body being found after all this time were slim. The odds were starkly against April, and agony ripped through Claire as she screamed out for her friend. She fell the rest of the way to the floor and lay on the cool wood, feeling untethered…floating. She dimly wondered if something inside of her had broken.

A sound was buzzing from the coffee table—her cell phone. She dove for the phone, desperate for answers, banging her knee on the coffee table. It was Detective Byrd.

"Is it her?" she answered, voice wavering with sobs.

"It's not her," Detective Byrd said, voice full of calm empathy. Claire didn't respond with words but instead with relieved sobs.

"It's okay," Detective Byrd said. "It's okay, Claire."

"Thank you," Claire said once her sobs subsided. "Do the Dells know?"

"Yes, we called them first," Detective Byrd said. "And we have more calls to make so I'm going to go. I'll check in on you later. Oh, and thanks for the email. We're trying to get video footage from the National Forest now."

"Thank you, Detective," Claire said. As she disconnected, relief and pride flooded her system.

The doorbell rang and Claire made her way to the door, opening it without thinking. Ryan stood in the doorway, taking in Claire's disheveled appearance with a look of concern on her face. Grease coated her hair from a lack of a shower and her eyes were red rimmed from crying. She wore the same clothes she had worn to the vigil and the bags under her eyes showed that she hadn't slept the night before. Ryan reached out a hand and wiped away a tear.

"You look tired," Ryan said as she stepped inside the house. "Have you slept?"

"I was busy," Claire said stupidly, not knowing what else to say.

"You have to take care of yourself, too, Claire. April wouldn't want you to stop sleeping."

"I know. I closed my eyes for a moment then I saw the body found in—"

"Body?" Ryan shouted. "What body?"

"It's not April," Claire said. "A body was found on the outskirts of town and hasn't been identified yet. Detective Byrd said it's definitely not April."

"Jeez…" Ryan trailed off. "I'm glad it's not her, but does that mean it's Bethany?"

"I don't know. I supposed it could be anyone."

For some reason, at that moment, the black truck from Claire's nightmare flashed into her mind, the headlights bright and the tires caked with mud. She looked down, mind traveling back to last night as she thought about the stuttering man.

"Where'd you go just now?" Ryan asked, bending down to catch her gaze.

Claire focused on Ryan but didn't really see her.

"The mud…," Claire muttered as she returned to the living room.

"The what?" Ryan asked, confused but following.

"The mud!" Claire shouted.

Claire sat on the couch and grabbed her laptop from the coffee table. Ryan sat down next to her, and Claire didn't register how close Ryan sat to her, completely caught up in her search. Their legs touched, and Ryan leaned into Claire's space to see the laptop screen better. Claire opened the folder with her pictures from the night before and clicked on one of the truck, making it full screen.

"The mud!" Claire shouted again, pointing to the mud on the tires. It also sprayed along the back of the truck bed as if the truck's tires had done some spinning. "There aren't many spots where you could get stuck in the mud like that. Mud that thick needs more space than Tree Park has to offer."

"I see," said Ryan, catching up. "Maybe one of the farms outside of town?"

"Exactly," Claire said, searching for *farms near Tree Park*.

The search results brought up a long list of farms in the vicinity, and

Claire's mind swam at the sheer number of possibilities. She took a deep breath, willing her mind to slow down. She knew this stuff; this was her area of expertise. She decided to start with the farms closest to Tree Park and fan out. She selected one and sent a link for another to Ryan, thinking it best if they split up the work and search. Claire and Ryan scrolled through websites and social media pages, scouring the information listed and checking the gallery of pictures for any sign of the stuttering man and his truck.

After they had checked three farms each, Claire wanted to give up. Why had she felt so excited about this lead? It was a stupid idea and would get her nowhere. She could feel her exhaustion catching up to her and her eyes began to close as she continued to scroll.

"You should rest," Ryan said, sympathy clouding her face.

She placed a gentle hand on the back of Claire's neck, rubbing her thumb in circles on the tense muscles. Claire melted under Ryan's gentle touch and leaned her head on the couch. A small groan escaped her lips; she hadn't realized how much tension she held. Ryan worked her magical fingers around the muscles of Claire's neck, and Claire felt herself slipping away from the conscious world. Her body grew weightless and warm.

"Oh my god!" Ryan shouted, startling Claire.

Claire sat bolt upright, eyes flying open as Ryan shoved her cell phone into her face. It took her a moment to focus, not sure what she looked at.

"That's him!" Ryan shouted.

Claire blinked hard as the image in front of her came into view. The website was old and hadn't been updated in several years. The top said, "Smithers Produce and Cattle" and below that was a picture of a family standing on the porch of a small farmhouse, miles of farmland extending behind them. None of the people in the photograph smiled, and their eyes appeared to be ghostly. In the photograph, the parents stood behind three children, two boys and a girl in the middle. Claire pinched her fingers on the screen to zoom in on their faces, stunned to see the stuttering man, though in this picture he was much younger than he had been at the vigil.

"Oh my god," Claire said, mind still trying to catch up. "We found him."

"*You* found him," Ryan said. "Searching the farms was your idea!"

"Oh my god!" Claire shouted with excitement.

Without even thinking about it, Claire put her hands on each side of Ryan's face and pulled her in for a kiss. The second their lips touched, she pulled back, aghast that she had kissed Ryan at all, let alone without consent. She stared at Ryan, horrified by the shocked look on her face. Claire felt like that moment lasted forever, her not speaking and Ryan looking stunned, before Ryan broke out into a small smile. She put a gentle hand on Claire's cheek and rubbed her thumb back and forth. Claire's insides melted with pleasure as Ryan leaned in and kissed her, lips soft but firm. A small electric shock traveled from Ryan's lips and into hers as she kissed her. Both women blushed as they pulled away from the kiss.

"I'm sorry," Claire said, embarrassed.

"Don't be. I've wanted to do that for so long." Ryan went in for another kiss, but the urgency of the stuttering man's identity hit Claire, and she stood up.

"We have to get this to the sheriff," Claire exclaimed.

She grabbed Ryan's hand and pulled her toward the door, snatching her keys and running outside. The two women jumped into the car and Claire backed out of her driveway, not caring if she ran over a reporter. People scrambled out of her way as she turned her car around and sped toward the Sheriff's department, hand tucked securely into Ryan's.

Chapter Sixteen

Brother Beau came to fetch April from the kitchen, face full of wariness. April stared into his eyes with a silent plea for escape. The slap from Mother Loretta still stung her face, and April felt like the air of the kitchen crushed her lungs. She wanted to get outside, desperate for a break from the insanity of this home. Brother Beau fixated on the red slap mark on April's cheek, and his eyes widened. As he approached, he shook with fear, and April noticed that Brother Waylon wasn't behind him.

Thank goodness it's only Brother Beau.

"A-a-are you ready?" Brother Beau said, keeping his gaze down at his feet as he stood next to April's chair.

"What?" Mother Loretta shouted, causing April to jump. "No one can understand you when you mumble, Brother Beau!"

Brother Beau recoiled at Mother Loretta's shouts and took a tentative step toward the door. Mother Loretta let out a cackle, laughing at her son for his fear. The tension between the mother and son thickened the air of the room and April could feel the burn of it on her skin. Brother Beau hesitated in the doorway, and Mother Loretta's expression sparkled with mockery.

"Are… you… ready?" Brother Beau spoke again, enunciating carefully, terrified to stutter again.

April nodded, and Mother Loretta snapped her attention to her.

"We use words in this family," she hissed.

"Yes, Brother Beau," April said, shaking with fear. Part of April felt good adapting to their ways; it gave her confidence in her ability to stay alive. Another part of her burned with anger—she didn't want to live this way.

Do I really want to spend my final days living an inauthentic life and trying to survive? Do I want to stay true to myself and possibly cut my life short? Do I have a choice about any of this?

Mother Loretta leaned down to unlock April's cuffs, and she drew her arms into her chest. The red rings around her wrists had worsened, and parts of her skin started to break and bleed. April rubbed them, wincing at the stinging. She stood up, wobbling on her feet, and held the chair as she got a head rush. She took a step toward Brother Beau, but the look in his eyes gave her pause. He nodded toward Mother Loretta. Catching the hint, April turned around and faced her new mother.

"Goodbye, Mother Loretta," she said down to the floor, afraid.

"I'll see you for dinner, my dearest daughter," Mother Loretta crooned with a gentle touch of April's throbbing cheek.

April turned to Brother Beau, and when he grabbed her hand, she felt taken aback. Every time she'd walked around before, she was either handcuffed or held around the wrists. This felt like he was embracing her in a new way. She didn't like it, but she did hope it meant Brother Beau trusted her. Perhaps his trust in her would lead to him letting her go. She squeezed his hand as they left the house and walked to the barn.

The paralyzing cold caused April to stumble the entire way. The dress the family forced her to wear barely covered her, and her skin felt freezing. By the time they arrived at the barn, her body shivered so hard that she had trouble standing and started curling into herself. Brother Beau led April into the barn, where he turned on a space heater and positioned her in front of it. Her shivering now out of control, she crouched down in front of the heater and tried to keep her breathing steady. Brother Beau rummaged around in buckets on the ground.

April lost touch with Brother Beau as she closed her eyes and willed her body to soak in the heater's warmth. Her shivering slowed, and she realized the barn had grown quiet. Eyes flying open at the chance she had been left alone, she lost her balance and fell backward, knocking into him. His stance faltered a bit at her hit, and he reached out a hand to steady her.

"Are you s-s-still dizzy?" he asked as she looked up at his face.

She pulled herself up and scooted closer to the heater, nodding. April's stomach churned, causing waves of nausea. The smell of the sugar and spices of Mother Loretta's baking had set April's stomach expecting food, and it now protested that she hadn't fed it. Brother Beau stood in silence for a few moments, allowing her to warm up and stop shivering.

"M-m-m-m," Brother Beau stuttered, trying to find his words as his face twisted in frustration. "Mother Loretta will want you to care for the livestock. That's Sister Jolene's job, or at least *was*."

April looked from her freezing blue fingernails to the barn stalls. She could hear the horse shuffling in the stall and remembered the name from her first trip to the barn. Other than her noisy barn mate, April hadn't seen any other livestock.

"Windy," she whispered into her hands, thinking that she may have found it a cute name in other circumstances.

Windy. Faster than the wind, she thought. *Maybe he's my key to getting out of here.*

April prayed her face had not given away her thoughts. She forced herself to stay focused on her fingers and rubbed her hands together, hoping it would hide the thoughts of escape.

It didn't.

"W-Windy is old," Brother Beau said. "He can't carry riders; his back is bad."

April shifted her gaze up to Brother Beau's face and could read the warning of caution on his face. He read her like a book.

"Come on," he said, nodding for her to follow him toward the stall.

April stood and followed, not afraid of him but wary of her surroundings. He opened the stall and reached in to hold the horse, gesturing for April to take the door. She moved in front of it and allowed it to rest against her side, peering past Brother Beau to the horse. Not only was Windy old, but he was a pony and probably couldn't have carried her weight, even in his glory days. He stood still, chewing on a piece of hay. Brother Beau stepped out of the stall and grabbed a small red bucket and stool. April stepped into the stall and he handed her both objects.

April took the seat with gratitude, her weak body shaking, and sat down with a thud. She clamped her hands to the stool, hoping that she wouldn't sway and fall from it. Brother Beau launched into a lesson on the different brushes in the bucket, stopping to take time for the information to set in. He spoke in a serious and firm tone, meeting April's gaze full-on, which made her uncomfortable—he normally avoided eye contact at all costs. Such seriousness about grooming tools brought an involuntary and disconnected laugh to April's lips. She cackled like a madwoman and surprised herself.

"Am I going to be quizzed on this?" she asked, but her laughter soon died. Brother Beau's eyes widened, and his hands shook in fear.

"Mother Loretta doesn't appreciate if you are lacking farm knowledge, and we will all be punished accordingly. It's very dangerous not to know what you're doing on a farm."

He spoke clearly and without stuttering. She nodded and looked at the brushes, willing the memory of his lesson to stick in her swirling mind.

"Which one is first?" he asked, and April grabbed the correct brush with only mild hesitation.

"And how do you use it?"

April didn't speak and brushed the rubbery comb in firm circles on the pony's side. She couldn't apply much pressure, and her weak muscles shook with exertion. He gave little pointers here and there, but overall, observed her progress over her shoulder. April zoned out, reviewing the information in her head as she rhythmically brushed the pony. The soft feel of the warm body under her hands and the quiet and happy grunts from the pony gave her a sense of peace that she thought she would never find again. She allowed herself to disconnect and simply exist within the flow of the strokes of the brushes. Part of her wished time would cease, and April let her vision blur around the edges.

"Sister Jolene... Sister Jolene?" It took April far too long to realize that Brother Beau meant her.

"Oh." She turned to Brother Beau.

"You can move on to the next brush," he said, stutter seeming to remain improved, and April wondered if he was growing comfortable around her.

April stayed quiet and obeyed. As she got into the rhythm of brushing again, her mind drifted to thoughts of Sister Jolene. April hadn't seen another girl in the house or on the farm. The fact that the family called the girls they took 'Sister Jolene' indicated that she was gone, whether temporarily or permanently. April wondered if she ever existed or if she had hallucinated the portrait on the stairs. Curiosity, lack of nourishment, and whatever lingering drug in her system prevailed, and she spoke without thinking. "Who is Sister Jolene?"

Brother Beau stiffened behind her.

She froze, stunned she had asked and unsure of what would come next. She continued brushing the pony, though overtly aware of Brother Beau behind her. She wondered if he would ignore her question when he spoke.

"Y-y-you are, Sister Jolene," Brother Beau responded through tight lips, stuttering resuming.

"No, I'm not, I'm April," April replied, hearing the annoyance in her voice at Brother Beau's attempt to divert the conversation.

"I-I-I know who you were before, April Dell." April shuddered.

He knew who I was before? Did he choose me deliberately for the job of his sister? How long has he known me—watched me?

"But it doesn't matter because now you are my s-s-sister."

"I'm your sister and the other girls were too? How is that possible?" April sobbed and Windy whinnied. Brother Beau looked frightened and pushed himself against the stall door, slinking away from April.

"Who? Is? Sister? Jolene?" she repeated.

April held Brother Beau's gaze, and his bottom lip trembled as his thoughts raced across his anxious face and tears threatened to spill.

"No one!" he shouted and pushed the stall door open, fleeing the small space.

April jumped down from her stool, ignoring Windy's protests at the sudden loud sounds. She stumbled and used the walls as a guide for keeping her upright.

"Please, just tell me!" Her voice cracked in her dry throat.

Brother Beau turned, eyes blazing now with anger and not anxiety.

"You can't tell me what to do—y-y-y-you can't take advantage of me!" he shouted back, surprising April further.

This poor man.

April felt like she was losing touch with whatever cruel reality held her captive.

How can I feel bad for the person who quite possibly ended my entire life, or at the very least life as I knew it before this wretched farm?

Anger fumed inside of her, and she threw the brush to the ground, startling poor Windy once more, who pulled against his leads.

"S-s-she was our sister." Brother Beau's quiet voice almost couldn't be heard.

April froze. The real and raw sadness painted across his face touched her heart, and she softened again, despite her frustration. He looked down and picked at the raw and chapped skin surrounding his fingernails. He spoke as if in a daze.

"She was our little sister and Mother Loretta's favorite child, her dearest daughter. She was beautiful and funny and was the glue that held our family together. When she was around, Mother Loretta always smiled, Father Preston didn't drink, and even Brother Waylon was happy. I've always been sickly, Mother Loretta says I was born with a bad disposition, but when Sister Jolene was here, that didn't seem to matter. Sister Jolene took care of me and made me feel whole. She was the most caring person I've ever met. She was born to be a caregiver but frustrated by it. She wanted to 'keep up with the boys' as she would say and was always pushing herself to be something she wasn't. I think she didn't want to end up a housewife like our mother, though she never told me that."

April listened with rapt attention, eating up every potentially lifesaving detail that came out of his mouth. He had never spoken this many words to her. She tried to make mental notes of questions about the story, like Father Preston and his whereabouts.

"It was a cold morning in January three years ago when we lost her. Mother Loretta, Sister Jolene, and I were baking in the kitchen—a pie that we could take to church with us the next morning. A lady at church fell and broke her hip, and Mother Loretta wanted to cheer her up. Sister Jolene wasn't much of a baker and begged to be allowed to do farm work with Father Preston and Brother Waylon. I think it bothered Mother Loretta that Sister Jolene wasn't as domestic as she was, but she never said anything. Funny thing about families—you can learn so much about them by what isn't said. Mother Loretta wanted to make Sister Jolene happy and decided to let her go. I didn't mind at all; I enjoyed the alone time with Mother Loretta and preferred a quieter room than the other two did. Sister Jolene went bouncing out of the kitchen, and we watched her trot out to the barn like a foal in the spring. Mother Loretta and I continued baking and humming sweet songs, no idea what was coming right at us."

He paused, pained by this memory, and April didn't push, thankful he told his story at all.

"Father Preston thought she was in the kitchen with Mother Loretta and me, and Mother Loretta and I would have never guessed that Father

Preston was running the tractor in the snow. Later he told us that he had just replaced the carburetor and was driving it across the land behind the barn to make sure everything ran smoothly before storing it once more for the rest of winter. The snow must have deadened the sound of it because we could usually hear the tractor running from the kitchen. Sister Jolene came bouncing around that barn just in time for us to see my father..." Brother Beau trailed off, unable to say exactly what they saw.

April couldn't imagine the horror of watching his little sister die, let alone something as gruesome as being run over by a tractor. She reached her hand out and placed it on his arm. He looked down at her hand as if shocked but didn't remove it.

"She didn't make it," he said.

April craved more information, desperate for the rest of this broken family's story, but they heard Brother Waylon's footsteps outside the barn. April snapped to attention, picking up the brush and resuming her grooming of Windy, fear now re-activated.

"Time's up," Brother Waylon said.

April returned the brush to the bucket and handed it to Brother Beau. Brother Waylon stepped aside to allow them to pass. When April left the stall, he grabbed her and placed the handcuffs around her wrist. The cold metal bit into her skin and April winced.

"Come along, then," Brother Waylon drawled.

He turned and walked, clearly testing April's resolve. She was determined to keep up with Brother Waylon and avoid getting on his wrong side—Sister Jolene certainly would have been able to keep up. She did her best to match his pace, and Brother Beau fell in line behind them, rushing to catch up after closing up Windy's stall. Halfway between the barn and the house, surrounded by sunlight and snow, April chanced a backward glance at Brother Beau.

"Thank you," she mouthed wordlessly. He dipped his head in acknowledgement.

He didn't have to share the story with her. He could have screamed for Brother Waylon to take care of her disobedience at any time. She was grateful he had instead chosen to tell her what he did. April wondered how many other women he had done the same for, if any at all. She faced forward again, focusing on keeping her pace even with Brother Waylon's.

How am I going to avoid having Sister Jolene's tragedy become mine?

Chapter Seventeen

Heather sat at her desk, pretending to work on paperwork but instead staring at the paper before her. She had done some difficult things in her time on the police force, but nothing could compare to this. She would never forget the look on Bethany's parents' face when she told them the news. Nausea rolled through her stomach as she wrote about the experience for the case file. It all felt trivial and like a waste of time. What was the point of paperwork if Bethany was gone? Nothing would fix this situation. Heather failed to find Bethany alive and the weight of that weighed on her shoulders. Nathan assured her she had done all she could, but Heather couldn't accept that.

My job was to save her, and I didn't—what more can I say? Same thing happened with Autumn... and maybe April, now too. She had to work hard to shut down thoughts of Autumn. The image of Autumn's lifeless body at the bottom of that building replayed in her mind. *The white bra and frilly pink underwear. How could I let two years go by with everyone thinking that my sister had taken her own life? I knew the truth.* Sitting across from Nathan for the past hour had been brutal.

She could have spoken up, told Nathan she had concrete proof of Autumn's murder, but couldn't bring herself to do it, to open herself up to his disbelief. As she stared at him, heartbroken, he looked up and met her eye.

"Alan over in tech found some interesting footage. He sent us a message." Nathan glanced at his phone on his desk.

He fixed her with a concerned look. Guilt and annoyance flooded her. He didn't have to look at her with such pity. She said nothing, only stood and walked toward the tech lab. Nathan followed, not speaking.

The lab was small and dark, with no overhead lights turned on. The plethora of computer screens illuminated the pathway, and Heather blinked as her eyes adjusted. They made their way to the rear of the room and stopped at a table with three wide screens sitting on top. Alan sat at an L-shaped desk, and the screens glowed with an eerie shade of blue, giving him an otherworldly appearance as it reflected on his skin. He stared at the screen on the right and typed furiously, focused and still.

Nathan cleared his throat, but when Alan didn't stir or stop clacking his keyboard, he tapped Alan on the shoulder, startling him from his concentration.

"Ahh," Alan breathed out as he turned. "Hey guys, I've got the footage."

He clicked on his computer screen and pulled up a video. "So, this was taken by Mr. Hackett, the owner of the market in April's neighborhood. Claire went by there this morning and he hadn't seen anything but called the office once he remembered that he could pull footage from the security cameras he installed. He added it after that break-in two weeks ago, so we lucked out. The street was empty for hours because of the storm, but then it picked up this."

The corner store and the street in front of it lit up the screen, though snowfall blurred the image. The time stamp on the video read 12:36 am, matching the timeline that Mrs. Dell had given the detectives regarding her phone call with April. Both the corner store and the streetlamps lining the street stood dark. Thick snowflakes fell, blanketing the scene.

"Power outage," the tech guy said. "Luckily this system has a battery-powered reserve in case of power outages."

Suddenly, the video lightened as approaching headlights came into view, and a large, black truck pulled in front of the corner store. The truck parked and a moment passed before the passenger side door opened, and a man got out. The man walked with a heavy limp toward the entrance of the store. He cupped his hands around his eyes and leaned toward the shop's glass door. Finding it closed, he turned, glanced down the street in both directions and then got into the truck. The truck sped off, and the video darkened again, the giant snowflakes coming into view.

"And that's it," the tech said.

"Any way we can see a close-up of that man?" Nathan asked, and Alan clicked into a different folder on his computer. On the second monitor he pulled up a picture of the man. The grainy picture couldn't hide the man's identity.

"See who it is?" Alan said, voice tinged with a bit of excitement at his discovery.

"It's the man from the vigil," Heather said, stunned.

This was more than she could have asked for. This man attended April's vigil and got caught on camera in the area of her disappearance around the same time. He also spoke with a stutter, which connected him to Bethany's case as well. This man had done something to these women—though he had an accomplice in the driver of the truck.

"Anything on the driver? He wasn't alone," Heather asked.

"Unfortunately, this is the best shot I could grab, the angle is so weird. I'll have a talk with Mr. Hackett about better placement of his security system so if he gets robbed again, we don't face the same issue," Alan said, getting off track as he searched through his files for another photo.

The picture filled the screen and Heather frowned, disappointed. Nathan leaned in for a closer look, but it didn't help. The still image featured the windshield, which was dark. A figure sat behind the wheel, but the angle obscured any details of the person's identity. Instead, it looked as if a demon or apparition drove the truck.

"No dice," Nathan said, sounding dejected as well.

"You're right, but I think this is enough for a warrant," Heather said. "Has anyone identified him?"

"No, we haven't," Alan said.

Heather left that job up to the tech analysts so Nathan and she could go and talk with Bethany's family. The conversation took the entire morning, and she hadn't yet investigated on her own. Guilt plagued her. *I need to do more for April.* She had to live with the fact that she hadn't saved Bethany and Autumn, and she certainly would not live in a world where she didn't save April as well. There was no choice but to find her alive.

"We'll get on it," Heather said, patting Alan on the shoulder.

"I've gotten his picture from the vigil to the local news stations. Maybe that will bring in an identity. Someone must know this guy." Alan turned to his screen.

"Good," Nathan said. "Thanks, Alan."

Nathan tapped Heather on the shoulder and nodded, indicating that he wanted her to follow him. They started to walk to the main squad room when Alan called out. "Uh, guys! This just came in."

They returned to Alan's desk, where he had video footage pulled up of a road at dusk.

"That's near my place," Heather said, confused. The clip showed the area outside her apartment above the bookshop.

"And look what's about to drive by," Alan said. Heather watched, dumbfounded, as the same black truck from the snowy video drove by and turned, headed straight for Heather's apartment. "Heather, I think this is the man who left that creepy box on your doorstep," Alan said.

"When was this?" Heather shouted, feeling her breath go out of her.

"Friday, around dinnertime." Alan pointed to the date and time stamp at the bottom of the video.

"That's when I was pulling the double. I didn't get home until Saturday morning and the box was waiting at the door when the bookshop opened that morning," Heather said.

"But why would the same man who took April and Bethany have an item of Autumn's?" Nathan asked, looking at Heather. He watched her closely, testing her reaction.

Heather felt faint, and not only from the lack of food. "Because he took Autumn, too," she said, staring into the darkness of the lab.

"Send that to me, and only to me, understood?" Nathan said to Alan, face serious and voice firm.

Nathan ushered her from the lab and into the squad's lunchroom. The only other detective in there quickly vacated upon seeing her stunned and pale face, leaving them alone. She sat down and stared down at her hands, mind swimming with the stuttering man's face and Autumn's undergarments. He left the box on her doorstep—wanted her to see Autumn's shirt covered in blood, and he had done something to Bethany and April, too. He had killed Autumn. Heather felt violated, her trust in her own safety shattered. She realized Nathan was talking to her, but she hadn't heard a thing.

"Sorry," she interrupted. "What?"

"I said, let's keep this between us for now," Nathan continued. "If the sheriff finds out, he'll take you off the case, and we can't have that. I know what this means to you, and I know what it would do to you if you couldn't be the one to solve this."

"Nathan," Heather said, biting her lip, "you could lose your job."

Guilt exploded in her chest again. Not only had she failed Bethany, but now had confirmation that she failed her sister as well. Nathan wanted to protect her, which would lead to even more failure.

"I would rather lose my job than lose you," Nathan whispered.

"Then I have to tell you something before you get any deeper into trouble," Heather said, biting her bottom lip as if to keep the words in her mouth.

"What is it?" Nathan asked, eyes swimming with concern.

Heather told him about seeing Autumn's crime scene photos and about the bra and underwear that both Bethany and Autumn had worn. Nathan never saw Autumn's crime scene, had opted to support Heather in that moment, and thus didn't know. Quietly, he stepped from the lunchroom, leaving Heather with her thoughts while he investigated. It felt like mere seconds before he returned, face pale and eyes wide.

"You're right," Nathan whispered, crouching down next to Heather in her chair. "But it doesn't change anything. What the sheriff doesn't know, won't hurt him. He'll take you off the case when he figures out the connection, and I won't be responsible for taking this away from you."

Nathan grabbed her hand. They had always been close, but their closeness seemed to have expanded over the past few days. The warmth of his hand seeped into her skin. Her heart beat faster and for the first time, she allowed herself to acknowledge the feelings she had for him. This wasn't physical, this wasn't friendship, this was love. *This is real love*. She loved him so much that she couldn't fathom a life that didn't include him in every way possible. But she couldn't deal with that now.

"I can't thank you enough, Nathan."

"The day I moved to Tree Park was the best day of my life because it brought me to you, the person who means most to me in this world, my partner," Nathan said with a sad smile.

"I shouldn't be that person, Nathan," Heather said, continuing to look down. The complications of their relationship felt overwhelming to her.

"Why do you do that?" he asked. "Why can't you accept reality for what it is? People love you and care about you, and you can't stop that!"

She didn't have the energy for this two days ago, and she certainly didn't have the energy for this now. It didn't matter what conclusions she had or had not come to—she simply couldn't do this.

"What about what I want, Heather? You aren't the only one here!" Nathan shouted and Heather didn't like it.

"It doesn't matter what you want," she shouted back, raising her head and standing up. "We can't do this, whether you want it or not, whether I want it or not. It can't happen, Nathan!"

"Says who? Work? A job is a job, Heather, but a person is so much more than that. You have to know by now that I love you!"

There it was. All spilled out onto the tiny lunchroom table like a glass of lemonade. Feelings on the table, the official crossing of the line they had spent all this time dancing around.

"Nathan..." Heather breathed out, both devastated and overjoyed by his admission.

Heather knew he had feelings for her; she could see that even before they had shared their near kiss, but she had no idea that he loved her. She hadn't stopped to consider that Nathan's feelings for her went just as deep as hers were for him. She had stupidly thought that Nathan's feelings were surface-level and not serious, and she had practically told him that they didn't matter. How could she be so cruel to the person she loved? Heather felt shame like she never had before, words lost to her. Nathan shook his head at Heather's silence and looked down at his hands.

"So, it's like that, huh?" Nathan sounded more defeated than he ever had in their entire partnership.

"No, Nathan, it's not that I don't have feelings—"

Someone shouted from the squad room. Nathan didn't look at her before storming from the lunchroom to check things out. She took a deep breath before following, still reeling from the conversation. Nothing went as she planned, expected, or hoped, and Heather felt more than burnt out; she felt like a pile of ash. She pushed open the heavy door, surprised to see Claire and Ryan standing in the squad room, both flush in the face and breathing hard.

"Claire?" Heather said, crossing the room and taking Claire's arm. "What is it?"

"We...found...him...," Claire panted, out of breath.

Ryan nodded to Heather and handed her a cell phone. The website on the screen displayed the stuttering man as a child on his family's farm.

"Oh my god." Heather filled with tension and excitement. "Someone get

Alan in here! Great work, ladies!"

Nathan ran to the tech lab to fetch Alan while Heather directed Claire and Ryan to a small interrogation room to wait for her. She went to her desk, calling the Sheriff out from his office as well. Sheriff Steinman poked his head out at the excitement as Alan ran in.

"I ran a search on the farm's name," he said. "It's owned by the Smithers family. Parents are Loretta and Preston Smithers, children are Beauregard, Waylon, and Jolene Smithers."

"I'll get working on a warrant," the sheriff said, catching up and rushing to his office.

Heather looked at Nathan, who stared at the website once more.

"Wait a minute," Nathan said. "That's the woman and man we interviewed about the truck!"

Heather grabbed the phone and zoomed in on the face of the mother.

"You're right," she said. "We were there a few days ago."

"April and Bethany could have been there while we were there." Nathan looked pained.

"We could have saved her." Newfound pain spread throughout her body.

This was it, concrete evidence that Heather had failed Bethany. She stood on the porch while they tortured women in that house. A wave of anger washed through her. Her vision went red around the edges, and Heather wanted to punch something.

"They will not get away with this, not again," Heather hissed, balling her fists.

"We won't let them," Nathan affirmed.

"And we can't wait."

Nathan nodded and ran to the Sheriff's office to tell him where they were going.

"He said he's working on the warrant and will call us when it's ready, but we can stake out the property for now. He said to be very careful without the warrant; we don't want to flub this."

"We won't," Heather promised, grabbing Nathan's hand and squeezing it. He withdrew his hand from hers as if she disgusted him.

"Don't," he warned and walked away from Heather, not waiting for her to catch up.

Her heart stung but she pushed it aside; she needed to focus on April. Her life hung in the balance, and one wrong move could lead to her death, just like Bethany's, just like Autumn's. Heather wouldn't have another death on her conscience, not even if she had to die herself.

Chapter Eighteen

April sat in Sister Jolene's bedroom, watching the setting sun. Brother Beau returned her to the room about midday. Although he avoided her gaze and refused to speak with her, he fed her lunch. April wondered if he worried he had told her too much about his family, and she replayed their story repeatedly in her mind—the details rolling through like a tumbleweed. Such tragedy had struck this small family, and their devastation rippled out from the farm, touching the town. April wondered if her parents experienced the same devastation in her absence.

How could they go through such loss and then inflict that on others? I'll never understand...

April tried to imagine her parents hurting other people's children out of grief for their own daughter gone and couldn't fathom that as a possibility. She knew that no matter the outcome, her parents would never stop fighting to ensure no other families went through something like this again. The vast difference between her true family and her captive one blew her exhausted mind, and chills rushed up her spine.

Tired of thinking about everything, April took off her shoes and socks and lay on the bed, rearranging her shackles to be more comfortable on the raw skin of her wrists. With actual comfort impossible, she closed her eyes, knowing there was nothing else to do. She tried to imagine pleasant images and stop thinking of this deranged family. Her mind calmed and slowed, and images of her family and friends floated through her head. Perhaps she had adjusted to her captivity, or perhaps her emotions had shut off. She didn't know, but she felt muted inside.

She drifted in the quiet place between sleep and consciousness when a loud crash from below startled her back to the present. A jolt of adrenaline forced her upright, and she hugged her knees close, dreading the possibility that this could somehow involve her. Mother Loretta shouted, and her voice rang up the staircase, clear as a bell. "HOW DARE YOU!" Another crash boomed through the house.

Fear shot through her body. Her cheeks flushed, and her mouth went dry as she strained to listen to the commotion, desperate for more information.

"Why did you take Sister Jolene so far away?" Mother Loretta continued to bellow, "Sister Jolene is to be kept here! Why have you done this to us?"

Another thud, this one duller than the last, and Brother Beau shouted in pain.

"YOU STUPID INGRATE! Do you not appreciate all that I provide for you? I keep you fed and alive, and this is how you repay me?" Mother Loretta howled with rage.

April could tell Brother Beau had done something wrong, but she wasn't sure what. Had Mother Loretta found out about Brother Beau telling their story? Desperate to find out, she slid quietly to the floor. She lay as close to the wooden panels of the floor as her restraints allowed her to. She listened, closing her eyes. She willed her ears to become her eyes as the thudding and crashing continued below. The sounds moved closer, though not up the stairs, and her desperation grew. Brother Beau called out in pain once more.

"M-m-mother, please!" he pleaded.

"Shut up!" Brother Waylon yelled. "You created this mess—now you'll take yer punishment."

April shuddered at the idea that Brother Waylon beat Brother Beau like he had beaten the last Sister Jolene. April feared that Brother Beau's thin and weak body couldn't handle it.

"Why did you do this to my dearest daughter?" screeched Mother Loretta. "Why did you take Sister Jolene so far away? She is mine, and she stays here!"

Mother Loretta's words ran together through her sobs. Brother Beau's voice came out as a gargled scream while Brother Waylon beat him. She winced as each blow landed and Brother Beau's pained shouts echoed up through the floorboards. Mother Loretta claimed he had taken Sister Jolene far away, but she also called April Sister Jolene, and she was upstairs. April wondered if she would ever make sense of the situation. Everything went quiet downstairs, the only sound Brother Beau's crying.

"Sister Jolene stays HERE! She is buried HERE! Am I CLEAR?" Mother Loretta's voice cracked from the strain of screaming for so long.

Brother Beau chanted, "Yes, Mother Loretta," repeatedly, and it was the only sound in the room for a while.

Brother Beau must not have buried the last Sister Jolene here with Mother Loretta's actual daughter.

Mother Loretta sounded genuinely confused as to why Brother Beau would break the rules, and April figured this was not something he normally did. What had driven him to break her rule? Was he trying to get himself killed? *Maybe he is sick of the life he was born into.* Suicide by family could be an easy way out for him, and she felt immense sadness that someone's life could be so tragic.

The next time Mother Loretta spoke, her voice sounded haunted and free of tears. "If you ever do this again…" she trailed off, leaving her threat up to the imagination.

Mother Loretta's loud shoes clacked across the kitchen floor and toward her living room. Brother Waylon's loud footsteps followed behind. The downstairs fell silent, and April wondered if Brother Beau had lost consciousness. She sat listening, afraid that a tiny movement from her would trigger the fight again. Too frightened to move and make noise, April sat frozen on the hardwood floor. Time stopped, minutes became hours and time became endless. April thought they might be done when the shouting resumed.

"NOOOOOOO!" Mother Loretta roared. "How have I raised such disobedient children?"

She jumped at the sound of Mother Loretta's voice breaking the silence, terrified that this time she had somehow done something wrong. Mother Loretta had said *children*, indicating that her words were no longer aimed toward Brother Beau alone. That also could have included April, or as they knew her, Sister Jolene. April heard the heavy footsteps of Brother Waylon running toward this side of the house as a hard object crashed down the hall. Mother Loretta wailed again, but no formulated words came out of her mouth, only shrieks and screams. April heard another voice cut through the commotion, and it took her a few moments to understand where it came from.

"A person of interest has been identified in the case of missing museum worker, April Dell," the female voice announced throughout the house.

April's mouth went dry at hearing her name. It must have been on the television, though she had not seen one in the house.

"Shown here is Beauregard Smithers who likely has information about the disappearance of April Dell, and police are looking to speak with him. Police have advised that he speaks with a stutter. If you, or anyone you know, has any information about April Dell or the man shown above, please call the sheriff's office at the number listed on your screen."

She took advantage of the noise to crawl into the bed and pull the covers over her head. Somehow, the police had gotten Brother Beau's picture and now showed it on the nightly news. The television drowned out Mother Loretta's wailing, and April grew cold with fear. The loud television below diminished her sense of hearing—she didn't know if anyone headed her way. She whimpered like a dog that had been run over by a car and left in the street to die. She knew her fate but couldn't move against it. Items continued to collide with the walls below as Mother Loretta bellowed, and the television changed topics. April's ears rang in a high-pitched screech. She felt like her insides would explode, and she could have sworn someone had lit her body on fire.

The locks on her door clicked as someone opened them, and the door swung open, smashing into the wall. She threw the blanket off her body at Brother Waylon, her only line of defense, as he stormed into the room. She let out an involuntary scream as he approached, nose bleeding and right eyebrow sliced open. He grabbed April's arm and roughly twisted it. She couldn't fight against his brute strength as he undid the restraints.

"Please, no," April whimpered, to no avail.

"Shut up!" he hissed, spit and blood flying into her face as he punched her in the side of the head. She saw stars twinkling before her world went black. She was dimly aware of her body being lifted and then tossed onto the ground.

When April's eyes opened again, she couldn't see. Panicked, she sat up and felt around, whimpering.

Why can't I see? What's wrong with me? She thought back to the blow to her head and winced.

She felt her temple, sore and bruised, but it didn't bleed. Because her hands were no longer bound, she tapped the ground and found that it was cold, wet, and hard. She crawled forward on her hands and knees, feeling in front of her for any hints when she bumped into something. The "something" groaned softly, and April gasped as she jumped, startled.

"W-w-who's there?" Brother Beau called out, and her tense muscles eased.

"It's April," she replied. "I can't see anything."

"Oh, Sister Jolene. We're in the c-c-cellar—it's sealed tight as can be on account of the rats that were getting in," Brother Beau explained. "I thought I was alone. When they tossed me down here, I didn't h-h-h-hear you."

April breathed a sigh of relief that she hadn't gone blind. "I must have passed out. Your brother whacked me pretty hard in the head after the fight downstairs." She rubbed her throbbing temple.

Brother Beau remained silent, and April sat still, waiting for whatever came next. She heard him sigh with a loud puff of air.

"I never w-w-wanted any of this, you know," he said, voice said and quiet.

April nodded, though he couldn't see it. Her eyes adjusted to the dark, and she could barely make out his form sitting next to her.

"When Sister Jolene died, everything fell apart." His stutter died away, and April listened intently. "We were never a normal family. I mean, look at our names."

"It is odd," April confirmed, wrapping her arms around her legs for warmth. The air felt as cold as it had in the barn.

"It is. Mother Loretta preferred the old-fashioned use of proper names, just as her ancestors on this very farm had done. Thought it might bring more prosperous growth to the land if we emulated the great farmers of old. I don't think she was right about that. I think her superstition killed Jolene just like children of old who died in farm accidents. That's nearly unheard of these days."

"I think I've only seen stuff like that on the old Westerns my dad used to watch," April said, smiling to herself at the memory of her father and his cowboy movies. Her smile faded with the thought that she may never see him again.

"Yeah, most equipment has all these new fancy safety features to prevent it. Anyway, we had a small funeral here when she died," Brother Beau continued, "We never interacted much with the townsfolk and we stopped attending church services, so no one ever knew Sister Jolene was gone. Mother Loretta felt it proper that we honor her here, and we buried her here, too, right alongside our ancestors."

April wondered how big the farm was and how long this family had owned this land.

"Once she was in the ground, Mother Loretta lost her mind. She started running through the house screaming for her 'dearest daughter' and ruining our rooms, trying to find her. That's when Father Preston started to drink."

"That's your father?" April asked, no longer shy. She needed to know more about "Father Preston".

"*Was* my father," Brother Beau said in a flat and disconnected voice. "I guess the alcohol took the edge off his pain after we lost our sister, made it easier for him to ignore Mother Loretta's behavior. He would drink himself drunk and pass out on the couch while Mother Loretta searched until her body gave way, and she slept on the floor of whatever room she had been searching."

April tried to imagine her reaction to seeing her parents like that; one lost in a cloud of anguished grief and another lost in the drink, and she shuddered. Brother Beau must have been terrified.

"After months of this, Father Preston started to get aggressive. He would grab Mother Loretta by the arm and force her to sit down. He would smack her from time to time, but nothing that left true marks. Oh, how she would scream and fight him, but farming made him a strong man. He was stronger than Brother Waylon, if you can believe it."

"I can't imagine that," April said. Brother Waylon was the strongest person she ever met and her fictional image of Father Preston, muscles rippling through his shirt as he roared with anger, terrified her. "Did he hurt you, too?"

"He never hurt a single one of us until Sister Jolene died. After that, he hurt whatever was in his way. That's how we came to lose all our livestock. He would stumble from the house in a blind rage and start wailing on whatever living creature he could find. Mother Loretta wasn't in a place to keep up the farm, and we slowly shut down our operations. Broke Brother Waylon's heart to see his beloved farm dying—he's never been the same since."

"That explains why he looks so dead behind the eyes," April muttered.

"Uh-huh," Brother Beau confirmed. "One night, nearly a year after Sister Jolene had died, Father Preston had enough. He started beating Mother Loretta like he never had before. We were in the kitchen cooking when

Mother Loretta began screaming for Sister Jolene and started rummaging through the cabinets, and Father Preston walked straight in and hit her, right on the top of her head, with his bottle of beer. I stood there, screaming, begging him to stop as the blood ran down her face. I was afraid of him. I never bonded with him; my father thought I was a 'sissy,' and I didn't like that much, so I stuck with Mother Loretta and Sister Jolene, though my mother doesn't care for me too much, either."

"She treats Brother Waylon differently," April said. "I saw it when she locked you in with me after I didn't come to dinner." April remembered the horrible look on Brother Beau's face when he realized she had locked him in.

"She always has, though it was better when Sister Jolene was still with us," Brother Beau said. "Anyway, Father Preston was hurting Mother Loretta that night, and I couldn't help her. He hit her over and over and over again. I didn't hear Brother Waylon come into the kitchen. He must have really been creeping and crawling, and by the time I saw him, the knife was already in Father Preston's neck. He died right there on the kitchen floor, all his blood pouring from his body from the hole in his neck. I can still smell the blood sometimes." Brother Beau stopped, and April could hear his shiver.

She opened her mouth to speak, but no words came out. She couldn't imagine witnessing that. *Will he continue talking to me?* She wished she could have seen what expression was on his face as they sat in the freezing dark.

"It's easier not to think about that anymore," Brother Beau said, and April could tell he lied. It sounded very much like something he thought about all the time.

"What did you guys do with your father?" April asked, pushing him with her curiosity.

"Brother Waylon helped me get Mother Loretta into bed, and I nursed her back to health. It was nice, somehow, to be able to take care of her the way that Sister Jolene took care of me. I like to think that she's proud of me, wherever she is. I still don't know how Brother Waylon got the kitchen clean. I'm pretty sure he never cleaned a thing in his entire life, but when I came downstairs the following morning, the kitchen was spotless, and Father Preston was gone. I never saw him again, and I was never brave enough to ask Brother Waylon what he'd done with him. Shortly after, Mother Loretta removed his portrait from the staircase wall and scratched out his name as if trying to block him from our memories."

Brother Beau sniffled, and April thought he had started to cry. She had never experienced this level of trauma. This broken family created a deep level of sadness in her. *How can the world be like this?* Her breath caught in her throat as she realized how much damage this had done to her own family. Her mind flashed to the effects this whole ordeal must have on not only her parents but also her roommate and co-workers, and her stomach turned to lead.

"So why did you take me? And the other girls? It sounds like your mother only wanted her daughter, and not some random girl," April asked, curiosity and anger bubbling inside of her.

"Mother Loretta never recovered. We spent months and months trying to take care of her and bring back the mother we had before we lost our sister. That's when Brother Waylon came up with the idea to replace Sister Jolene. He wanted Mother Loretta to wake up and find her 'dearest daughter' there, so he forced me out with him, and we took the first girl he could find. I-I-I didn't want to do it, you must know that I didn't, but I had no choice. I had w-w-w-watched my brother kill my father, and I feared that I was n-n-n-next."

April heard Brother Beau take a long, deep breath, the air shaking as it came in and out of him. She knew he didn't want to partake in this plot, but hearing the concrete proof devastated her even more.

"And you know the rest of the story—the cop's sister on drugs and the girl who fought too hard," he finished.

April pondered these two girls, now broken and dead, one at her own hands. That's when it hit her—the cop's sister—Autumn Byrd. She had killed herself like everyone believed but under such wildly different circumstances.

Her heart broke for Autumn and Heather. April vowed to tell Heather the truth if she ever saw her again.

"Why me?" April asked, wondering for the millionth time why they had chosen her.

"Because you're different. You care about people and are kind. You are beautiful inside and out. You embody everything we want Sister Jolene to be…everything she was," he said, and April imagined his eyes shone with love for her.

She wished she hadn't asked this question. Chills traveled up her spine. *The brothers must have watched me for a long time before taking me.* April didn't know if she would ever get out of here, but she did know that she would never feel safe again.

Chapter Nineteen

The drive was long, and Heather remembered how it felt the first time they had done this. That drive had been awkward, and Heather had thought things couldn't possibly get worse. What she wouldn't give to go back in time to that drive and warn herself about all that would come, not only in her personal life but her professional one. This time, however, the drive was awkward in a different way, somehow a more uncomfortable way.

They sat down the street from the property, waiting. After about twenty minutes of unbearable silence, she couldn't take it anymore. The tension felt borderline dangerous.

How can we execute a search warrant in a potentially life-threatening situation like this? It wouldn't work, and that frightened her.

"Can we talk?" Heather asked, feeling vulnerable and placing her hand over his, hoping he didn't react as he had in the squad room.

Nathan's hand felt warm under hers. She wished she would never have to take it away from his. She couldn't read his expression. His gaze followed her arm up to her face, where his eyes met hers. The look in his eyes pleaded with her not to hurt him again. Instead of replying, he pulled his wrist away and let out a long, loud breath.

"I can't do this right now," he said, staring out the windshield. "We've got a lot of work to do."

"I get that," Heather said, nodding. "But how can we get work done if we can't even speak to each other?"

"I can talk to you about work just fine," Nathan guffawed.

"Nathan, come on," Heather said.

"No, Heather, you come on. You've made it very clear how you feel, and I'm just done with all of that. Let it go," Nathan said, sounding resigned.

"But you didn't give me a chance to make it clear how—" Nathan's phone started ringing.

Sheriff Steinman's contact appeared on the screen in the center of the dashboard. Heather selected the answer button for Nathan, and he spoke.

"Sheriff? Got the warrant?"

"Got it!" Sheriff Steinman said. "It states that I must be present during the search, so don't go in the house without me."

"Alright," Heather said. "Should we wait at the driveway or on the edge of the property?"

"Alan got a hit on the truck. It's registered to Preston Smithers, so I want you guys to approach the family and ask about it. Feel out the situation and see what we're working with. Alan's emailing the registration so you have something to present to the family."

"Sounds good," Nathan said. "We'll update you once we establish contact. Should we alert them that you're on the way?"

"No, keep them in the dark until I arrive. I don't want them to take any rash action out of desperation. Don't want to put you two in danger, either."

"Okay," Heather said. "We'll be on the lookout for the email from Alan."

"I will. See you both soon. I'm about thirty minutes out. Stay safe."

The phone clicked off, and Heather and Nathan's tense and awkward silence resumed. She wanted to continue the conversation but the moment had passed. Nathan said he could communicate with her regarding work, and that was about to be put to the test. If she felt like he kept her at arm's length when they confronted the family, then Heather would take further action, but for now she sat back as he drove toward the house. As Nathan turned down the long driveway onto the property, Heather took in the surroundings to see if she could find anything new.

"Still no cars and still no black truck," Heather said, swiveling her head in every direction to double check. Nathan also glanced around and confirmed. He parked and the partners each looked at their phones, the email from Alan waiting for them. The registration clearly showed Preston Smithers' name printed on the new owner line. They couldn't refute it.

"Let's do this." Heather opened her door and Nathan followed suit.

This time, Heather avoided the sight of the small graveyard and instead studied the rest of the property. The farm seemed massive to her, though she knew larger ones existed. The snow melted in some spots, and she could see patches of brown through the stark white. Heather noted no farm equipment in sight—strange, even at this time of year. No livestock or horses either, despite the barn to her right. Something felt amiss.

As they made their way to the familiar wooden door, Heather tensed in anticipation. The sun started to set and the sky behind the house turned brilliant shades of orange and yellow. The beauty of the scenery struck her. Heather put her hand on the gun on her hip as Nathan knocked on the door.

As they waited, Heather's mind wandered to her father. She thought about his death and tightened her grip on her gun. He hadn't been prepared for what happened to him, and she wouldn't make the same mistake. She imagined his final call a million times, wondering what must have gone through his mind and how he must have felt, and shuddered. This situation could get her killed, just like her father, and that frightened her. No amount of preparation could have readied her for this actual moment—the confrontation of potential killers. A gust of chilly wind blew by, whipping her hair as Nathan knocked again. The knock echoed through the house, but no other sounds came from inside.

"Sheriff's office!" Nathan bellowed, and Heather could finally hear footsteps approaching from the other side of the door.

The same woman who answered the door during their first visit opened it now too, but her strong-looking son didn't come with her. She wore the same old-fashioned clothing, though something was different. Her gray dress appeared wrinkled, and a large stain of some kind covered the bottom. Heather couldn't tell what she had spilled on herself.

Motor oil? Coffee? Blood?

The collar of her dress hung open, missing several of the buttons. Strands escaped from her tight bun all around her head, giving her a sort-of halo. Deep wrinkles lined the bags under her eyes, which were bloodshot and glassy. The woman looked exhausted.

"Can I help you?" she said, the ire in her voice evident.

"I'm not sure if you remember us, but I'm Detective Longville, and this is my partner, Detective Byrd." He gestured at Heather.

"Yes," the woman replied.

"We're looking for Preston Smithers in relation to his black pickup truck. We believe that the truck was used in the commission of a crime," Nathan said, matter of fact, and showed the woman the registration on his phone. The woman refused to look at the phone and instead kept her cold and distant gaze on Nathan's face. She appeared bored and annoyed with his line of questioning.

"That man doesn't live here anymore," the woman said as she moved to close the door. Nathan stepped forward a bit, keeping the conversation going.

"Are you Loretta Smithers?"

"I don't believe that is any of your business," the woman hissed, narrowing her eyes at Nathan. Heather could feel the tension building and stepped forward, wondering if she might respond better to a female detective.

"If he isn't here, Mrs. Smithers, where has he gone?"

The woman didn't answer but instead stared at Heather as if trying to figure out where she knew her from. The woman remained silent and Heather grew uncomfortable under her piercing gaze. Heather looked to

Nathan for support, and he started to speak when the same man from their first call came out from behind the door. He dressed the same as before, but this time bruises covered his face, and a cut sliced above his eyebrow. The wounds looked fresh.

What happened to him?

"Can I help y'all?" he asked, southern drawl thick in his raspy throat.

"Yes, we're looking for the Smithers residence regarding a police matter. Can you confirm if Preston Smithers lives here?" Nathan asked.

"That man ain't here, as my momma just told you."

"Okay, thank you for confirming that information. We're looking for a black truck that may have been used to commit a crime. The same one we were looking for the last time we came," Heather said. "Do you happen to know if Mr. Smithers took the truck with him? Or did he leave it behind?"

The woman at the door stopped her bizarre staring and seemed to come back to life. "We told you last time that there is no such truck here. Now, if that will be all, I'd like to formally request that y'all do not return about this matter again."

The woman started to close the door and Nathan opened his mouth as the man stepped in front of his mother, shielding her.

"My momma said we are through, so we're through. If you don't leave our property, then we'll have to force the matter. Now, *go*," the man hissed gruffly and slammed the door in Nathan's face.

Heather and Nathan walked down the stairs, staying aware of their surroundings. Heather knew the sheriff should arrive any moment, but she had hoped things would have gone differently. She didn't think these people were going to willingly give over one of their own, but she hoped they would at least have some sort of breakthrough.

"I guess we'll tell the Sheriff that they aren't going to be willing when he arrives with the warrant," Heather said as they walked to the car. She switched on her flashlight, shining it on the uneven ground as darkness settled.

"Yeah, doesn't seem like this is going to be an easy one," Nathan said.

Heather stopped at the car, staring at the barn and silo. *Damn. We are so close. I can feel it.* As she went to switch her flashlight off, the light glinted off something on the ground.

"You coming?" Nathan called from inside the car. "We should probably make it seem like we're leaving so they don't get suspicious."

"One sec," Heather said and turned to walk toward the barn, picking up her pace to a half run.

"Where are you going?" he hissed, confused. He stepped from the car and watched her but didn't follow.

She bent down to investigate and didn't hear the front door of the home swing open until Nathan called for her. Without checking the object, she scooped it into her gloved hands and shoved it into her pocket.

"What do you think you're doing?" the man shouted as he came out of the door and onto the porch, holding a long shotgun.

Nathan made a move toward Heather, creating a barrier between this man and her. She could feel his anger at her random, reckless behavior through his body language.

"Just admiring the property before leaving," she said, keeping her hands shoved into her pockets as she made a beeline for the car.

"You need to git on now, and I mean it," the man snarled, gun steady in his hands.

Heather could see that he did, in fact, mean it. She nodded, and both she and Nathan got back into the car. Nathan put the car in reverse and turned around. The man aggressively followed, walking behind until he could no longer keep up. Nathan turned onto the main road, leaving the farm out of sight.

"What the hell was that?" Nathan's voice came out an octave higher, stressed and frustrated.

"Sorry, I thought I saw something," she said as she emptied the contents of her pocket.

It was a watch with a small face that had a crack running through the center. The hands had stopped, presumably when it was broken. The band was made of high-quality leather, though cracking with age in some spots. Heather flipped the watch over and found an inscription.

She read the inscription out loud to Nathan. "Arlene's Bake Shop, Est 1963."

Nathan pulled over the car and looked between Heather and the watch, flabbergasted. "That's April's watch," he said, stunned.

"Let me find the picture Lucy Dell sent us," Heather said, laying the watch on the center console between them as she took her phone from her other pocket. She didn't want to take any chances of being wrong.

She found the picture of April's watch and Nathan leaned over to look at her screen. Heather held the real watch next to the picture on the screen.

"Perfect match," Nathan whispered. "How did you see it all the way out in the snow?" he asked, looking up at her.

"I really don't know," Heather said. "Something reflected from my flashlight then I felt pulled toward it. I can't believe it's hers—you know what this means, right?"

"I do. We better call the sheriff back now."

Nathan wasted no time, and they called the sheriff together, filling him in on the details of the interaction at the door, Heather's finding, and the man's weapon.

"Great work, detectives," Sheriff Steinman said. "I'll have someone at the station confirm the identification of the watch. I'm about ten minutes out, and then we'll get this ball rolling."

"We're on it, Sheriff," Nathan said, signing off.

As Nathan and Heather waited the ten long minutes for the Sheriff's arrival, they watched the sky together, changing from dark purple to black, with stars appearing overhead. Heather knew the answers she sought for her sister lay on that farm, and she was beyond ready to receive them.

Will we all make it out of there alive?

Chapter Twenty

After the detectives rushed out of the station, followed shortly thereafter by the sheriff, Claire and Ryan simply sat, unsure of what to do next. Detective Byrd had ushered them into an interrogation room and then forgotten them. Claire understood the major break in the case, and they didn't have time to talk about her methodology for locating the stuttering man, but somehow, she felt shafted. She'd done the work the detectives so clearly couldn't do and then they left her behind like trash. She didn't expect them to take her out on the call to the farm, but she expected more than this.

Claire had spent a lot of her life feeling like this, and she hated every second of it. In the trailer park, the kids at school called her "trailer trash," causing Claire to wish she could erase her family and her home from her life. College was the same—she still felt like garbage, less intelligent than those around her. She failed at making friends in her youth, failed at her college courses, and now failed as an amateur detective as well.

At first, Ryan and Claire sat in silence. Part of Claire waited for Detective Byrd to return, though she had watched her dash out of the building through the interrogation room window. Ryan respected Claire's emotions and kept a supportive hand on her arm. As time passed and it became clear that

Detective Byrd forgot them, Claire felt sick to her stomach. She couldn't stop images of horror from the farm from haunting her mind, and being cooped up in this interrogation room didn't help. She imagined April trampled to death by a horse, laying in the snow with a slit throat, and burning to death in a fire. No matter how many times she tried to push the thoughts from her mind, images of dead April forced their way back in.

Her lack of sleep caught up with her in a bad way, and she accepted two cups of coffee from a secretary with gratitude. Claire guzzled it, despite the horrible taste. The woman offered shy apologies and assured the women that updates would come soon. Claire thought that unlikely but nodded and smiled at the secretary. No point in ruining the nice lady's day just because her day went terribly. She alternated between pacing the room and sliding to the floor from exhaustion.

"Maybe we should go home so you can rest?" Ryan asked.

"I won't leave until I know she's okay," Claire responded flatly, and she hoped Ryan understood.

How can I go home and take care of myself when April can't do the same? She would wait in this interrogation room until they had news, even if that meant sleeping on the cold, hard floor. April would do the same for her.

She closed her eyes for a moment. She hadn't fallen asleep, but she wasn't quite awake either. She could feel Ryan's anxious energy beside her. After what felt like hours, the Dells arrived, and Claire's heart sank to find that it had only forty-two minutes had passed.

The Dells' disheveled look caught her off guard, and Claire shuddered to think how she must look, too. Mr. Dell appeared gaunt. His clothes hung from his frame, limp and lifeless. His gray peppered hair now turned fully white. The wrinkles in his face seemed to have sunk deeper into his skin, and he looked like he might be at death's door. *My father wouldn't care if I went missing. Hell, he probably wouldn't know if I did.* She had tried her best to continue a relationship with him, but she wouldn't track down someone who didn't want to be found. She wished she had a family to lean on right now, but the only person she identified as family was gone.

Mrs. Dell, on the other hand, looked more swollen than she usually did. Red splotches covered her skin, giving her the appearance of having a serious ailment. Pink rimmed her tired eyes, and she breathed in labored and jagged breaths, despite walking slowly through the precinct. Mrs. Dell's normally anxious energy had taken a sour turn and she threw herself on a chair with an exasperated breath. Mrs. Dell looked as terrible as her husband, and Claire's heart broke all over again for April. It would have devastated her to find her parents looking like this. Claire and Ryan shared a worried glance, and Claire tried not to cry.

"Claire, Ryan," Mr. Dell said in greeting, voice flat.

Claire stood from her position on the floor and moved toward the Dells, thinking she might hug them, but their closed-off demeanors stopped her. Ryan took a step toward Claire and laid a gentle hand on her arm.

"They found her watch!" Mrs. Dell shouted, her voice coming out as a strangled squeak, and Claire had a hard time deciphering her words.

"They found what?"

"Her watch," Mr. Dell said. "At least, we assume they found it, because they called and asked us about it."

Claire's pulse quickened. "April's watch?"

"Who else's?" Mrs. Dell cried. Mr. Dell rushed to his wife's side and placed a hand on her shoulder, but Mrs. Dell shrugged it off.

"Don't touch me!" she shouted again, and Mr. Dell pulled back as if he were afraid she might hit him.

"Breathe, Lucy, like the doctor said," Mr. Dell said, trying to sound calming but instead sounding agitated, exhausted, and afraid.

Ryan grabbed Claire's hand and held on tight, as if trying to keep Claire from floating away. She started to ask more questions about the watch but stopped. She didn't want to make things worse. The walls collapsed in on Claire as she felt the air in the room grow thicker. An ache built in her chest as she struggled to breathe. Her face grew hot and flushed, and Ryan watched her closely.

"Are you okay?" Ryan whispered.

Claire couldn't respond. All of the air had left the room.

"We'll be right back," Ryan announced as she pushed Claire out of the room.

Ryan led Claire to the rear of the station, and Claire avoided the sympathetic glances that followed her throughout the building. She hated being the missing girl's roommate. When they finally emerged from the sheriff's station, cold air smacked her in the face. *If they found her watch on the farm but not April, what does that mean?*

"Breathe with me, too," Ryan said, grabbing both of Claire's hands. "Watch me and breathe with me."

Claire did her best to follow Ryan's deep, long breaths but she couldn't keep up. Ryan's chest moved impossibly slow with her calm breaths and Claire's refused to cooperate. Instead, her lungs inflated and deflated so rapidly that she swore one of them had a hole and leaked air. She sank to the ground, wrapped her arms around her head, and let out a pitiful wail. Claire heard a nearby flock of birds take flight at her sound, and she wished she could join them. She'd focused so intently on trying to find April that she had never once stopped to think about what might happen when they did.

She knew the possible outcomes—find April alive, find April dead, or never find April—and she didn't like any of them. If they found April alive, life would never be the same, April would never be the same. She didn't know how to be there for April if she did come home. If April could live through this ordeal, certainly Claire could live through it too, but she didn't know how to take care of someone broken by the horrors of life.

I wish it was me instead of April. She's too good for this and I'm just trash.

But what if they didn't find April alive? What if they couldn't save her? Claire couldn't imagine burying her best friend and living the rest of her life without her. Hell, these few days without her were the most miserable of her life and she had stopped taking care of herself entirely. She needed April to survive—no one could convince her otherwise. Where would she go without April? Being stuck in this town without her was its own death sentence. She knew that she could never truly prepare for whatever came next, but she owed it to herself to try. If they had found April's watch, that meant she'd been there at some point.

Claire supposed the worst outcome of all would be to know that April had been on that farm and still not find her there. If April lived or died, it would give closure, but if they never found her, no one could ever move on. Her breathing slowed as she thought through these possibilities, and Ryan smiled.

"Hey, that's better!" she said. "Nice and slow breaths."

Claire nodded. "What if I never see her again?"

Ryan wrapped her in a hug. "You don't have to think about that now. We don't know what's going to happen."

"I know that, but what will I do?" Claire said, unable to move away from the line of thinking.

"You'll get through it. We'll get through it together."

Claire buried her head deep into Ryan's chest and nodded. She supposed she would get through anything, regardless of how it felt, and it would feel easier with Ryan by her side. "Thank you," she whispered.

"Anything for you, Claire," Ryan said, kissing Claire gently on the forehead.

Claire savored the feeling of Ryan's lips on her skin, hoping that this wouldn't go away when things settled down. She spent so long wanting Ryan, and this was the worst possible time to start a relationship, but Claire couldn't help herself. She hoped this thing—relationship or whatever it was—wasn't temporary or budding from a place of desperation, but one of true love and honest feelings. Ryan shivered, and Claire stood up, pulling Ryan up with her.

"Let's get warm," Claire said, holding out her hand.

Ryan took her hand, and it felt as if it had always belonged there. They made their way into the station, hand in hand. Claire didn't know if the stares they got on the walk to the interrogation room were because she was the roommate of the missing girl or because women didn't often hold hands in Tree Park, but Claire didn't care. She was proud to be with Ryan, and she hoped Ryan felt the same way. She looked into Ryan's eyes and her heart skipped a beat. Life didn't stop because one person went missing, as much as she would have liked for it to. Before returning to the interrogation room, she leaned in and kissed Ryan on the lips, smiling.

Mrs. Dell sat in her chair sobbing into her hands and Mr. Dell stood behind her, scrolling through his phone. Mr. Dell looked up as they entered and blushed at their hand holding. Mrs. Dell didn't look up from her sobbing and Claire felt grateful for that. Ryan essentially came out to her town by holding Claire's hand and she dreaded how people might react, especially Mrs. Dell. Mr. Dell cleared his throat through his blush as he held out his phone for Claire to look at. She dropped Ryan's hand and grabbed the phone, frowning as she saw the same website she had located earlier on the screen.

"Does April know him, Claire?" Mr. Dell asked.

"Not to my knowledge," Claire replied. "If she did, I didn't know about it. I never saw him before the vigil."

"Me neither," Mr. Dell said. "Though I keep trying to force my brain into making a connection that isn't there. I feel like if I knew him, I could better help my little girl."

Claire nodded in understanding. She zoomed in on the picture of the family and scrolled her fingers to look at the property behind them.

"I guess that's where the police are right now," she said to Mr. Dell, who leaned forward to glance at his phone screen.

"Yes," Mr. Dell continued. "I feel so useless sitting here so I thought I would do some 'Googling,'" he said, using air quotes, "but I've come up dry. Only the website that you found."

In the hustle and bustle of discovering his identity, Claire hadn't thought to try to find out more about him. Ashamed, Claire handed Mr. Dell his phone and pulled out her own. She typed "Smithers Farm" in the search bar and scrolled through the page of results, Ryan reading over her shoulder. The outdated farm's website gave no useful information, and the button for placing orders didn't work. Several online reviews reported that orders had gone unfulfilled, tarnishing the farm's reputation. Every review before three years ago glowed, a stark contrast to the more recent ones.

"None of them have social media that I can find, and it appears that their website is outdated. They may have shut down operations at their farm, which makes sense if they are committing crimes," Claire said to Mr. Dell, who seemed impressed that Claire had gained all that information in a matter of minutes.

"How did you find that so fast? Must be a youth thing," Mr. Dell asked, laughing a bit at his own age.

"How can we know anything about them if they aren't on the internet?" Mrs. Dell looked up from her sobs, surprising the rest of the room.

"I'm not sure there's much to find," Claire said. "I guess we just have to wait for the detectives."

Mrs. Dell nodded, and Claire felt sorry and worried for her. Ryan wrapped her arm around Claire's shoulders as she locked her phone and stuffed it into her pocket. It was going to be a long night.

Chapter Twenty-One

April didn't know how long she'd stared into the darkness before a sliver of light appeared at the top of the cellar stairs. She'd heard shuffling and doors opening and closing for some time now and grew anxious at the idea that someone might come for her. Her brain shut down, the anxiety too much for her frazzled nerves. Brother Beau's injuries prevented climbing the stairs and attempting an escape, but April simply hadn't considered it a possibility. She felt stunned when the door opened without being unlocked. Lost in the pitch black of the cellar, April never considered a way out. Something inside her had disconnected in that darkness, and she didn't care about what happened to her.

I guess I'm ready for the end.

Part of April welcomed death and wanted it to come quickly, but another deep piece of her would never accept it. She didn't move as feet stomped down the stairs, knowing they belonged to Brother Waylon. She didn't resist when his rough hands yanked her to her feet and toward the stairs. Her feet dangled as he dragged her up the stairs. The light coming from the upstairs portion of the house blinded her and she closed her eyes.

Whatever will happen will happen. I don't even think I care anymore.

Brother Waylon brought April into the kitchen, where he shackled her to the same chair from her time with Mother Loretta before. Mother Loretta paced the room and glared at April when she came in. There would be no sweet words or gestures this time. She mumbled to herself, seeming to come apart at the seams. Her poise had faded and now she looked like a crazy witch. Brother Waylon paused in the doorway and watched his mother's pacing.

"Mother Loretta, it'll be alright—we'll git Sister Jolene back," he said in the sweetest tone of voice April had ever heard from him.

Mother Loretta paused in her looping track and slowly turned to face Brother Waylon. His boyish smile did not stop his mother from letting out a banshee scream. April's body instinctively tried to cover her ears at the sound, but her bound hands couldn't move. She buried the ear closest to Mother Loretta into her shoulder, hoping the scream would die out soon. As the scream ended in a guttural gurgle, April chanced a glance at Brother Waylon, who shook in his boots, literally.

"My dearest daughter is gone, you imbecile," Mother Loretta said, her voice thin, like a ghost. "I will never have her back. I will never feel her kiss on my cheek, and I will never brush her soft hair. I will *never* see my dearest daughter again."

Brother Waylon's eyes widened as he stared at Mother Loretta, who crumpled to the floor. Her dress fanned out around her legs, and she sobbed openly. April stayed quiet, partly captivated by Mother Loretta's raw display of grief and partly flabbergasted by the softer side of Brother Waylon. April watched in stunned fascination as Brother Waylon took a few tentative steps into the kitchen and toward his mother. He crouched down and laid a gentle hand on her back.

"Oh, Mother Loretta, don't cry," he said, southern drawl elongating each word as he spoke.

Mother Loretta remained frozen under her son's gentle touch, and April felt emotionally affected by the gesture. At the end of the day, no matter how insane this family was, they were in mourning. April's heart nearly jumped out of her chest as Mother Loretta released another banshee shriek, striking Brother Waylon straight in the mouth and knocking him to the floor in surprise.

"Stop, stop!" he shrieked as Mother Loretta stood over him, kicking his body with all her might.

"It should have been you and not her!" she shrieked, continuing to kick him.

April let out an involuntary yelp at the brutality of Mother Loretta's actions, drawing attention to herself.

"As for you, you sick imposter!" Mother Loretta hissed, ceasing her kicking and turning her attention to April.

Brother Waylon crawled toward the kitchen door and paused in the threshold, watching. She met Mother Loretta's gaze and April flooded with a fear that she had never experienced before. As she tried to look bold and unafraid, she thought, *I hope my death is quick*. She had lived enough of this hell to know she couldn't do it forever, certainly not as long as any of the other Sister Jolenes had. She understood now why Autumn had taken her own life, and April thought she might do the same if she got the chance.

"Feeling brave, are you?" Mother Loretta sneered. "Well, my dearest daughter, let's see just how brave you are."

Mother Loretta lifted her hand as quick as a cat, and April flinched, remembering the sting of Mother Loretta's last slap.

"That's what I thought," Mother Loretta said, turning to Brother Waylon. "Bring my other son to me."

With that, Brother Waylon left the room, and Mother Loretta resumed pacing through the kitchen, mumbling to herself. When Brother Waylon returned, he carried Brother Beau over his shoulder like a sack of potatoes. April imagined his brother couldn't weigh much in his sickly state, and Brother Waylon made it look effortless. He tossed Brother Beau to the kitchen floor, stopping Mother Loretta in her tracks. The fall to the ground knocked Brother Beau's wind from him, and he coughed, curling into himself.

"Poor baby," Mother Loretta said with a sick smile. "Are you still not feeling well? You've been nothing but a burden your whole life. It should have been you instead of my dearest daughter, too. I'd trade a hundred sons to have Sister Jolene back!"

Mother Loretta didn't beat Brother Beau as she had Brother Waylon, but instead spat at him. The spit landed on his cheek, and he reached out to wipe his face, whimpering. April looked at Brother Beau, crumpled on the floor, and pitied him. It must have felt unbearable to have Mother Loretta as a caregiver.

"Guns," Mother Loretta hissed at Brother Waylon as she created a new track, pacing to avoid Brother Beau's crumpled body.

Brother Waylon left the room again and when he returned, he carried two long shotguns. He leaned them against the kitchen counter, out of reach of both April and Brother Beau. Mother Loretta's gaze flicked to the guns as she went back and forth, but she didn't stop or grab one. Brother Waylon stood next to the guns, and Brother Beau appeared to pass out.

April tried to focus on the guns, but her vision swam. She squeezed her eyes shut, willing herself to stay present and fight the waves of nausea now flooding her body. Behind her eyelids, April saw rapid moving images, memories of the life she lived before being brought to this farm.

This really is the end.

She thought of her parents and the sweet love they had given her from the second they held her in their arms. She thought of the opportunities they had afforded her and the sacrifices they had made. She thought of how that love could turn sinister in this type of grief but knew that her parents would use the pain of April's loss to bring something good to the world. She knew the story of Sister Jolene's family would not be the story of her own, and she took solace in that fact.

She thought of her roommate and her lack of faith in herself. She thought of how Claire had taught April what it meant to be young and free. She thought of all the times Claire protected her and knew she would punish herself for being unable to save April now. She thought of their good times and their sisterhood. She knew Claire's strength and resiliency would see her through. She had braved her way through other tough times in life, and this wouldn't break her either. A tear slid down her cheek at the thoughts of her best friend, desperate for one more moment with her.

She thought of her job at the museum and the children she gave tours to. She knew that museum guides were a dime a dozen, but she hoped her replacement would feel as passionate as she did. She thought of her future as an art curator and could see cracks forming throughout that dream. As the idea shattered, April didn't feel sad—instead, she felt free. She accepted her fate and let go of the expectations she once had. She couldn't change this family's choices, but she could embrace the last moments of her life with grace.

Will I die as Father Preston had? In this kitchen, blood exploding from my neck, at the hands of Brother Waylon?

She shuddered and hoped Mother Loretta hadn't noticed. She peeked through her lowered eyelids as Mother Loretta's mumblings grew louder. She caught snippets of words and phrases, and the woman sounded as if she had finally lost her mind.

"Jolene… gone, gone… dearest daughter… everyone will die… will I die… retribution…."

Things stayed this way for a while—Mother Loretta pacing and whispering, Brother Beau passed out on the floor, and Brother Waylon holding his stance next to the guns, waiting for orders. April started to fall asleep in her chair, head drooping. She jerked upright, trying to keep herself awake. The sky had darkened, and she kept her focus out the window.

What is it like to die? Will my soul float out of my body and into the realm above? Will my body's energy flow from my dead self and into something else around me? Will I be born again? Am I doomed to haunt the world forever, a ghost of this family's trauma?

April's fear reignited as some instinctual circuit within her brain sent flares and distress signals to the rest of her being. Her pulse quickened, and her breath came in shorter bursts as her mind settled into total panic. She didn't want this. She didn't want to die. Her situation felt hopeless, but her mind searched with desperation for a loophole.

Maybe I know something that can help me escape.

April knew she couldn't handle this life as long as the last Sister Jolene had, but maybe she could take it long enough to make a break for it. She tried to slow her breathing and thought about each member of this family. Mother Loretta worshiped her "dearest daughter" more than anything in the world, Brother Waylon took on the role of fierce protector to his sister, Brother Beau cherished his sister's good care of him, and Father Preston couldn't cope with the loss of his little girl. Sister Jolene had been kind and caring but daring and bold.

That's it—I need to emulate those qualities, right here, right now.

She looked from Mother Loretta to Brother Waylon, but neither looked at her. She cast her gaze down to Brother Beau's prone form and noticed something felt different.

Had he moved?

His eyes remained closed and his breathing even, but April swore he had moved several inches to the right. She blinked hard, and his eyes met hers. She startled but didn't dare make a sound. He wordlessly put his finger over his lips in a shushing movement before dropping his hand and closing his eyes once more. He had a plan, and she needed to distract the others to help him accomplish it. She tingled with anticipation as she broke the tense silence.

"I know how much you all loved Sister Jolene, and I know I'm not her," she said, unsure of what to say next. Mother Loretta stopped pacing and stared at April with anger. Brother Waylon stood up straighter from the counter and looked at April with disgust.

"I can't ever be her, but maybe I can be part of this family in a different way. Maybe we could all grow to love each other and depend on each other the way you did before," she finished, surprised at the turn her words had taken and hoping it would make a difference. It was her last hope. The two continued to stare at her, lost for words, and April noticed Brother Beau shift a few more inches to the right.

"You think you can just come into this family and be a part of it?" Mother Loretta asked in a shockingly steady tone. She didn't sound angry, only dumbfounded.

"I think I could. I think we could all be a part of this together," April confirmed, meeting Mother Loretta's eye.

Mother Loretta's gaze softened into a look of sadness, surprising April. She took a tentative step toward April, who continued to meet her gaze.

"Are you really buying this, Mother Loretta?" Brother Waylon asked, voice laden with incredulity. "Don't let her fool you. She's just another harlot from the street. She can never be a part of this family, especially not the way Sister Jolene was."

Mother Loretta paused and looked at Brother Waylon. When her eyes returned to April, they held a more sinister look.

"My son is right—you're an outsider. You aren't one of us." She took another step toward April.

"I could be one of you! I could learn. Brother Beau taught me how to groom Windy, and I already know how to bake and clean. Please, give me a chance, Mother Loretta, please," April pleaded, and Mother Loretta's eyes softened again.

April knew her tricks worked as she appealed to the side of this mother that grieved, desperate for a daughter. Mother Loretta now stood as close to April as she could get. She crouched down to look directly at April.

"I could be your dearest daughter," April offered.

Mother Loretta put her hand on April's cheek and rubbed circles with her thumb.

"My dearest daughter," Mother Loretta said, a sad smile on her lips and a single tear rolling down her cheek.

"How dare you disrespect Sister Jolene that way," Brother Waylon spat as he picked up a shotgun and pointed it at his mother. Mother Loretta straightened and used her body to shield April from Brother Waylon.

"I am the matriarch here, and I make decisions about the members of this family, not you, Brother Waylon. Stand down," she said.

Brother Waylon did not stand down and instead cocked the shotgun. "Either I take her out by herself, or I take you out with her. The choice is yours, Mother Loretta."

He aimed the gun at Mother Loretta's midsection. If he shot now, the bullet would travel straight through Mother Loretta's stomach and into April's head. She swallowed hard at the possibility and tried to see Brother Waylon from behind Mother Loretta's form. Mother Loretta raised a hand to her son, about to speak, when a piercing sound broke the silence. In the distance, sirens cut through the air, and everyone in the room, except Brother Beau, looked toward the kitchen window. April watched with renewed hope as flashing blue and red lights reflected off the barn and lit up the property.

"YOU AREN'T WELCOME HERE!" Mother Loretta screamed at the window, pushing past Brother Waylon and grabbing a shotgun.

Brother Waylon lowered his gun and looked at his mother, terrified. April chanced a stealthy look at Brother Beau. He had moved farther away, and his hand dug quietly into the corner cabinet. April saw him surreptitiously take a handgun from the cabinet, close it without sound, and tuck the gun into his shirt. The gesture only took one moment, and Brother Beau's clean movements shocked her. His normal weak and shaky demeanor had vanished. Brother Waylon and Mother Loretta whispered to each other. Suddenly, a voice boomed out from the front door, and an echoing knock pounded on the front door.

"Sheriff's office, open up!"

April whimpered as she recognized the sheriff's voice through the door, allowing hope to pulse through her body. She could taste the freedom—

either through death or rescue from this farm, and she welcomed whatever happened next. The sheriff banged on the door again. April slid her arms up and down within her restraints, trying to figure out a way to break free of them.

"We have a warrant," the sheriff bellowed. "Open up!"

Mother Loretta and Brother Waylon stared at each other. Brother Waylon gave a curt nod to his mother as she placed a hand on his cheek, exactly as she had done with April.

"I'll protect you, Mother Loretta," Brother Waylon whispered to his mother as he kissed her forehead.

"I love you, son," Mother Loretta responded as she fired a shot at the door to the kitchen, warning the sheriff they would not be opening up and they would not make this easy.

Chapter Twenty-Two

"Shots fired, everyone down!" Sheriff Steinman shouted as he threw himself down to the porch.

Heather and Nathan followed orders and hit the ground at the bottom of the stairs of the porch. The remaining four officers in the yard also fell to the ground as everyone waited for another shot. Nathan reached out and grabbed Heather's hand, and gratitude flooded her system. After a few moments of quiet, Sheriff Steinman crawled to the edge of the porch steps, slinking down them and meeting Heather and Nathan in a crouched position.

"Looks like you were right about them putting up a fight," he whispered, glancing at the house.

"Not happy to be right about this," Heather replied.

The three crawled their way to the fleet of police cruisers blocking the driveway. They needed to regroup and get the inhabitants of the farmhouse talking. They had no other choice with a hostage inside.

Heather thought of her father, who never seemed to leave her mind while on this farm. She wondered what had gone through his mind at the bank robbery. *Had he felt nervous, or was he confident in his ability? Did he think about the fact that his life could end? What did he think as the bullet hit him and he fell to the ground?* Heather shook away the memories and focused on the task at hand.

"Does the warrant cover the entire property, Sheriff?" she asked.

"It does, which will take a lot of time to comb through once we're done with the family. Look at all that land. Why?"

"I think the officers should start here, with this graveyard, once we notify the family. I have a sinking feeling that there's something to find in there," Heather replied.

The sheriff instructed a pair of officers how to proceed, once able to do so. Heather imagined what kinds of bodies might lie buried under those graves and suspected that maybe Preston Smithers hadn't gone that far after all. She moved on from the small cemetery, hoping this family wasn't smart enough to hide evidence somewhere on the vast property. They hadn't seemed like career criminals, and hopefully, they made errors that could make this investigation easier. Heather shuddered as she imagined them dumping Bethany's body near the woods of Tree Park, dumping Autumn outside of the bowling alley.

Sheriff Steinman grabbed the megaphone, and the group took a few steps closer to the house. "This is Sheriff Steinman of Tree Park. We have a warrant to search the property; come out with your hands on your heads," he shouted as his words echoed through the empty farmland.

Heather waited with bated breath and strained her ears, trying to hear anything from inside the house. Nothing. As they waited, a scream tore through the silence.

"HELP MEEEEE!"

"That's April Dell," Heather said to the sheriff.

The sheriff nodded. "Let's try calling the home phone. Heather, take the lead on the phone call." Nathan pulled out his cell phone, put the call on speaker, and held it in the middle of the group.

"We are calling your phone," the sheriff shouted into the megaphone. "We want everyone to stay safe and want to do this in a way that works for everyone. Please answer."

The world went quiet again, only broken by the sounds of a shrill phone ringing inside the house. After an impossible number of rings, a click sounded through the receiver. Someone had picked up.

"Hello, this is Detective Byrd; we met on your porch," Heather started.

"We want you to leave our land," said the man's voice from the door, gruff and quiet. "That's all we want—no one gets hurt if you leave."

"Can you tell me who I am speaking with?" Heather responded, trying to buy time.

"No, I cannot, who do you think—" Another voice cut him off.

"We said you need to leave… are you soft in the head? Imbecile." The voice belonged to the woman from the door. With another click, the call ended.

Nathan had studied something intently on his phone and now held it up for the Sheriff and Heather to read. The station had sent information detailing the family's names—Preston and Loretta, mother and father, the twins, Waylon and Beauregard, and the youngest, Jolene.

"Loretta told us that Preston took off years ago, but perhaps we can appeal to the safety of her kids," Heather said as she called again.

This time, Loretta answered. "What?" she hissed. "We already told you to leave us alone!"

"I just want to talk about your family, your kids—Waylon, Beauregard, and Jolene," Heather said. "Would you come outside so we can talk?"

Loretta paused for a few moments before speaking. "How do you know about my daughter?"

Nathan looked at Heather in confusion and whispered, "All we have on the girl is a birth record. What is she talking about?"

"I think she's gone. Dead," Heather whispered, hand over the receiver. "She sounds like a mother pining for her baby girl."

"I lost someone too," Heather said. "I know what it's like to miss someone so much that your insides turn rotten, and your world loses all color. I would love to have a chance to talk with you about her, please."

Mother Loretta paused again, and Heather heard a commotion in the background. She looked at the sheriff, eyes wide, but the sound of struggles only intensified.

"HELP ME! PLEASE!"

"That's April Dell," Heather whispered to the sheriff and Nathan. "I would know her voice anywhere after watching all the videos on her phone. We've got to get in there, Sheriff."

Sheriff Steinman nodded and spoke into the phone's receiver. "Sheriff Steinman here. We're going to have to come in now. We would like your cooperation but don't need it, ma'am."

"I've got a gun on the girl, so if you try any funny business, she dies! Send the lady cop only." Mother Loretta sounded angry and hung up again.

Nathan looked between Heather and the sheriff. "No way, right?" Nobody responded.

Heather looked at Sheriff Steinman, and he nodded, sure of his decision. Heather had training and fieldwork for these situations.

"Nathan," Heather said. "She requested me. I did all those classes for a reason. This is who I am and what I do."

"No way!" Nathan shouted again. "We should call out-of-town resources—you shouldn't have to do this!"

"We already called for backup," the sheriff said, "but we need to get in there now, or they'll kill April. We have no choice, Nathan."

Heather tried to grab Nathan's hand, but he moved away. His eyes flashed with terror and pain, and she thought she could see tears swimming in them before he started to walk to the patrol cars.

"Please, Nathan, don't do this," Heather hollered, but the Sheriff interrupted her.

"I hate to break whatever this is up, but April may not have much longer," he said.

Heather nodded and did a brief radio check.

"Nathan, before I go—" She stopped when he held up a hand.

"Tell me after," he said, continuing toward the patrol cars and meeting with the other officers, preparing to run into the house should Heather need backup before the additional resources arrived. Nathan didn't bother to turn and look at her, and although she didn't want the image of him walking away to be the last, she had no choice.

Heather reviewed some safety tactics with the sheriff, though her attention zeroed in on the house itself. No more shouts or cries for help had come from the house, but that didn't mean something terrible wasn't happening inside.

"If I don't make it out—" Heather started, but the sheriff cut her off.

"Heather, bah, don't talk like that," he said, tightening the straps on her bulletproof vest further.

"Sheriff, please," she said, trying to be serious, and he nodded.

"If I don't make it out, tell my mom I love her and make sure she's taken care of."

"Of course, you know I will, but you're going to be fine. We've got backup on the way, so we need you to keep the situation in there as calm as you can while we wait for their arrival."

"And will you tell Nathan that I love him, too?" Heather said, blushing. "I know he said to tell him after, but I can't take the chance of him never knowing."

"So, it's like that, huh?" Sheriff Steinman said. "Fooling around under my nose?"

"No sir, we haven't broken any policy, but it didn't stop the feelings from blooming. Please—you'll tell him?"

"I sure will, but remember, history doesn't always repeat itself. You've learned valuable lessons from Sheriff Byrd, and you'll be fine." Sheriff Steinman clapped Heather on the shoulder. She straightened, pushing away the nervousness.

Heather began her trek to the house. She walked with slow and deliberate steps, taking deep breaths at every chance she got. She imagined her father walked beside her, holding her hand as tightly as he could. She climbed the porch steps, each one creaking under her weight, keeping an eye on the surrounding landscape.

Nathan stood, ready to charge into the house after her. He dipped his head in a nod as he covered his heart with his hand. She mimicked the expression, covering her heart, and smiled. Turning sideways, she pushed the wooden front door open. It creaked, and she stepped over the threshold. When the door closed, she thought, *Will I ever see the outside world again?*

Chapter Twenty-Three

April's ears rang so loud she thought she might have lost her hearing entirely. The sounds came through muffled and muted. After firing the warning shot and speaking with the sheriff on the phone, Mother Loretta returned to her trance. Brother Waylon's anger flared in a way that April had never seen before. Fumes practically shot out of his ears and nostrils as he stood, panting. While Mother Loretta talked with the police, Brother Waylon crept toward April.

By the time Brother Waylon's fist cuffed April on her ear, she didn't have time to register what had happened to her. An explosion of pain burst in her head and she wondered if she'd been shot. Brother Waylon loomed over her, scowling with anger and cackling in laughter. She shuddered. She could taste the freedom—things couldn't end, not now. She shrieked, praying that the officers could hear her through Mother Loretta's phone. When that didn't stop him, she tried again.

"HELP! Please!" April shrieked as long and as loud as humanly possible before Brother Waylon's fist swung into her lip.

The taste of blood filled her mouth as pride flooded her chest. She didn't know if the officers heard her, but she wouldn't go down without a fight.

Mother Loretta threatened to kill her as she raised her shotgun to April's temple. The cold metal cooled her skin, and April leaned into the gun. She must have been concussed.

"Detective Heather Byrd, Sheriff's office," April heard a voice call from the hallway.

"In here. Come in slow and give me any weapons you have," Mother Loretta said.

Moments later, Detective Byrd, or Heather, as April knew her, entered clad in tactical gear, including a bulletproof vest. She made immediate eye contact with April, her face showing deep concern. Heather passed her gun to Mother Loretta and tried to stand as close to April as possible.

"You think I'm stupid, lady?" Mother Loretta hissed. "The radio, too. You're with us now; no contact with them allowed."

April watched as Heather reluctantly handed over her radio and turned to April.

"Are you okay?" she asked.

April's brain swam, and she couldn't formulate an answer. She wanted to tell Heather that she was okay, but the words wouldn't connect with her mouth. Her mind wanted to tell Heather something else, too, but she couldn't find it within the fuzzy recesses of her mind.

"Don't speak to Sister Jolene!" Mother Loretta shouted, now turning the gun on Heather, who raised her hands.

April felt so confused. Her head pounded as she tried to keep up with the insanity and her eyes drooped, head lolling to the side.

"Sister Jolene?" Heather asked. "Who's Sister Jolene?"

April could see Heather's confusion as she looked from Mother Loretta to April and then around the room to Brother Beau's crumpled form. Mother Loretta roared, and Brother Waylon approached from his place in the shadows of the kitchen door.

"Don't contradict Mother Loretta," he said through his teeth. "Sit down."

Brother Waylon pushed Heather's shoulders, but she stood her ground.

"I'd like to stand if that's possible," she said and turned to Mother Loretta. "I apologize for the miscommunication about this young woman here."

Heather stood firmly in place, allowing one hand to rest on April's confined arm. April appreciated Heather's quick thinking as Mother Loretta calmed down some, and Brother Waylon stepped back from the detective. April shut her eyes, savoring the safe feeling of Heather's presence.

"I would like to talk to you, however, about the matter that brought us here," Heather said. "My people are not going to be able to leave until they've completed their duties. A judge has ordered this to be carried out. Now, I'm sure this is all a misunderstanding, and if this is, in fact, your daughter Jolene, then my officers will be out of your hair in no time."

Mother Loretta seemed to contemplate this information. She clearly wanted the police to leave but she was aware enough to understand that April was not her daughter. She turned her blank stare toward Brother Waylon, saying nothing.

"You can tell your people to leave, or we will shoot both you and the girl," Brother Waylon said, grabbing Heather's radio and holding it in front of her.

"They aren't going to leave. Maybe we can make another deal?" she asked, refusing to take the radio from Brother Waylon.

Brother Waylon put the radio on the counter and pulled a pair of handcuffs from the back pocket of his jeans.

"You've forced my hand," he hissed at Heather, trying to catch her wrist.

Heather resisted Brother Waylon, and April watched in awe at her lithe strength and agility. She wished she could have had those qualities too. Brute strength won out and Brother Waylon wrestled the detective to the floor, handcuffing her right hand to the chair that trapped April. Brother Waylon then turned to his mother, whose whimpering grew louder and busied himself with trying to calm her. Heather cast a warm glance up at April, which she appreciated immensely.

"Don't worry," Heather whispered. "We're going to be okay."

April tried to nod, to acknowledge she heard Heather, but her neck wouldn't cooperate. Instead, she rolled her head in a weird swinging motion before giving up. April started to lose touch with reality.

Is any of this real? Where am I?

A thick fog surrounded everything as April tried to maintain consciousness. Heather watched her with worry, calculating her injuries.

"Let's talk privately," Mother Loretta whispered to her son, catching April's attention and reigniting her desire to stay awake. They were leaving the room.

"If you two move, you know what will happen," Brother Waylon threatened, pointing his gun at April and then shifting it to Heather.

Brother Waylon guided Mother Loretta from the room, though April could tell by their footsteps that they had stopped just outside of the door. April knew she would need to keep her voice low, barely above a whisper. She tried to remember what she needed to tell Heather as a hand gripped her arm on the other side of the chair. Startled, April's head snapped to attention.

Brother Beau. His hand rested gently on her arm. *He has a gun—should I be afraid of him?*

"A-a-are you okay?" Brother Beau said in a quiet stutter.

"You," Heather said, the word hissing through her teeth.

Brother Beau looked past April to Heather chained to the chair next to her. His face blanched white at the sight of the detective, but strangely enough, he smiled.

"I-I-I'm glad you found us, Detective. I was hoping my clues would help."

Heather looked stunned as she stared at Brother Beau, mouth agape.

"I knew it was you," Heather said, "but what I don't know is why."

"I don't want to be a part of this anymore," Brother Beau said in a low voice.

He truly means it. He fed information to the sheriff's department. He may have saved her life. That's when it hit her—what she had so desperately wanted to tell Heather.

"Autumn," April said, word muffled by heavy lips, but clear enough.

She watched as Heather's face changed from a look of confusion to fear to sadness.

"She was here?" Heather whispered, voice tinged with grief.

"She was here," he confirmed with a sad nod. "But I never w-w-w-wanted that. It was Brother Waylon who had the idea. I can't live with the guilt anymore."

"You did the right thing," Heather replied to Brother Beau.

"I-I-I hope so," Brother Beau said, eyes filling with fear as he shifted his gaze toward the door to the kitchen. "Someone has to stop them. That's why I left the box at your doorstep."

Mother Loretta's voice rose, and Brother Beau scrambled back to his place on the kitchen floor. He collapsed in a heap and resumed his false fainting. April wished she had said something, thanked him for his help in her rescue, but the moment had passed. Brother Waylon and Mother Loretta came through the door.

April glanced over at Heather, who fiddled with her sleeve in an awkward motion. *What is that?* Finally, she registered the object. It was a handcuff key Heather had hidden in her clothing. She made a swift movement to unlock herself but kept her hand on the chair as if still bound. She made a soft shushing noise to April as Brother Waylon and Mother Loretta turned their attention to the pair. April thought Mother Loretta might speak as a loud sound interrupted them.

"Detective Byrd," the radio sitting on the counter shouted, "Detective Byrd, come in, Detective Byrd."

April could see Heather contemplating reaching for the radio but thought otherwise. Brother Waylon grabbed the radio and smashed it to the floor, plastic bits shattering and a terrible screeching sound emitting from the speaker before it died altogether. He turned his gaze toward April, a new sheen of craze reflected.

Please, please, let us survive.

"We've decided what to do with this little situation of ours, and I'm quite pleased with the result." He sneered as he raised his shotgun to April's forehead.

"Say goodbye," he said, a cackle breaking out of his lips as he pulled back the top of the gun.

April closed her eyes and thought of her father's warm embrace as the sound of a gunshot rang through the kitchen. Instead of a blinding pain and the end of time, April instead heard a shrill cry coming from Brother Waylon. She opened her eyes in time to see him fall to the ground, blood pouring from a wound on his upper thigh.

Brother Beau stood, leaning heavily onto the counter, holding the handgun out in front of him. He had shot his brother in the leg and saved April's life. Gratitude for him washed over her as she watched him crumple toward the floor, unable to hold himself up in his weakened state. She imagined it took everything he had left to pull the trigger. The door splintered as officers swarmed into the room, shouts of "Down, down, down!" echoing in the small space.

Mother Loretta screamed as she raised her shotgun and fired at Brother Beau. The bullet whizzed through the air, past April and Heather, and hit Brother Beau's throat. April let out a strangled scream. She watched as Brother Beau's blood flowed from his neck in waves. April thrashed, desperate to get to the man who had saved her life, but the chair held her firmly in place. She held his eye as Brother Beau cried out, blood pouring from his body. In a matter of moments, his face went slack—it was over. He died just as Father Preston had—blood flowing freely from his neck on the kitchen floor at the hands of a family member.

Officers swarmed and suddenly Heather stood in front of Mother Loretta and Brother Waylon, gun aimed at the pair on the floor. Brother Waylon continued groaning and rolling back and forth but allowing his mother to help him.

"Don't move," Heather shouted as she kicked away the two shotguns from the reach of the mother and son on the floor.

Mother Loretta looked up in horror as she realized her mistake. Brother Waylon writhed in too much pain to notice anything other than his hurt leg. Sheriff Steinman ran to support Heather, flanking her on the side with his gun held up, matching hers. Another officer pulled Mother Loretta to her feet, cuffing her hands behind her back. April didn't see anything else that happened as a male detective, someone she dimly recognized but wasn't familiar with, crouched down to free her. He, too, had a handcuff key tucked into his outfit, and luckily this family all used standard handcuffs with universal keys.

The second the detective freed her, April flew to Brother Beau's body, throwing herself on him. She had to tell him thank you, desperate for him to feel how much he didn't deserve this life or this death. Strong hands pulled her off Brother Beau, and she resisted, thrashing and hitting, fearing Brother Waylon had captured her once more.

"You're safe, you're safe," the detective repeated, pulling April from her trance.

She took one look at the detective's face and her body gave way. He wrapped his strong arms around her as he lifted her. April reached out and grabbed Brother Beau's lifeless hand, desperate for one last chance to say goodbye. As she felt his fingers slipping away from hers, his blood now coating her skin, she wailed in agony.

"Thank you," her mind whispered the words she could not get past her screams.

By the time April reached the ambulance, the world spun in an all too familiar way, and she lost her grip on reality.

In the dark space behind her closed eyes, April swore she saw Brother Beau.

He held a cowboy hat over his chest and smiled at her.

"I'm so sorry," she said through her tears as she reached out for him.

Brother Beau grabbed her hand, his grip surprisingly warm and firm, nothing like his hand had truly felt. "Don't be—I'm free," he said.

Tears fell down her cheeks as she smiled at the broken man who had risked everything for her.

"You set me free," he said, and April could feel the gratitude flowing from him.

Brother Beau turned and walked away, fading into the darkness as he placed his cowboy hat on his head. His pain was gone, his stutter was gone, and April was free, too.

Chapter Twenty-Four

Claire sat with April's parents and Ryan in silence for what felt like hours, though she had no idea how much had passed. After their failed attempt to gain more information about the Smithers family, the group fell into an awkward and tense silence. Claire contemplated striking up a conversation multiple times, but somehow it felt wrong. After a long time of imagining what she might say in her mind, her eyes couldn't stay open, and her head dropped onto Ryan's shoulder. Ryan wrapped her arm around Claire's shoulders and she slept the lightest sleep of her life. Her mind rested yet also remained alert. She could hear Ryan's fingers tapping away on her phone, could hear Mr. Dell pacing, and Mrs. Dell's quiet cries.

Constant interruptions from the precinct disturbed her as well. The secretary who had brought the coffee earlier had checked in a few times to see if the group needed anything, but each time they had declined. Every time she heard the door open, her eyes flew open, and she looked up, sure there would be news of April. Instead, the woman's face remained apologetic and sympathetic, and Claire's frustration grew with each intrusion into their anxious space. She supposed she ought to eat something; her stomach growled and hurt, and she knew she couldn't keep anything down. April's parents also refused sustenance, making her feel better about her own refusal.

Hurried feet outside of the interrogation room door snapped Claire back to attention. She sat up so abruptly that Ryan startled, and Mr. Dell stopped in his tracks. The door burst open, and the secretary came into view, face flushed. Everyone stood up at once and Claire felt like the air had rushed out of the room as she held her breath.

"They've got her; they're on the way to the hospital," the secretary said. "Family and roommate only, though."

Mrs. Dell moved as if she might faint, falling forward and grabbing onto the back of the chair in front of her. Mr. Dell stepped in behind her, supporting her large frame with ease.

"Is she okay?" Claire asked.

"I don't know. I have an officer set to drive you to the hospital. He went for the car and will pick you up outside."

The Dells left the interrogation room hand in hand, running as fast as their broken bodies would allow. Claire looked at Ryan.

"Go," Ryan said and kissed Claire on the lips.

"Thank you for everything. I couldn't have gotten through these past few days without you," Claire said, blushing.

"Oh, you could have," Ryan said, laughing. "Text me when you know something and call me when you get home, okay?"

"I will," Claire said with another kiss before she dashed after April's parents, grabbing Mrs. Dell's other hand to support her to the car.

Claire helped each of April's parents into the car and slid into the backseat next to Mr. Dell. The sirens above their heads wailed as the officer raced to the hospital on the other side of the national forest. The night sky sparkled above them. Normally Claire found the gorgeous array of stars above Tree Park refreshing and calming, but today she found it daunting. Her brain had gone into a clouded overdrive, and she couldn't stop imagining what April would look like.

Maybe she only has one arm or a shaved head or a body covered in bruises.

Maybe she's in a coma fighting for her life. Maybe she'll die before we arrive.

Lost in her thoughts, she couldn't remember the long drive.

The officer pulled up to the hospital and the vehicle had barely stopped before Mr. Dell jumped out to the sidewalk and helped Mrs. Dell out. Claire followed as quickly behind as she could, but she could feel a chasm building between them. Though she had held their hands every step of the way, Claire was not family, and they focused on each other now. As the Dells reached the desk, Claire hung back, widening the gap between them.

"April Dell!" Mr. Dell shouted at the nurse. "Please! Where's our daughter?"

The nurse looked at her computer, locating April's room. The Dells ran down the hallway, Claire following more slowly as a doctor stopped them in the hall.

"Mr. and Mrs. Dell? I'm Doctor Beauly. I'm the one who has been treating April since she arrived."

"How is she?" Mr. Dell asked.

"She's fine, hurt but not badly. She's dehydrated and has several cuts and bruises. She looks much worse than she is, so prepare yourself for that. She has a concussion and seems to be suffering from shock, which is not uncommon in these situations. We've given her a sedative to help her calm down and rest. We'll hold her until we're sure she is physically and mentally sound enough to go home. I expect her to be here for at least a few days. Police officers will also be visiting to update you on the case and talk to April once we've cleared her for such activity. Do you have any questions?" the doctor asked. He had good bedside manners, and Claire was glad for that.

"Can we see her?" Mr. Dell asked.

"Of course, but remember that she's sedated. She won't wake for some time, and that's normal."

The doctor led the family down a series of hallways, never questioning Claire's placement with April's parents, assuming that she belonged with this family. Claire felt grateful she didn't have to wait in the lobby.

When they arrived at April's door, her parents rushed inside, each grabbing hold of one of her hands, but Claire remained in the doorway. Mrs. Dell sobbed, her head resting on her daughter's forehead, and Mr. Dell kissed April's hand. Bruises littered April's hands, and her knuckles appeared swollen. It was definitely April lying in that bed, but she was almost unrecognizable. Black and blue shadowed her face, and she had a large gash on the side of her temple. A deep cut split her lip, and a fresh bruise darkened the surrounding skin. Dried blood covered her ear, and matted hair framed her face. April looked paler than she had just a few days ago, and though Claire thought this impossible, thinner too. She did, however, look peaceful in her sleep, and she savored the small moment.

Claire stood for a while, watching April's parents acclimate themselves to their daughter's injuries. Dread and emptiness built in her stomach, but her mind focused only on her crumpled friend in the hospital bed. As she stared at April, she wanted to reach out and pull her into an embrace but knew she couldn't. That's when it hit her—Claire didn't belong here. She wasn't April's real family.

Claire turned and numbly followed the hallways back to the lobby without saying anything. She sat in one of the chairs and stared at the television mounted on the wall, not seeing the show. She had built up her relationship with April in her mind over the past few days. Claire had actually started to believe that they were sisters. She felt foolish and she didn't know what to do next. She contemplated calling Ryan to come pick her up, but the shame she felt prevented that. Ryan probably wouldn't understand the bond between April and Claire, and she couldn't risk Ryan confirming that. She thought about calling a cab, but going home without April felt wrong too. She froze, waiting for a better idea to hit her, no matter how long that may take.

She sat still, staring at nothing, when someone sat down next to her. Annoyance shot through her that a stranger sat so close despite the myriad empty chairs. She cleared her throat to say something and looked at the person next to her. It was Mr. Dell.

"Why aren't you with April?" Claire squeaked out, voice hoarse and throat raw with emotion as tears streamed down her face.

"It's scary seeing her like that, huh?" Mr. Dell said, patting Claire's knee.

She wiped away the tears and took a deep breath, willing her voice to stabilize.

"I tried to be prepared for it, but I'm really not," Claire said, voice shaking despite her efforts.

"Is that why you left?"

"I figured I would give you some time as a family," Claire said sheepishly, feeling bad for having left without saying goodbye. She didn't consider that the Dells would have noticed her absence.

"Claire—you are family. We wouldn't have found April without your work in tracking down the Smithers farm," Mr. Dell said. His voice took on a lightened tone and Claire imagined his students liked him a lot.

"The police would have found them eventually." Claire looked down at her hands. She told the truth—the police would have solved this case without her.

"That may be true, but would it have been in time?"

Claire looked up at Mr. Dell, stunned by his words. She hadn't stopped to consider that the police might have discovered the farm too late. If she hadn't done the work to find the family, perhaps April's parents would have to identify her body right now instead of nursing their daughter back to health. Claire couldn't find words and cried harder.

"There, there," Mr. Dell said, wrapping his arm around Claire's shoulders. "You've done a good job. We have our girl back and now we can celebrate that."

"Is she going to be okay?" Claire asked, wiping her nose on the sleeve of her shirt like a small child.

"She is, though I suspect it will take some time. She's going to need her family for that. Her sister included," Mr. Dell said with a supportive smile. "And I suspect that if she wakes up without seeing said 'sister', she is going to be a very grumpy girl."

"You should be with your wife and daughter right now, not me," Claire said through a weak smile.

"Did April ever tell you about the first time she told me she thought you were her long-lost sister?" Mr. Dell asked.

Claire shook her head, looking at Mr. Dell with wonder.

"It was on her first Thanksgiving break home from college. She spent the entire break in a funk, and it was clear she didn't want to be home. Mrs. Dell and I tried not to have hurt feelings, but I did, so I eventually confronted her about it. She said that living with you had felt as natural as living with me, but now that she had spent that time with you, it felt like something was missing from her life to be away from you. She said that she thought you might be 'soul sisters' and destined to be best friends." Mr. Dell smiled sadly at Claire.

"I felt the same way she did," Claire said. "That's why we decided we would never live apart. Even when we're married and grown, we'll find a way to be with each other as much as we can."

"I know we haven't always been welcoming to you, Claire, but I think all of this changed that." Mr. Dell drew Claire into a hug. She allowed Mr. Dell to envelop her in his safe arms.

"I'd really like that, Mr. Dell," she said into his warm chest.

"Well then, how about we go back to April's room?"

"I would love that, too." Claire said, wiping another tear away. As the two walked to April's room, Claire grew lighter.

April might be home soon.

She didn't know what the next steps held for April, but she knew she would be there for her, no matter what. April had never stopped supporting Claire in anything she had done, and Claire would jump at the opportunity to do the same for her sister. She had watched enough true crime shows and listened to enough true crime podcasts to guess at what came next. First, physical healing and dealing with the investigation. Second, therapy and medication to learn how to live in her new reality. Then finding the path forward for her life, whether still graduate school or something else.

Maybe now is the time to step onto my healing path. She had never been through anything remotely as traumatic as April's past few days, but her past affected her, nonetheless. She should set an example for those she loved and get herself mental health help. Claire suspected that if she could heal her own mind, bigger things might be in store, and she made a mental note to call Detective Byrd. Claire had a purpose to discover, and she thought it might be right here in Tree Park's sheriff station.

Chapter Twenty-Five

April's mind had grown fuzzy after her rescue, but scenes came back in those terrifying recurring flashes. She hated that. A flash of ambulance sirens blaring as trees rushed by, a flash of several doctors and nurses at the hospital fretting over her, a flash of screaming and fighting against Mother Loretta but realizing it was only a doctor, a flash of an IV in her arm delivering the sweetest of relief. Overall, she didn't remember much. The sedative caused a dreamless sleep, and she welcomed the emptiness with open arms. She settled into the void and very much wished it would never end. This nothingness felt amazing after everything that happened.

When April finally awoke, she jolted upright, convinced that her rescue had been a dream, and she was still in Sister Jolene's bed. She scratched and clawed at her wrists, terrified when suddenly and a woman loomed over her bed.

Mother Loretta! She's going to slap me! She swatted at the woman, screaming, as a distant part of her brain noted people standing in the doorway. *Oh God, I'm not on the farm anymore—it's my family...* A nurse stood over her and after a sharp sting on her arm, everything faded again, slipping back into her dreamless bliss. She floated there for long enough that she thought she might never come out of it.

The next time April woke, her brain had caught up enough to remember that she was in the hospital. Instead of sheer panic, pain overwhelmed her body. Her head throbbed, her ear ached deep into her skull, and her teeth felt loose behind her busted lip. She sat up slowly, groaning and wishing her sleep would return. Her parents both slept in chairs next to her bed, and April felt relieved. She wasn't ready to face them. As if hearing her reluctance telepathically, April's mother breathed deeply, stretching her body as she sat up. Her eyes flew open at seeing April sitting up, and she jumped out of her chair, rushing for the bed.

"April?" She grabbed her daughter's arm and looked her up and down as if checking to make sure it was her before pulling her into the lightest hug April had ever felt.

"Mom," April whispered as she let her mother squeeze her body despite the pain in her muscles.

April dreamt of this embrace since the moment the brothers stole her, but somehow it didn't feel how she expected. She wanted to feel safe and secure, but instead, she felt close to nothing at all. Her father awakened, too, and April reached out her hand for him. He took her hand and squeezed it with tenderness, but April still felt nothing at all.

Something inside of me is broken. A huge part of her had expected to die on that farm, and that part of her had shut down entirely. *Will I ever be able to put things back where they belong?* Though she had been hopeful when the officers arrived, a part of her had died on that farm, just as the previous Sister Jolenes had.

Her parents talked to her, at her, her mother smiling through her tears and her father putting on a brave face, but she couldn't focus on their words. The sound of Brother Beau's strangled gurgles as the blood in his body drained from the bullet hole in his throat reverberated through her mind. She squeezed her eyes shut, willing the sound to vacate her mind, but instead images of his death scene flashed behind her eyelids. Those were worse than the sounds and her breath quickened as panic set in.

I can't do this. I can't be alive.

She couldn't live in the world after this had happened to her. Her blood was supposed to be splattered all over the kitchen floor. She was supposed to be 'Sister Jolene' and live and die on that farm. She wasn't meant to be saved.

She let herself drift again, trying to escape into the void.

Maybe I'm stuck in a version of hell where I'm doomed to be alive when I was supposed to have died. She watched as her mother and father faded away into nothing and she could finally be at peace once more.

She couldn't get Brother Beau's sacrifice out of her mind. He had wanted to escape the hellish life on that farm, but it shouldn't have been through death. The dream of dying in that kitchen with Brother Beau settled in her mind like fog settled into a forest. She could see herself curling into a ball on the floor next to him, both having been shot and bleeding out together. She desperately wished that she weren't in this hospital and didn't have to face what was coming next.

Is my life more important than his? Am I destined to do something great with it that now he would never have the chance to do? Will I ever be okay? April felt like the life she had lived a few short days ago was someone else's entirely. She thought about her home with Claire, her job at the museum, and her parents—but that life didn't belong to her anymore.

The April who the brothers stole out of the snow in the middle of the night no longer existed. She would never be the same person again. She stopped taking sedatives then, figuring that her waking moments were no better than her unconscious ones. She stayed in the hospital for two days and then the staff talked about sending her either home or to a psychiatric hospital. She didn't want to be trapped anywhere else and figured it would be best to bite the bullet and stay in the present world. Instead, she would push away the panic and stare blankly out of the window of her hospital room. She looked out into the bright morning sky and wished she could transform herself into a bird, fly straight out that window and into the sun, never to be seen again.

She spent much of that day staring at the television, hoping her visitors would think she was engrossed in it and not entirely disconnected. April's mother's hand never left hers, but to April it felt like a dead animal laying across her palm and not the loving touch of a mother. April knew Claire had visited several times, though she never caught her awake. When she finally did, Claire had rushed into the room and wrapped April in an embrace, crying tears of joy. She did her best to be present and pretend to be excited to see Claire, but she knew Claire could see right through her. She could see the heartbreak in Claire's eyes at April's muted reaction to seeing her. She could see the stolen glances between Claire and her parents, the concern beaming between them, but she couldn't seem to find her way out of the darkness. Everyone assured her that it would be okay, that she would get help, that she was safe, and that she would heal, but indifference reigned. She would never trust safety again.

The next time she woke up from a nap, Heather sat beside her, the room empty. April looked around, stunned that her parents had left her. Heather saw her face and mistook her expression for one of distress.

"They're grabbing a bite to eat. I promised to sit with you until they got back," she said.

April chuckled. She felt an immense amount of relief with them absent and her entire body relaxed.

"I needed a break anyway," she said to the detective. She had charged into literal gunfire to save April, and she would never be able to express her true gratitude. April still didn't know if she wanted to be alive, but she hoped one day that might change.

"Thank you," April said. "I didn't have a chance to say that."

Heather looked at her with empathy in her eyes and not sympathy. For the first time, April didn't feel like a victim.

"When my sister went missing, everyone treated me like I was broken, and I hated it. I wanted my life to go back to the way it was before, and when people treated me that way, it felt impossible to get back to who I was. It really created a dark cycle in my life," Heather said.

"Everyone thinks I'm crazy now or something. I can see it in their eyes—the fear that I might do something reckless at any minute. It's like they're afraid to be around me but obsessed with me at the same time and I hate it."

"They're worried about you—with everything you've been through, it's only natural, but I promise that I won't treat you that way, okay?"

"Okay," April said, grateful for Detective Byrd's kind words. "Did you find anything else out about your sister?"

"Not yet. Once the sheriff caught wind that I suspected my sister had died there, he pulled me from the case."

"I'm sorry, that must be hard," April said, knowing what it felt like to be out of the loop.

"It is what it is," Heather said with a shrug. "Detective Longville will be coming by later to conduct a formal interview, so rest up until then."

"You could use some rest, too," April said, noticing the bags under Heather's eyes for the first time. She looked like she hadn't slept in days and her curly, black hair stood in disarray. "You don't have to wait here for my parents. I'll be fine on my own."

"Oh, I am not upsetting your parents. I remember what your dad was like in high school! I also know that you would be fine on your own. You wouldn't still be here if you weren't a fighter," Heather said, smiling, but the smile faded.

April's heart hurt for Heather. "Autumn took her own life so the brothers couldn't. She knew what was in store for her and she didn't want to give them the satisfaction of choosing for her. She took control of her destiny in her final moments, and you should be proud of her," April said, voice growing thick with emotion.

Heather's eyes welled with tears. "Thank you." She kissed April's palm and the two turned to the television mounted up on the wall, content catching both of their attention.

"We have an update in the April Dell case," a serious young man reported.

"The sheriff has confirmed the identities of the persons arrested two days ago when police made a daring rescue of April Dell from an unmarked farm outside of town. Loretta Smithers and her son, Waylon Smithers, were taken into custody. Their identity was discovered after authorities tracked down a suspect who appeared at a vigil held for Ms. Dell."

"It was actually Claire who discovered Beauregard's identity," Heather said to April, who felt both shocked and not shocked at the same time. It was just like her true crime loving best friend to help solve her case and the thought made her smile.

The newscaster continued, "That man has been identified as Beauregard Smithers, and he died on the scene, though the manner of death has not yet been released. After being briefly treated at the hospital for injuries sustained during their arrests, both Mrs. Smithers and her son were taken into custody until they make their plea before a judge."

The camera turned from a view of the newscaster to an aerial view of the farm. April watched, fascinated at how tiny the barn looked from the drone footage of the property. She could see tiny people the size of ants scrambling around the property, presumably searching for evidence. The farm had been her entire world when she was locked there—it felt so vast and deep that the rest of the world disappeared. Now, watching the footage of the farm, April realized that it was a relatively small property. She mused at how a simple change of perspective could alter someone's opinion of something so drastically.

"The Smithers family has also been linked to the case of Bethany Tyler, missing college student whose body was found in Tree Park just days ago. Sources have reported that the family is also being investigated in the now reopened case of Autumn Byrd, though the sheriff's department has not yet confirmed this information. Sheriff Steinman did make a statement at a recent press conference."

The screen switched to a video of Sheriff Steinman. "April Dell was recovered safely from the Smithers' farm thanks to the quick and brave actions of our Tree Park detectives. Our officers are working tirelessly to be sure that any evidence found on the farm is processed in a timely fashion. We will continue our diligent work and keep the public updated as new information becomes available. I want to assure the residents of Tree Park and the surrounding areas that all threats of harm have been neutralized and our community is rid of the evil doings of this family. I hope we can come together as a community to heal. Thank you all for your time."

April shut off the television. Heather's face had gone white, and she clamped her lips tightly together.

"It's hard knowing that Autumn was there but not knowing the details. I wish we'd had more time with Brother Beau."

Heather frowned at April, clearly confused at the use of the term 'brother' before Beau's name.

"The family all referred to each other that way, title before a name," April explained. "Anyway, *Beau* told me that his family had been doing this since his sister Jolene died in a farming accident a few years ago. He said they took girls to try to alleviate their mother's grief, but it obviously didn't work out that way. Autumn took her own life and Waylon killed Bethany just before I arrived."

"Beau's the one who called into the sheriff's station and told us where to find her. He also sent me a box with the shirt Autumn was wearing the night she disappeared. He came to your vigil, as you heard, and called in a tip about Bethany's case before she was killed, too. He was instrumental in this thing getting resolved," Heather explained.

April nodded, thinking for the millionth time that Brother Beau had saved her life and didn't deserve his gruesome death. She was about to say this out loud when her mother burst into the room.

"Darling! You're awake!" her mother crooned, bounding toward April.

"Yeah, but I don't feel well." She curled down into the bed, pulling the comforter up over her shoulders.

"Oh dear, you should rest." Her mother dragged a chair next to April's bed.

April sat up a bit as Heather stood and made her way toward the door.

"Thanks again, Heather," April said.

"Thank you, too, April. You have no idea what you've given me."

April felt Heather's words in her heart. She closed her eyes and rested back into the pillows as her mother ran her big hand over her hair. She realized she was coming back to herself, no longer only feeling numbness, as she drifted into sleep once more.

Chapter Twenty-Six

Sheriff Steinman forcing her to leave the farm had been one of the most challenging moments in Heather's life. She knew it would come if the Sheriff caught wind of what was going on, and she knew she couldn't jeopardize the case against the Smithers family, but none of that stopped Heather from wanting to be there. She was desperate to find a way to be close to her dead sister, and combing through every inch of the farm would have been a way to do that. After Nathan had whisked April away from the farmhouse and to the ambulance, Heather contemplated pretending that Beauregard Smithers had never told her about Autumn, but she knew what would happen if that ever came to light. Beauregard had died in the shootout in the kitchen, so he couldn't tell anyone the truth, but Heather knew she couldn't live with herself if she didn't share the story. An officer escorted her from the property without having a chance to say goodbye to Nathan. He had rushed back into the farmhouse after the ambulance departed, and Heather watched him go back in with sad eyes. Not only that, but she hadn't seen him since that day as he had been working around the clock and sleeping at the station.

Heather spent the first day after April's rescue sleeping. By the time she woke and left her bed on the second day, the realization that she hadn't had the chance to tell Nathan that she loved him hit her like a truck. *What if he never talks to me again? What if he hears me out but feels differently now?* She spent that second day crying on her couch while Luna purred in her lap, trying to cheer her up. *These tears are probably for Autumn.* She knew solving Autumn's case wouldn't bring her back, yet she was somehow disappointed that it didn't. She had spent so long telling herself if she solved Autumn's death everything would be okay, but now she only felt empty and alone.

Three days after her charge into the Smithers' Farm, the state police interviewed Heather about her investigation into Bethany and April's cases. She provided as many details as she could, though it annoyed her. She understood the department protocol to have a debriefing, but she knew it had to do with Autumn, too. They needed to understand how much damage Heather had done to the case in her reluctance to share her suspicions about her sister's disappearance with her sheriff. She never once mentioned Nathan's suspicions, wanting to protect her partner. This led to another day of self-loathing. *I should have been smarter about that as well. I was so focused on finding the truth for Autumn, I couldn't see anything else.*

Her father would be upset with her too, if he were alive. He had taught her a lot about life and policing, and one of the most important things she had taken from him was to remain true to herself. Her continued involvement with April's case meant she sacrificed herself. She was desperate to be true to her sister, desperate to keep that relationship alive even in death, and she had sacrificed her moral compass and quite possibly her job. Now, Autumn's justice could be at risk. Disappointment in herself and the imagined disappointment from her father took over once more, and she spent another day in bed.

Heather's grief confused her—she had grieved so much that she thought it was over. She knew her sister was dead, she had seen the crime scene photos and Autumn's body at the morgue, but a piece of her heart refused to accept that as reality. The grief for her sister, disappointment from her father, and devastation over the loss of Bethany mixed. She ultimately decided to take a leave of absence from work. She had to be true to herself, as her father had taught her, and now was the time for self-care and not for pushing herself.

Heather's phone dinged with a text message. *It's Nathan*, she thought, reading her screen. *He's coming over.* Fear gripped her, paralyzing her body. She wanted to tell him the truth about her feelings, but this would be a professional visit. She knew the majority of what had happened to Autumn; April had given her that sweet gift, but she dreaded the specific details. She didn't want to think about the events that led to Autumn's capture and subsequent suicide, and her stomach swam with nausea.

She had also avoided her mother. She'd made one brief call to alert her about the reopening of Autumn's case but hadn't given her any details. She had feigned professional responsibility but knew this excuse wouldn't last forever. But if she didn't tell her mother the sheriff would, and she didn't want more bad news coming from the police.

When Nathan knocked on her door, she contemplated ignoring it, pretending she hadn't heard him. But that wouldn't work. *I can't run from reality forever.* Heather looked through the peephole and then pulled the door open. His face told her what she already knew—they had confirmed the presence of her sister on the farm. Trying to keep her face neutral, she invited him in. He on the small couch, and she settled in beside him, tucking her feet up underneath her.

"Give it to me straight," Heather said, face serious. She wanted to hear the story from his perspective without giving away what April had already told her.

Nathan took her hands in his, an intimate gesture that caught her off guard, and looked her square in the eyes.

"We found evidence of her, and Beauregard Smither's journals also confirmed that she was on the farm. The family lost their youngest, Jolene, to a farming accident, and Waylon Smithers created a scheme to help their mother cope with grief. He murdered his father and began stealing women.

They happened upon Autumn by pure chance, hoping to find someone who looked like their sister." Nathan pulled his cell phone out of his pocket and scrolled to a picture of a beautiful young girl, brown hair and big brown eyes matching Autumn's perfectly. And Bethany's. And April's. Heather shuddered.

"Wow," she mustered while staring at Jolene, sad that she had died so tragically but also hating her for looking like her sister.

"Beauregard wrote that Autumn was very sick with detox after they took her, and Waylon beat her for it. By the time she had recovered from her lack of drug use, they had injured her body in ways that wouldn't have repaired itself without medical intervention. Beauregard wrote that he attempted to give her first aid, but he only knew about animal care and couldn't help Autumn," Nathan continued.

Heather had dreaded this, and her hands shook as images of her sister's sickness and injuries floated through her mind.

"How long?"

"Four months," Nathan said, squeezing Heather's hand. The intimate gesture triggered Heather's tears, and her vision blurred.

"Four months," she repeated in a whisper, aghast. Sixteen weeks, one hundred and twenty days, 2,880 minutes. She marveled that Autumn made it as long as she did.

"Autumn was being kept in an upstairs bedrooms. She couldn't walk at that point, so they didn't lock her up the way they did with Bethany and April. She crawled to a window, climbed out onto the sill, and threw herself to the ground. She probably wouldn't have died from the fall alone but she had sustained so many other injuries that her body couldn't fight anymore. Waylon had wanted to bury her on the property, but Beauregard feared that their mother might punish them if they learned the truth about what they were doing, so they gave her some animal tranquilizers and other substances that they had on the farm and dumped her where it might look like the suicide that it actually was."

Dizziness washed over Heather, and she gripped Nathan's hand tighter. Her mind spun with a million questions about the case, none of which were appropriate for a family member of a victim to ask. She supposed one day she might ask Nathan to tell her more about the brothers and their mother, about Bethany's time on the farm, but for now she had taken her detective hat off. She was Autumn's sister and nothing more.

"Aside from the stories in Beauregard's journal, we also found a trinket from each of the women they took. It seems that Beauregard was keeping mementos of the girls, trying to be connected to his sisters. He had kept one of April's snow boots, Bethany Tyler's necklace, and this," Nathan finished, scrolling to another picture on his phone.

It was a picture of a tiny gold ring with a sun at the top; the ring that Autumn's mother had given her for her sixteenth birthday.

"My beautiful sunny girl," Heather's mother had said as Autumn had opened the box. She had never taken it off, and Heather hadn't thought to look for it in the chaos of her death. Heather had supposed Autumn had lost it or pawned it for drugs and seeing it on the screen now started the flow of tears again. Nathan drew her close and Heather curled her entire body into his, letting the tears flow, wetting his shirt. After a while, the tears slowed and she sniffled with sadness and grief.

"We have to tell my mom," Heather whispered into Nathan's chest.

"I know we do," Nathan said. "The sheriff instructed me to inform her, but I wanted to tell you first. I owed that to you after everything we've been through together. I knew you'd want some time to process this on your own and also to be there when your mom found out. I know that your mother doesn't often afford you the space you need to grieve, and I figured this was one small thing I could do to make things better. It seems ridiculous now; nothing is okay."

This made Heather cry again, knowing that she didn't deserve Nathan after the way she had treated him. She had brushed off his feelings like they were nothing when in reality, they meant everything to her. She stood and stumbled over her own feet, rushing to her bathroom, fearful that she might get sick. Once in the bathroom, she splashed cold water on her face and did her best to take deep breaths. She gripped the side of the sink, willing the world to slow down and stop.

Nathan knocked quietly, but Heather had locked it behind her. The last thing she needed after everything that had happened over the past few weeks was for Nathan to take care of her more. She leaned her head against the cool porcelain of the sink as she thought about what to do next. An image of her father filled her mind, his smile bright and his eyes warm.

What would Sheriff Byrd do?

He would tell Heather to take care of the family she had left. Her father was gone, and her sister's death had finally been resolved, leaving only Heather and her mother. She may not be the best mother in the world, and she certainly hadn't supported Heather, but that didn't mean she wasn't her mother. That didn't mean that they didn't still need each other. Heather knew in her heart that she couldn't leave her mother alone to hear this news. Just as Heather had needed to hear it alone, needed her independence to cope, her mother needed a hand to hold and a shoulder to cry on.

Not only did she need to be there for the only family member she had left, but she also needed to decide who her true family was, and she knew that included Nathan. Heather took a deep breath and left the bathroom, feeling braver and more resolute than she had in a long time. When she stepped from the bathroom, Nathan sat on the edge of her bed, hands clasped and one leg jolting up and down.

"Are you alright?" He approached her and placed a gentle hand on her hip, as if to steady her. A fire lit in her stomach at his touch, and her body screamed out for him to touch her more. Her mind flashed back to their near kiss last week and how she had felt that invisible string drawing them together. She took a small step closer to him, feeling his heat flowing into her.

"I'm okay, only thanks to you, though," she said, feeling shy.

"I told you before—I'm here for you, even if I don't have to be," Nathan said, voice quiet.

"You don't have to be," Heather confirmed with a small nod as she placed her hands on his chest and ran them up and around his neck.

What she wouldn't give to pull the shirt from his body and rub her hands over his skin. Nathan gasped at her touch, and she could see he wanted the same thing.

"You said that you had something to tell me." He leaned closer. She could feel the heat of his breath on her face, and she yearned for his lips on hers.

"You have to know by now that I love you," Heather said with a sultry smile and Nathan laughed at hearing his own words echoed back by her.

"Oh yeah?" Nathan teased her.

"Yeah. I love you, partner," Heather said as Nathan's lips finally met hers, and she melted into his kiss.

His lips were as warm and soft as she had imagined, and all of her tension melted under their touch. Heather felt like she could kiss Nathan forever and wished they could stay in that blissful moment for the rest of their lives. She pulled away from the kiss and looked at Nathan, his smile bigger than any she had ever seen on him before. She couldn't help but smile back, giggling and blushing.

"I love you too, partner," he said, kissing her one last time before standing up.

Heather groaned but stood as well. They had work to do, and she didn't look forward to it, but at least she had her partner by her side through it.

Chapter Twenty-Seven

April woke with a start, gasping for breath and hand flying to her chest, startling the puppy next to her. The dog, a fluffy Bernese Mountain Dog, sat up and put its nose in April's face, licking her with its long, sloppy tongue.

"Cujo!" April said, laughing and pushing the dog away. One month had passed since she came home from the hospital, one month of healing and moving on.

Cujo settled down and curled up next to April, resuming his snoozing as April petted the fur along his back. When she first got home, she bought the largest puppy she could find. April hadn't been nervous to return to her home with Claire, but she dreaded those long nights that Claire worked late, and April knew that she would need something for security. So far, Cujo chased butterflies in the yard and never growled at anyone, but he at least gave April the semblance of safety. Long nights without Claire felt a little more tolerable with her little buddy to keep her company, and she never felt alone.

The choice of moving back home with Claire had been a no-brainer to April, despite her parents' apprehension. April's mother pleaded and nearly demanded that April stay with them and even went as far as to offer to pay to break her lease with Claire. April considered the offer but quickly concluded it would only worsen her mental health. She might feel safe in her parents' home, but it would also feel like a step backward. April's decision upset her mother, but she ended up calling April every hour and tracking her location on her phone instead.

This had stressed April. Before her kidnapping, April had worked on setting boundaries with her mother and trying to distance herself, and this pushed her so far back. Her therapist helped her to navigate everything, and she was thankful for the support. The hospital had started April on an anxiety medication and Claire researched therapists, so by the time she arrived home, she had everything set up that she needed. Given that Tree Park had no therapists or mental health care, April traveled to the nearest city to see her therapist. She loved the respite from her tiny town, even if she did have to drive an hour. She had once viewed Tree Park as a safe haven, but now the streets held dangerous shadows, and the town felt sinister. She had improved a lot over the past month, but felt nowhere near normal, and she often wondered if Tree Park held her back.

Therapy had been the perfect outlet, as Claire assured April that it would, and she felt so grateful for the resource. The sessions challenged her—April hated talking about her emotions, especially when it came to her kidnapping, but she found her them incredibly helpful, as well. She'd learned a lot about trauma and how to cope with her newfound anxiety, and she began to manage her feelings more and more. She now looked forward to leaving Tree Park for her three times per week appointments and knew that she would need to make a change sometime soon. April took a leave of absence from her job at the museum and didn't know if she wanted to return—the job seemed too close to home now.

April checked her phone on her nightstand to see the time, ignoring the several messages from her mother. Her therapist told her she shouldn't manage her mother's emotions and to only respond to messages when it suited her. April had always gone out of her way to make her mother comfortable, sometimes at her own expense, and it felt good to give herself permission to let up on that. April begged her mother to get a therapist of her own, but her mother refused to see her co-dependency and the problems it created, not only for herself but their family as well.

April stood in front of her mirror as she put on the black dress and boots that she had laid out the night before, running her hand through her short, blonde hair. The drastic change felt unfamiliar, but she was glad she had done it. Every time she looked in the mirror, she only saw Sister Jolene staring back, and she would do anything to make it go away. Changing her dark brown hair to blonde had helped, but if April looked too deeply into her own eyes, she could still see Sister Jolene. Her therapist explained this was a normal response to trauma, similar to the flashbacks that a veteran might suffer from after active combat.

April opened the door and left her bedroom, finding Claire waiting outside of it. Cujo bounded from April's room and jumped onto Claire's legs. Claire bent down to pet him, scratching behind his ears and talking to him in baby speak.

"What are you doing?" April asked, laughing at the pair as they loved each other.

"I couldn't wait to show you this!" Claire thrust an envelope into April's hands. It had the emblem for the police academy on the front.

"Is this what I think it is?" she squealed in delight.

"It is!" Claire shouted. "I got in!"

April screamed and jumped up and down, dragging Claire into a bouncing hug. Cujo jumped with them, barking with his own puppy excitement.

"I knew you would," April said as everyone calmed down.

Claire had met with Heather after April's rescue to discuss the next steps to become an officer. Loving true crime as she did, Claire found being on the outside of the investigation frustrating and terrible. Heather told Claire she had the mind of a detective, and Claire wanted to move forward with her life.

She applied to the police academy in the nearest big city. It hit April then that Claire would move away, and her heart sank. *How can I live without my best friend, my sister?* She tried to hide the emotions that came alongside her excitement and pride in Claire, but Claire saw right through her.

"You could come with me," Claire sang, grabbing April's hands.

"I don't know," April said, looking down at her shoes and clicking them together.

Claire's face turned sympathetic, and April hated that. She pulled her hands from Claire's and took a step back, rubbing Cujo's ears to say goodbye.

"Let's go," April said. "We don't want to be late." The two women left the house and got into Claire's car without another word about the police academy or Claire's move.

The short drive to the church crossed through main street, and time slowed, yet another consequence of April's trauma. When Claire drove through the exact spot where the brothers took her, April closed her eyes. She let her mind scan her body, feeling the way the dress hung from her frame, the way her shoes wrapped her feet, and the way her breath went in and out of her lungs. She focused on the rising and falling of her chest as they passed through the spot, keeping the flashbacks at bay. She silently thanked her therapist for teaching her how to stay grounded in the present instead of allowing her mind to fly to the past and traumatize her again. Yet no matter how much she practiced her coping skills, she couldn't stop Brother Beau from entering her mind.

Will I ever stop seeing the man who ruined and saved my life?

Part of her didn't want him to go away. Somehow, holding onto her connection to Brother Beau allowed her to remember the good in the world, and she saw it as a reminder of hope. She pictured his sallow face and dark green eyes, and she let him stay there as she focused on her breathing. Claire grabbed April's hand once they passed through the spot of the kidnapping, signaling to April she could open her eyes.

They pulled up to the church and rushed inside, trying to avoid the cold

February air. Inside the doors stood a giant photograph of Autumn Byrd. April paused for a moment to study the photo. They shared in the horrors of the farm and it forever connected them. She would have made the same choice as Autumn if the officers hadn't rescued her—she would have taken her own life. She laid a gentle hand on the photograph and tears filled her eyes as she walked into the chapel. Heather and her mother stood in the doorway, greeting the long line of guests. At the front of the line, Heather and April embraced, Heather smiling through her tears.

April gave Heather's mother a sympathetic glance but kept her focus on Heather. She didn't want to re-live any of the details of her time on the farm. Heather's mother asked April questions in her desperation to learn more about her daughter's time on the farm, and it made her uncomfortable. April's therapist had warned her this event might bring up new flashbacks, but she needed to be there—she needed closure for herself, as well.

Heather had taken a leave of absence from Tree Park's Sheriff's Office and April heard she might not return. Heather kept in close contact with April, probably to stay connected with her sister, but she enjoyed it. She didn't bring up Autumn and instead acted as a big sister, sending her dinner on rough nights and driving her to therapy before April felt confident enough to drive herself. Heather had helped April so much and she really hoped she wouldn't stop helping other people. She would understand if Heather never returned to police work, but she hoped she didn't avoid helping in every way. April knew that dating her partner, Detective Longville, complicated matters as well. He stood behind Heather, ready to step in, and April found it romantic.

"Thank you for coming," Heather said.

"Of course." April rubbed Heather's arm. "In a way, Autumn saved my life. I don't think Brot—I mean Beau—would have gone to the lengths he did to save me if it hadn't been for her."

Heather nodded as the tears fell down her cheeks.

"It helps knowing that her life meant something to more than just us," Heather said.

"She meant something to a lot of us. Look at all these people," April said. Heather turned to look at the crowded chapel and smiled. April gave Heather's arm one more pat before moving on.

As April made her way into the chapel, she saw her mother waving her arms in the air.

"Over here, April!" she shouted through the crowd, and her face reddened in embarrassment.

April glanced behind her to see Claire talking with Heather and Detective Longville and decided not to wait. She needed to stop her mother from charging through the chapel for her. She rushed down the aisle and entered the pew, sitting next to her mother, who pulled her into an aggressive hug. April didn't reciprocate and her mother crushed her between her strong baker's arms. Shifting and wriggling out of the hug, her mother frowned.

"You didn't text me back. I was starting to worry," April's mother said, almost twitching with anxiety.

"Sorry, mom," April said flatly.

Claire slid into the bench beside her, and April's father started a conversation with her, talking over April's mother and stopping her line of conversation. April felt so relieved.

April's father had retired early from teaching—the bakery made more than enough money to support the two of them. He spent his time reading and writing, with the hopes of publishing own collection of short stories one day. Her father's work took inspiration from her kidnapping and April hadn't felt brave enough to read it yet. It was never too late to achieve your dreams, and her father's work brought her pride. April's mother had hired help at the bakery as she couldn't work full time due to her anxiety. She often left work to check on April, or even try to find her, and that didn't bode well for maintaining a business. In their newfound spare time, April's parents had made a real effort to bond with Claire, and April appreciated this. The awkward tension that existed between them before her kidnapping dissipated, one silver lining of her horrible situation.

Ryan came bounding down the aisle and slid in next to Claire, planting a big kiss right on her lips. April smiled at seeing her best friend happy. She wished she hadn't missed the budding of their relationship, wishing could have been there for Claire to gush to after their first kiss, but glad that she had been there for the rest of it. Ryan seemed to be around all the time, and it gave April a sense of relief. She had always been an introvert with lower social needs than others, but her kidnapping had exacerbated that, and she couldn't handle leaving the house much. Ryan stepped in to fill the gap in Claire's social life, and it alleviated April's guilt and responsibility. Ryan smiled and waved at April, and Claire winked. April wondered how the pair would handle Claire's move to the city for the police academy and thought Claire hadn't told her of her acceptance yet. Though only an hour away, long-distance relationships could be complicated.

The memorial was beautiful. Heather spoke eloquently about her sister. With palpable grief in the room, April knew the majority of the crowd felt guilty. April herself had written Autumn off as a junkie and never thought twice about her disappearance and suicide. She took it at face value without stopping to think about the life underneath the tragedy and the family members it destroyed. She wished more than anything she could have one more conversation with Autumn. She imagined thanking Autumn for everything and apologizing for stereotyping her into something she didn't deserve. April knew many thought the same thing.

Several members of the audience stood to speak about Autumn, and as much as April wanted to participate, she didn't feel ready. No matter where she went in Tree Park, everyone looked at her with horrified awe or pathetic sympathy, and she couldn't imagine being met with the entire town giving her those looks all at once. Overall, though, April was glad that she attended, as conflicted as she had initially felt. She made a mental note to tell her therapist about how healing the experience felt for her as she followed her parents out of the church, Claire and Ryan hand-in-hand behind her.

When they all paused at their cars and made small talk, April grew anxious. She needed some alone time, her and Cujo, after being in the packed church for so long. Claire picked up on April's anxious cues and kissed Ryan goodbye, promising to call her later. Ryan made her way to her car as April hugged her parents, ignoring her mother's urging that she come home with them.

As they parted, April's mother turned and shouted to Claire, "Did you hear back from the police academy?"

"I heard this morning, and I got in!" Claire said.

April's parents pulled her in for celebratory hugs. They talked about how proud they felt and gushed over Claire's accomplishment as April's anxiety continued to build, filling her body with jitters and shakes. April felt like she might explode and didn't want to cry or hyperventilate in public.

"And I'm going with her!" April shouted, stunned but relieved to have said it out loud. She couldn't wait to get out of this damned town. This had lived in the back of her mind for so long and this memorial had sealed the deal. She couldn't build a life here outside of "the kidnapped girl" or "Autumn's successor", and she couldn't heal from her trauma without getting space from this part of her. Plus, she couldn't part from Claire yet, and she could find a job at one of the many museums in the city. April's mother gasped, her face stunned and slack with shock.

"We can talk about it later," April said. "Claire doesn't start for another five weeks."

April's mother didn't say anything. April's father pulled Claire in for one last celebratory hug and then hugged his daughter.

"I'm proud of you," he whispered, and April smiled, squeezing her father a little harder. Those four small words meant everything to her. Her anxiety reached its peak as she opened her arms to hug her still-stunned mother.

"I love you, dearest daughter," her mother said into her ear and April's blood ran cold.

She felt paralyzed and unable to move as her mother let go of her and her parents made their way to their own car. Claire, sensing April's emotions, ushered her to the car and helped her into the seat. April stared with wide eyes out of the windshield, reeling from her mother's words.

Did I mishear her? Does she intend to keep her here in Tree Park, no matter the consequences, just as Mother Loretta had tried to do for her girls? Is my mother becoming Mother Loretta?

April's pulse quickened and her breath shortened. Mother Loretta stood a few yards away, hiding behind a tree. Her dark green eyes glowed as she put her white, slender finger to her lips, silently shushing April. Her connection with reality snapped as she screamed. Claire dropped to her side, but she shook her head back and forth, hair swinging through the air. Dizzy, April slowed her shaking and peeked back at the tree, seeing nothing but shadows.

About the Author

Denver Wheeler (they/them) is a non-binary author from Williamsburg, Virginia. They studied psychology in college and graduate school, and run a small mental health counseling practice as well as actively practicing as a therapist. Denver's literary work deals with different aspects of mental health and how trauma can affect us all.

In their spare time, Denver enjoys reading, spending time with horses, and being with their husband and child. Denver is a proud member of the LGBTQIA+ community and incorporates this pride into their writing.